Malediction

Malediction

Duke C

www.urbanbooks.net

Urban Books, LLC
300 Farmingdale Road, N.Y.-Route 109
Farmingdale, NY 11735

ISBN 13: 978-1-64556-140-8
ISBN 10: 1-64556-140-2

First Trade Paperback Printing January 2021
Printed in the United States of America

10 9 8 7 6 5 4 3 2 1

Distributed by Kensington Publishing Corp.
Submit Orders to:
Customer Service
400 Hahn Road
Westminster, MD 21157-4627
Phone: 1-800-733-3000
Fax: 1-800-659-2436

Malediction: a magical word or phrase uttered with the intention of bringing about evil or destruction; a curse.

Part 1

Chapter One

Damien couldn't read another word. He quickly turned the page. This tragic story made him think of his ex-girlfriend, Kenya, who left him three months ago. He flipped through the classified section of the paper. No new jobs were listed. Many of the opportunities that were in print already had received his resume at some point. Damien became frustrated at the poor response to all the cover letters and resumes he'd faxed and emailed to almost every company that advertised in the *Chicago Daily*.

He flipped to the horoscope section of the paper. The two middle-aged women who wrote the respective horoscopes were smiling for the camera as usual. Their smiles (which were more like smirks) always told Damien their true feelings about what they were writing: "This section of the newspaper is bullshit, and we don't believe anything we have written about astrology."

Damien smiled as he read what the woman in the left column had to say about the people born in the sixth month of the year. According to the lady with the keen nose and long eyelashes, someone special was going to come into Damien's life and change it forever. He doubted that. She also wrote that his circumstances, and those of millions of others, would change for the better soon. The remainder of her short paragraph had nothing to do with Damien or his life.

He began reading his horoscope in the right column. The woman with the bushy eyebrows and the noticeable hair above her lip told Damien and whoever else read her column that they would become wealthy in the near future. That was contingent upon them keeping negative people and elements far away from them. Damien smiled until he read her last sentence.

"There will be more dark days and steep mountains to climb before the sun begins to shine in your direction," wrote the astrologist.

Damien didn't think that things could get any worse than they were already. He shook his head in disgust and turned to the sports section.

No story or headline really caught Damien's interest he folded the newspaper in half and threw it on the porch. Damien set his size-eleven shoe on top of the paper so it wouldn't blow onto the sidewalk or out into the street. He leaned back on the wooden bench and closed his brown eyes. In the last three months, his life had drastically changed for the worse. Damien took a deep breath and began to recollect how fast his world had turned upside down.

The wind continued to grow stronger as the temperature steadily declined. Damien pulled his White Sox cap down tighter on his head. Thunder roared and banged like a sledgehammer. The gray sky cast a dark shadow over the atmosphere. The rain was coming.

Three months ago, the weather was perfect for outdoor activities. The sun was shining brightly, and temperatures were in the high nineties. People in the neighborhood barbecued and played cards in their backyards while kids threw water balloons at one another and chased the ice cream truck down the street. Now it was cold and gloomy outside, and Damien was the only person visible. As quickly as the season had changed from summer to winter, so had Damien's life. Instead of sitting at his desk inside his cubicle at work, he was now sitting on his parents' porch all alone, trying to find a job and trying to figure out where he went wrong in his life.

Damien loved and respected his dad because he always told him the truth. He never tried to hide or sugarcoat anything. When he was about to become a teenager, he'd sat down with his father and listened to him talk long and openly about sex. The talk was awkward and weird at the time but very informative to Damien. After that graphic conversation, he felt as though he could talk to his dad about anything.

"Hey, kid. Wake up!" said a raspy voice coming from the foot of the porch.

Damien didn't realize that he had dozed off. He opened his eyes and saw the mailman standing with a stack of mail in his hands. He jumped up and grabbed the mail from Terry, who had been their mailman for over twenty years now.

"Good mornin', Terry," Damien said to the short and thin postal worker.

"Good afternoon to you too," Terry replied facetiously. He had a huge smile on his bearded face. Terry was always cheerful and pleasant. Not once could Damien ever remember seeing him with a frown on his face. He handed Damien the mail and quickly walked away.

The colorful trees blew in the howling wind. Damien jumped like someone had scared him, and he dropped the mail onto the porch. Someone had walked past him. He could feel them and hear them. Damien just couldn't see the figure.

Chapter Two

Laurence slowly turned his black Cadillac Escalade into the spacious driveway. Although it was drizzling and wet outside, the truck was still shining like the day he drove it off the showroom floor. You could see the twenty-two-inch chrome rims from a mile away gleaming and sparkling in the hazy night. Laurence could not function any other way. He was obsessed with keeping himself and everything that he possessed clean and organized. He didn't care how much rain or snow fell on the ground. Laurence was still going to have his car detailed inside and out. As a youngster he'd run with his father, who was extremely meticulous. That was why Laurence demanded everything around him to be clean and in order.

The automatic sensor light came on above the four-car garage as Laurence put the SUV in park. He planned on sitting in the car and listening to his music while he ate his food, so he left the truck running. This was a normal routine for Laurence. He never came home and went directly into the house. He loved to relax and unwind in the car while he grooved to one of his favorite artists. Tonight, he was playing Too Short, the foul-mouthed rap veteran from California. He loved Too Short because he rhymed at a pace where Laurence could understand every word he spoke, and the music sounded so good coming through his speakers.

Although Laurence was married, he still considered himself a player. That was why he loved listening to the

Oakland rapper's tales of sex, pimping, and street life. Other than Too Short, and some early Public Enemy, Tupac was the only hip-hop artist Laurence would play. When rap wasn't blasting from his speakers, Laurence was playing soul music from the seventies.

He turned the system up a notch and began nodding his head back and forth to the thumping bass line. Laurence reached into the white plastic bag on the passenger floor and grabbed his dinner. He set the hot carton of chicken wings and French fries on his lap. He had been out of town for more than a week and was craving a meal from Harold's Chicken.

As soon as he'd gotten back in Chicago, Laurence drove to the city to order some chicken from Harold's. His favorite was the wings topped with hot sauce and ketchup. Not only was the food delicious and satisfying, but being in the restaurant always brought back memories of his father. Before his father was brutally murdered, the two of them would have lunch at the Harold's on 109th and Halsted at least three times a week.

Laurence devoured his chicken and fries in less than five minutes. He smiled as he put the carton of bones and used napkins back in the plastic bag on the floor. He could vividly see his old man pointing his finger and telling him to slow down and stop rushing before a bone got stuck in his throat. He always told Laurence that he would have a hard time keeping a woman if he made love as fast as he ate his food.

Laurence reclined in his gray leather seat, the smile still on his face as he thought about his dad. He couldn't believe that his father, and best friend, had been taken away from him more than twenty years ago.

Laurence Alexander Cane was an intelligent businessman who put nothing before his business. His motto was "Business first and business second." He'd believed that everything else would fall into place after that. Whether it was right or wrong, he always did what was necessary to progress. Laurence's father taught him this strict rule of business before he reached junior high school. By listening to his dad's words of wisdom and carefully studying his every move, Laurence learned how to handle himself and deal with any problems that tried to hinder his growth. He considered himself to be strong enough to handle any issue or problem that presented itself to him. After the unexpected death of his father, Laurence knew that he was mentally strong enough to deal with anything. The situation he was in now was a different type of challenge, though. It caused Laurence to question his principles and integrity as a man.

Laurence was in a situation that made him angry and happy at the same time. He hated this feeling of mixed emotions. It was time for him to sit down with his wife and come clean about certain things. He had planned to talk to her several times over the past few months but kept putting it off. Laurence usually never had a problem expressing his feelings and telling the truth. No matter how brutal and cold that truth was, he almost always spoke his mind without hesitation. Now he had the unfortunate duty of telling his wife of ten years that he had a mistress and that this woman was seven months pregnant with his child.

He knew he should've told her four months ago when he got the unexpected news, but he just couldn't look his wife in the face and break her heart with all she'd been through, not being able to bear children herself. Laurence thought about going inside the house and telling his wife everything now, but then he quickly decided against it. After a busy week of meetings and flying from coast to coast, he was too tired to argue and explain anything right now to his wife. All Laurence wanted to do was have a cocktail or two and watch a good movie. In the morning, over breakfast, he would finally tell his wife that he was going to become a father for the first time.

The bass line thumped from the speakers while Laurence sang along with his favorite rapper. He hit the rewind button one more time and continued his one-man concert. It was midnight now. Laurence hoped that Lynn, his beautiful wife, was asleep. He wanted to go in the basement and unwind. He needed some time alone to think and meditate. A cigar and a double shot of cognac were calling his name.

Every day, Laurence was becoming more and more like his father. Laurence drank cognac and loved cigars like his old man. Making money was also his number one priority and focus in life, and he was married with several women on the side just like his dad was. The difference was that his old man, or Mr. C. as he was infamously known, had babies all around the city and an expensive cocaine habit. Laurence never tried any type of drug and had no intention of ever indulging in such a dangerous habit.

The night grew colder, and Laurence was exhausted. It was time to get some rest. He snatched the key out of the ignition, grabbed his cell phone off the wood-grain dashboard, and slowly opened the door. The interior light came on, and the sound that let him know that the door was ajar began to hum. Laurence picked up the Harold's Chicken bag from the floor and jumped out of the SUV. He shut the door and ran inside the five-bedroom home. Laurence was too tired to grab his suitcase or any other personal belongings that he needed. Those things could wait until the morning. The light drizzle that was falling earlier was now a vicious downpour.

Lynn was in bed dreaming just as Laurence had hoped she would be. He kissed her on the cheek and then on her soft lips. Her eyes never opened. She must've been in a deep sleep, because she usually would wake up when Laurence came home. He smiled and walked downstairs to the spacious basement. He turned the light on over the bar.

Laurence was relieved that Lynn hadn't woken up, because if she had, she might have tried to start an argument with him. He noticed that lately his household wasn't as peaceful as it had been in the past. Every time Laurence came home, he had to hear her fuss and yell about something. Many of his wife's complaints were about the lack of time they spent together. She didn't seem to understand that in order for her to live like a queen and have the luxuries that she possessed, her husband was not going to be home too often. Laurence was out making sure that they maintained the lifestyle they were accustomed to living.

Laurence placed his black leather coat neatly across one of the barstools. The designer coat shone in the dim light because of the water that was slowly dripping from it. He took off his matching ostrich belt and laid it on top of his coat. Laurence left his cell phone on the bar. Whoever called him tonight would get nothing but an automated greeting. He slid his platinum watch off his wrist and set it next to the phone. Laurence then unbuttoned his silk gray shirt and set it neatly on the back of another stool. After he removed his socks, he would be ready to lie down and relax. Laurence had already taken off his charcoal-colored Stacy Adams shoes at the door. Any person entering his home had to remove their shoes at the front door because of the beige carpet that ran throughout the living room. He and his wife were no exception to this rule. Laurence grabbed a thick cigar and a shot glass from beneath the bar. He also grabbed a short and wide bottle of cognac that was resting by the sink before he casually walked to the entertainment area.

The home that Laurence had constructed after his wedding was as quiet as a library. The sound of the rain crashing into the three-story home was soothing and somewhat of a stress reliever for Laurence. He fell onto the Italian leather couch and poured himself a drink. For some unknown reason, the first shot always went down a little rough. He cleared his throat and filled his glass to the top again. The top-shelf cognac flowed smooth as water this time around. Laurence poured another shot, then set the glass and bottle on the square-shaped coffee table that was sitting in front of the burgundy sofa. He grabbed his cigar out of the marble ashtray that his wife bought for him while they were on their honeymoon in Italy. Laurence dipped the Cuban cigar in his drink, lit it, and then took a long and hard pull. He was in heaven, at least for the moment.

There were no phones ringing, no meetings with lawyers and accountants, no noisy clubs, and no wife in his ear complaining. This was definitely a peaceful moment for Laurence. It was just him, his cocktail, and his sweet stogie he slowly puffed on. The only other thing that would make this night perfect was a good movie. Laurence already had one in mind. He wanted to watch something with plenty of action and violence in it. The majority of his film collection consisted of horror, action, and gangster movies. Laurence grabbed the universal remote off of the coffee table and turned on the television and all of its components. He got up and walked to the wooden DVD shelf while steadily blowing smoke out of his mouth.

Training Day was going to be the flick of the night. Laurence pulled it out of the alphabetized DVD rack. He kept his movies and CDs in alphabetical order so he could find any disc without having to look all over the place. Every aspect of his life had to have order, or he wouldn't be able to function. Laurence slid the disc inside the player and sat back down. He turned the volume and bass up on the surround-sound system. The action seemed more real when the bass was booming and every sound from the movie was in stereo. Laurence was a movie buff, and watching his seventy-inch screen was a form of escape for him. He had the area soundproofed for that reason alone. The volume on the system could be at a ridiculous level, and his wife wouldn't be able to hear any of it from upstairs. When Laurence invited some of the guys over to play poker, billiards, or dominoes, they could make as much noise as they wanted and play the music as loud as they wanted, and it wouldn't disturb Lynn at all.

Smoke from the Cuban cigar floated throughout the air. Laurence drank another shot of cognac. He set the empty glass on the table, then fell back on the plush leather couch. He closed his burning eyes. Laurence continued to take pulls from the stogie as he listened to the powerful bass and sound effects that were coming from the sound system.

He was now somewhere between a state of meditation and a state of inebriation. Laurence wasn't quite daydreaming, nor was he asleep. He listened to the movie as he watched a blackout take place in his mind. Nothing could be more relaxing and self-gratifying than what he was doing right now. Not even a full-body massage on an exotic island from a beautiful woman could compare to the way he felt at this moment. The older he became, the more Laurence began to appreciate and value his quiet time alone. Exhaling smoke into the dark room was a form of therapy for Laurence. It was as if he were letting out all of his frustrations and problems that were bottled up inside. He was also relieving stress and tension at the same time. Nothing could disrupt his time of peace and meditation. Laurence wouldn't allow anything or anyone to come between him and a quiet night of rest.

Then, out of the nowhere, the telephone rang.

The disturbing phone rang again. Laurence opened his cloudy eyes and stared at the cordless handset that was sitting at the end of the beige marble table. The phone continued to ring. The annoying buzzing sound reminded Laurence of the fire alarms that he and his friends used to set off in grammar school.

The ringing suddenly came to a halt. Laurence smiled, but he was extremely upset that someone would be disrespectful enough to call his home in the middle of the night. He took a deep pull from the cigar and turned his attention to the screen. Denzel was lying on the floor smiling and talking while his partner aimed a shotgun in his face.

Laurence took one last pull from the Havana. It was as sweet as a plum and as strong as a bottle of Old Grand-Dad. He put the cigar out and set the ashtray on the table. Laurence then grabbed the bottle of cognac and poured what little was left into his shot glass. The glass was full to the rim, causing the alcohol to spill on the table. As soon as he grabbed the glass, the telephone rang again.

Laurence drank the shot of whiskey down and slammed the glass on the table so hard that it bounced up and fell on the wooden floor. Surprisingly, it didn't break. He gazed at the ringing phone with anger and contempt. If looks could kill, the cordless phone would've been buried underneath six feet of dirt. Laurence thought about grabbing his Smith & Wesson and blowing the annoying phone into pieces, but he quickly dismissed that idea due to the fact that it was insane and slightly over the edge. The phone rang for the fourth and last time. Laurence jumped up and snatched the phone from the edge of the table.

"Who the fuck is this?" Laurence barked at the unknown person on the other end of the line.

"It's me, your sista," replied the soft voice to Laurence's abusive question.

There was complete silence on the phone for a moment. Laurence hadn't spoken to his sister in over four years. The last conversation they had ended with him screaming and cursing at her and then Laurence telling her that he never wanted to see her again.

Renee, who was three years younger than Laurence, had slammed the door as she left and cried after the explosive argument. Finally, tonight, she'd decided to swallow her pride and pick up the phone and call her big brother. Renee knew that if she didn't take the initiative and make the first call, they'd spend the rest of their lives in silence. She knew how stubborn and evil Laurence could be, and she knew that he meant every word he said about not ever wanting to see her as long as he was breathing.

"Laurence," Renee said loudly. She didn't know if he was still on the line.

Laurence took a deep breath and sat back down on the sofa. Renee was the last person in the world he wanted to hear from. The sound of her voice irritated and frustrated him. But he was drunk and wanted to stay in that mode, so he decided to stay on the line and listen to whatever it was that she had to say.

"What do you want?" Laurence asked. His tone was so calm that it scared Renee for a moment.

"How are you?" Renee replied.

"Tired and drunk," Laurence said. His eyelids were going up and down like an elevator now. If Renee didn't say why she was calling in the middle of the night, she was going to quickly get the dial tone. Laurence was on the verge of passing out. The alcohol and fatigue came crashing down on his body harder than the pouring rain was pounding down on the roof.

"What you been drinking?" Renee asked rhetorically. Her big brother only drank dark liquor, and more often than not, it was cognac. He'd been drinking it since he was a teenager running the streets with his father.

"I know you have a reason for calling me this late. Why are you botherin' me?" Laurence said slowly. His eyes closed, and he began to drift into a world of darkness.

Renee hadn't realized how late it was. For three straight days she'd sat in the hospital, talking to and helping take care of her weak and ailing mother. "Mama is . . . she is very sick."

Laurence opened his burning eyes. His mother's condition must be serious, because he could hear the pain and fear in Renee's voice. Deep down inside he empathized with her, but he was so distanced from his mom that it was hard for him to show any type of emotion. "What's wrong?"

"She has cancer. Lung cancer," Renee said. Tears welled in her big brown eyes.

"Lung cancer!" Laurence stated with disbelief.

Renee began to cry. "And the doctors are only giving her less than a month . . . to live."

"When did she start smoking?" Laurence inquired. He closed his eyes again. He knew that it wouldn't be long before he dropped the phone and began snoring.

"You know she never smoked. Her fuckin' husband chain-smokes, and that's how she got . . ."

Renee couldn't talk anymore. She began to sob even harder. The thought of her mother dying in a hospital bed with tubes running from her petite body was devastating. Her pain turned into anger. Renee never liked her mother's husband, but now she despised the man. She'd pretended to like him only because she knew how happy he made her mom. Now she couldn't stand to look at his face or even be in the same room as the burly man. When he was at the hospital visiting her sick mom, Renee made sure that she was on the other side of town. Renee knew that it was wrong to think such cruel and evil thoughts, but she wished that it were the husband dying from a terrible disease instead of her loving mother.

"I should have killed him a long time ago," Laurence whispered. He hated his mother's husband with a passion. If it weren't for his sister convincing him to leave the man alone, his mom would've become a widow for the second time in her life.

Renee didn't respond to her brother's statement. In the back of her mind, she wished he would've taken care of the man who married her mother after her father was murdered. That was of no significance now. The only thing that mattered now was their mother being happy and as comfortable as possible in her last days. Renee wiped the tears from her face and tried as best she could to compose herself. She had something important to tell Laurence.

"Mama wants to see you," Renee said as she sniffled. She assumed that, given their mother's condition, Laurence would be more than willing to visit the hospital.

Laurence replied without hesitation, "I'm busy." He opened his blood red eyes and glanced at the screen. The end credits were rolling. He sat up and grabbed the remote control off the table. He turned everything off: the TV, the surround sound, and the dim light hanging over the bar. The basement was as dark as Interstate 65 after the sun heads west. Laurence didn't know if Renee was still on the line. There was just silence. He was hoping that she had finally hung up the phone so he could dive into dreamland. Laurence was about to hit the OFF button on the cordless handset when he heard Renee yelling and cursing.

"You selfish son of a bitch! Your mother is on her deathbed, and all you can think about is yo' fuckin' self!" Renee shouted.

"Fuck you, Renee," Laurence shouted back. He couldn't believe how such a perfect night of peace and relaxation was turning into a night of hell and frustration.

"No, fuck you! I see you haven't changed at all. You should be ashamed of your . . ." Renee was too frustrated and angry to finish cursing at her brother. She inhaled deeply and exhaled slowly.

"Don't ever call me. Forget I fuckin' exist," Laurence yelled into the phone. He was squeezing the phone so tight that his hand began to tremble.

"I only called you to tell you your mother—"

Renee didn't get a chance to finish yelling at Laurence. He hung the phone up in her face. Then he jumped up and threw the handset across the room as hard and fast as a pitch from a major-league baseball player. The phone crashed into something and produced a loud cracking sound before falling to the floor. Laurence felt relieved. He fell back down on the leather sofa, anticipating some much-needed sleep.

Laurence closed his burning red eyes. He was now having a difficult time falling asleep. He couldn't stop thinking about his mother being sick. The last time he saw her she was beautiful and in great shape. But that was almost twenty years ago. Laurence couldn't believe that so many years had gone by without him speaking to his mom. He blamed their lack of communication on her and the man she'd decided to marry less than two years after his father died. His mother betrayed his dad, whom he loved and deeply admired, and he could never forgive her for such an act of disloyalty. Laurence knew that his dad had women all over the city, but he just couldn't understand why his mom would even think about marrying another man. In a heated discussion, she'd told him that she had to live her life and that it was none of his business who she married or chose to sleep with.

Laurence stayed away for several years until Renee had finally convinced him to make peace with his mother. Laurence would talk to his mom once or twice a week. Renee and Laurence would take her downtown for lunch a few times out of the month. They all would laugh, cry, and reminisce about everything from their father to growing up with a mother who believed in whipping ass first and asking questions later. Everything was going great between Laurence and his mom. That all ended the day she decided to invite him to her home for dinner.

The thought of sitting at the table with his mother's second husband made Laurence angry. He thought long and hard before deciding to go, against his better judgment. It was no secret that he hated her husband, but Laurence wanted to make his mother happy, so he showed up at her home. Besides, how could he tell her no when she was making his favorite dish of macaroni and cheese with barbecue chicken?

"Hi, son," Laurence's mom said with extreme joy. She wrapped her arms around him and held him. She was excited that Laurence had finally showed up to her home for dinner and that he accepted her husband. At least, she wanted to believe that her son accepted him, even though she knew in her heart that he never would.

"Good to see ya, Ma." Laurence kissed her on the cheek.

"I love you," his mother said. She held him tighter as she looked into his eyes. She couldn't believe how much he resembled his father nowadays.

"Love you too," Laurence replied. He stared at her in disbelief. She didn't seem to be aging. She looked as young as she had when he and Renee were kids. Her frame was still small and curvy, and her peanut-butter complexion was still smooth and flawless.

Laurence took off his brown leather jacket and handed it to his mother. She hung it up in the closet behind the front door. "Your sister should be here in a minute," she said.

Laurence didn't respond. He knew in a matter of seconds he'd be officially introduced to the "new" husband, even though the marriage was going on six years now. He was uptight and a little nervous. A drink would calm him down and help him relax. The thought made him realize he'd forgotten to bring his mother a bottle of red wine. That was her drink of choice. He'd been so preoccupied with the sick thought of meeting her husband that he had driven past several liquor stores without even thinking about stopping. Laurence apologized to his mom for walking into her home empty-handed.

But Mother couldn't care less about a bottle of wine. The only thing that was important was that he was in her home. Her husband had plenty of alcohol anyway.

Mother grabbed Laurence by the hand and walked him through the living room and into the dining room, where the food would be served. The walls in the living room were covered with abstract art and cultural art. Scented candles were lit around the room, but he couldn't smell them because of the overwhelming aroma of barbecue chicken and sweet cornbread. The money green furniture sat on a beige carpet, and a huge flat-screen television was mounted on the wall to complete the decor. Tall and short plants covered the remaining areas of the dining room and living room. Walking through the house made Laurence think of the old cliché "The more things change, the more they stay the same." His mother was still a woman of style with exquisite taste in art, clothes, and furniture. She should've been an interior designer instead of an accountant, he thought.

Laurence and his mom strolled into the dining area and stopped. Her husband was sitting at the head of the table, drinking a bottle of beer. There was an awkward moment of silence. Mother squeezed her son's hand so tight that her entire arm began to tremble. Sweat began to drip from her forehead as well as her armpits. She was much more nervous than she'd expected. The two men she loved were finally going to meet each other. Mother looked up at her firstborn child and noticed that he was staring at her husband with contempt.

Laurence gazed at the man with the thick black beard and neatly trimmed Afro like he'd stolen a million dollars from him. He wanted to slap the beer out of his hand and throw the husky guy out of a window. Laurence already knew that the night was going to be long.

"Are you gon' introduce me to our guest, baby?" the husband asked. He sucked down what was left of his beer before standing.

"Yes, I am!" Mother quickly responded. She walked Laurence over to meet her spouse.

Laurence and the husband exchanged greetings. They shook each other's hand while glancing up and down at one another. Laurence was trying to break the man's hand while shaking it. The husband squeezed just as hard and winked at him with a sly grin on his round face. Laurence couldn't even fake a smile. He jerked his hand away from the husband and turned back toward his mother.

"You boys sit down. I'll bring the food out," his mother said nervously. She could sense the tension in the air, so she thought it would be a good idea to play some soothing jazz music. Some Miles Davis or Wynton Marsalis would lighten the mood.

"Let me help you, baby," the husband suggested.

Before they vanished into the kitchen to bring out the food and silverware, Laurence asked his mom where the bathroom was. He had to have a talk with himself. If he didn't, he was sure that he would lose his temper and do something to the husband that he'd live to regret. Before his mom could open her mouth, the husband was already pointing and telling him where the bathroom was.

"Thanks," Laurence said dryly. He stopped himself from telling the husband that he wasn't talking to him and that he should mind his own damn business. Laurence was slowly losing control. This man had done absolutely nothing to him except marry his mother, and he wanted to kill him. He needed to be alone for a moment so he could collect himself and simmer down. Laurence walked into the bathroom and shut the door.

If you were in a bad mood or feeling depressed over some obstacle that life threw in front of you, then stepping into the bathroom could become some form of therapy for you. The strawberry-and-watermelon-scented bathroom was extremely bright and colorful. When Mother had decorated this rainbow-colored room, her intention was probably to add some sunshine and energy to the day of whoever walked in. The shower curtain was baby blue, with canary yellow and fluorescent pink stars splashed all over the linen. The bright pink towels hanging on the silver rack were accented with small lemon-colored towels folded into triangles. The plush rug and toilet seat cover matched the shiny yellow stars spotted all over the shower curtain.

Laurence smiled as he looked around the room. His mother loved colors, bright ones at that. He turned and stared in the mirror. What he saw was an angry man who was beginning to let his rage get the best of him. His eyes were turning red like they always did when he was on the verge of losing his temper.

"*Just go out there and eat and go home. Don't say a word,*" *Laurence said to the man in the mirror.*

He turned and gazed at the door. His mother had the jazz station playing. Some good music usually made him feel better when he was angry or having mood swings. The music wasn't going to put him in a pleasant mood tonight. He was hoping that it would make the time move faster, though. He turned back to the sparkling sink and turned the faucet on. Soothing cold water on his face helped him relax a little. Laurence splashed on another handful, then turned the faucet off.

"*If you leave now, nothing's goin' to happen. But if you stay . . .*" *Laurence didn't want to finish his sentence. He knew exactly what would happen if he didn't leave right away. There would be blood. Someone would get killed. The hatred he had in his heart for his mom's husband was growing by the second. He wasn't sure how much longer he could suppress his anger and rage.*

The melodic doorbell rang. It was so loud that for a moment it drowned out the soft jazz music. Renee and her husband had joined the party. Laurence could hear their voices just as clear as he could hear Miles Davis coming through the speakers. Why hadn't he left before his sister arrived? He banged on the sink with his fist. Renee was not going to let him leave this house, no matter what explanation he came up with. She would tell him whatever he had to do could wait. Then she would put her heartbroken face on to make Laurence feel bad that he ever suggested such a thing. Renee was a master of persuasion. She always got what she wanted and when she wanted it. She was spoiled rotten, courtesy of her father, and she was just as stubborn as her mother.

There was no way out. Laurence stared at his reflection. The man in the mirror was beginning to scare him. He was losing control. Some wicked and evil spirit was taking control of his mind. Something bad was bound to happen.

There were two thumping knocks on the bathroom door. Laurence heard them but didn't react. He was in another world. Murderous and evil visions were racing across his mind faster than drivers speeding around the track in the Indy 500.

"The food is ready," Mother told Laurence. "Come and eat."

"Here I come," Laurence replied. He bent down and turned the sink back on, then soaked his face again with the brisk water. He then stood up and wiped his face with his right hand. The devilish grin on his wet face made him question his own sanity. Yes, he was slowly losing his mind. That didn't really bother Laurence at the moment. What bothered him was that his mother's husband was still breathing. The smile on his face quickly turned into a frown. Laurence was disgusted with himself. He couldn't look at his image in the mirror for another second. He hit the light switch on the wall and walked out of the bathroom.

Everyone at the table bowed their heads as Renee blessed the food. Mother and her husband sat at the head of the square table, while Renee and her husband sat between them on one side and Laurence sat by himself on the opposite side. There was very little talking at the table while everyone fixed their plates and ate. The food was so delicious that nobody could concentrate on anything other than their plates of macaroni and cheese, barbecue chicken, cornbread, and sweet potatoes. Renee broke the ice by making small talk. She talked about her plans for grad school and how she and her spouse planned on having three children. Her husband was short and skinny with a mustache as full and thick as Richard Pryor's. Laurence didn't know her mate and really had no intention of ever knowing the man. All that mattered to him was that his younger sister was happy and being taken care of.

Laurence ate his dinner like he was in the military or in some juvenile eating contest that was going to win him nothing but a blue ribbon. His mother glanced at him and smiled. She couldn't be happier. Both of her children were in her home, having dinner for the first time in years. She fought hard to hold back tears of joy that were beginning to surface.

"That was delicious, baby!" the husband exclaimed. "I'm stuffed like a pig." He pushed his empty plate away from his huge stomach.

Laurence looked at him out of the corner of his eye like he had called his mother a degrading name, like bitch or whore. He thought about sticking his fork into the man's fat neck.

Renee saw the evil look that Laurence gave the husband. She knew he despised the man, but the look Laurence gave him was of pure disgust. Renee knew that she would have to get her brother away from the husband before . . . She really didn't want to think of what could happen. She made eye contact with Laurence and smiled at him. It was the type of smile that said, "I know exactly what you're thinking, but don't let your emotions get the best of you."

"Thank you!" Mother said to her spouse. "I hope you all enjoyed it."

Everyone praised Mother and told her how good the food was. She had a huge, bright smile on her glowing face that showed her perfectly aligned white teeth. Tears began to fall from her big brown eyes like soft raindrops falling from the sky. She'd fought hard all night to hold back the tears of joy, but now they were flowing, and she couldn't stop them. Renee jumped up and wrapped her arms around her mother. Her eyes *began to water too. Their spouses looked at them and smiled.*

"Let's clear the table, Ma," Renee said while wiping tears from her face.

Mother stood up and rubbed her hand gently across her face. Her makeup was still flawless. They grabbed all of the empty plates and headed into the kitchen. Soft jazz still played in the background. When the ladies returned from the kitchen, they would be serving Mother's famous banana pudding for dessert.

"Bring me a beer, honey!" the husband requested. He reached down beside him and picked up a glass ashtray that was sitting on the floor. He then pulled out a cigarette and a purple lighter from the pocket of his white collared shirt.

Laurence and Renee's husband turned and stared at the husband like he was a fool. Neither of them smoked, and they assumed that he wouldn't be rude enough to blow smoke in their faces at the dinner table. How wrong they were.

"Bring my sons out a beer too, baby!" the husband playfully shouted. He put some fire on the end of his long cigarette and inhaled slowly.

"What the fuck did you just say?" Laurence whispered. He stared at the husband like a boxer looking into the eyes of his opponent before round one.

"He was jokin'," Renee's husband said.

Laurence gave Renee's husband a "shut the fuck up, because I wasn't talking to you" look. The short man with the thick mustache wanted to tell Laurence to calm down, but he decided against it to avoid any confrontation. He turned to see what the husband's reaction would be. To his surprise, he was smiling and puffing on his cigarette like it was the last one he'd ever taste.

"I'm not your fuckin' . . ." Laurence said to the smiling husband. He was too annoyed to finish talking. Whatever evil spirit that was lurking deep inside of him was now beginning to show its ugly face.

Laurence jumped up so fast that his wooden chair fell backward and flipped once before crashing into the wall. The husband's narrow eyes were now big as golf balls. He tried to put his hands up and defend himself, but it was too late. Laurence was already swinging at his bearded face with the thick glass ashtray. There was a loud pounding sound when the husband's 300-pound frame fell to the floor. Blood squirted from his forehead and ran down his face onto his long-sleeved shirt. The husband made a grunting sound as his eyes slowly began to close.

"Stop it, stop it! Please!" Mother screamed as she and Renee ran from the kitchen.

Mother's words fell on deaf ears. Laurence swung the ashtray again at the husband's bleeding head. This time the ashtray cracked in half. The harsh impact of the blow knocked the husband completely unconscious. Renee's husband grabbed Laurence by the arm in an attempt to restrain him. He wasn't quite strong enough, though. Laurence swung him around and threw him into the wall.

"Laurence," Renee screamed. Tears fell down her face again.

"Get out! Get out, just go," Mother yelled as she fell to her knees. She began to wail when she saw her husband lying stiff as a board with blood pouring from the deep gash in his head. By his lack of motion and sound, Mother could only presume that the worst had happened.

"Get the hell out of my home, and don't ever come back," Mother yelled at Laurence. She held on to her *husband with every ounce of strength she could gather in her body.*

"Call the police," Mother said to Renee. "Do it now."

Laurence stood watching the woman who'd carried him for nine months. How could she protect and worry about her husband and not him? What mother would abandon her child like this? Laurence didn't say another word. He headed for the front door. His mother and sister continued to cry as he walked out of the house. Laurence slammed the door behind him. He didn't know if he would ever see his sister or mom again.

It was almost four in the morning. Thinking about his mother and how she chose another man over him infuriated Laurence. He had no intention of visiting her in the hospital. She probably couldn't care less if he showed up anyway. He did promise her that night that he would kill her husband, and he meant it. Laurence planned on keeping his promise. That fat bastard would finally pay for ruining his family and turning his mother against him. Laurence smiled as he drifted into a world full of darkness and dreams, or in his case, nightmares.

Chapter Three

Soul music blared from the speakers as the bartender prepared to close for the night. The tall and voluptuous lady sang to herself as she cleared the bar of empty beer bottles and dirty glasses. Closing time was less than an hour away, so she moved swiftly to get everything cleaned and put away for the next business day.

Damien and Alex had been drinking in the lounge for more than three hours. They drank ten shots of 1800 apiece and four Long Islands between the both of them. Damien was broke. He hadn't worked in months and had less than $25 left in his savings account. Money was not an issue on this rainy October night, though. Alex had plenty of money to spend. He had $5,000 in the left and right pockets of his baggy Sean John jeans. He discreetly showed his big brother the stacks of cash that were sealed together with rubber bands.

Damien said, "What the hell you do, rob somebody?"

Alex glanced at Damien and smiled. It was one of those smiles that said, "I have a secret, and I will never tell you or anyone else." Alex turned toward the busy bartender and ordered two more shots of tequila. She obliged his request with a smile on her face. The brothers drank the shots down without limes or salt. Alex took the conversation away from him by asking Damien about his love life. "What up wit' you and Kenya?"

At first, Damien didn't say a word. He put his head down and stared blankly at the clean bar. He didn't want his little brother to see how hurt he was over Kenya. "She left me," he said finally, still staring at the wooden bar. "Called me one mornin' and said she didn't wanna be with me. Said she was in love with another man and that she was pregnant by him."

Suddenly, Damien stopped talking and dropped his drink onto the floor. Glass shattered everywhere. His eyes were glued to something in front of him.

"Hey, you a'ight? You look like you seen a ghost or something," Alex said.

"I could feel someone staring at me, right in front of me."

"What? That girl got yo' mind all messed up. Or maybe you had too much to drink," Alex suggested.

"That's it! You boys have had enough. Time to go," the tall barmaid proclaimed.

The brothers walked half a block to Damien's truck. The two-minute stroll seemed to take them an hour. All they could think about was going home and diving into bed. Being cold and drunk was a miserable feeling. Damien assumed that the freezing air would wake him up, but it didn't. The night wind blowing into his face just made him dizzier.

Before Damien and Alex hopped into the truck, an SUV pulled up right behind them. Alex immediately recognized the driver. The owner of the pearl white Cadillac Escalade jumped out of the shining SUV. He was wearing a long brown leather coat with matching leather cowboy boots. The woman sitting in the passenger seat stayed in the car and continued nodding to the music that was playing.

"Yo, Ken!" Alex yelled. He tried to stand up straight but couldn't. Alex leaned sluggishly against the passenger door of his brother's truck.

"Alex, long time no see," Ken said with a smile. He walked up to Alex and shook his hand, then gave him a one-arm hug. The strong stench of liquor on Alex's breath made Ken frown and quickly step back.

Damien climbed into the driver's seat. He was dizzy and nauseated. He didn't know whether he would vomit or pass out first. His first attempt at putting the keys in the ignition failed. Damien slowly picked the keys up from the floor and tried again. No luck. They slipped out of his hand and bounced on the floor again. He had a hard time finding them this time. He ran his hand across the carpet several times before finding them by his left foot. He slowly and carefully inserted the key into the ignition before starting the truck. The radio blasted on at a disturbingly high volume. Damien turned the radio off and turned the heat up. He blew the horn at Alex.

"You 'bout to open a shop?" Alex asked Ken. He didn't know how much longer he'd be able to stand on his legs.

"Yeah, the grand openin' is tomorrow. You should come and check it out," Ken replied. He pulled out a black business card from his coat pocket and handed it to Alex.

Alex stared at the card. The alcohol caused him to see three cards instead of one. He stuck the card in the back pocket of his baggy jeans. "You need a barber? 'Cause my brotha can really cut."

"Actually, I do," Ken answered. He didn't know why he answered Alex. He could see and smell just how drunk he was. His red eyes were closed before he could finish telling Ken that Damien knew how to cut hair. Ken held Alex's shoulder while he opened the car door for him. He could see Damien hugging the steering wheel with his face buried in his coat. They were never going to make it home in this condition, Ken thought. He helped Alex climb into the truck by holding him up and pushing him inside.

Damien jumped up from the steering wheel. He thought he was in bed. He was disappointed when he realized he was still sitting in his car. Damien put the truck in gear and slowly drove home.

Chapter Four

The strong winds and bitter-cold air of yesterday were gone. The pouring rain was heading south, and the dark gray clouds that loomed in the sky were now snow white. The bright sun shone across the blue sky as if it were the first day of summer. Laurence sat in his spacious kitchen reading the newspaper while the sun beamed through the windows and patio door. The radio sitting on the counter was tuned to the old-school soul station. The digital clock on the electric stove read 6:30. The morning hours had a creepy way of quickly passing by, Laurence thought.

Laurence had had a difficult time sleeping. The thought of his mother having cancer disturbed his sleep. At 4:30 he'd decided to get up and get his day started. Laurence shaved and took a long, hot shower. He slipped into his money green silk pajamas and headed for the kitchen. Laurence turned the radio on, then made a pot of coffee. He read the newspaper and sipped his coffee while waiting for his wife to come downstairs and make breakfast.

After reading the sports section of the paper, Laurence poured himself another cup of coffee. He liked his coffee with lots of cream and very little sugar. He thought about throwing a pinch of whiskey in but decided to wait. He was hungry, and the alcohol would do nothing but suppress his appetite and make him want to drink more.

He sat back down at the glass kitchen table and sipped his piping hot coffee while reading the newspaper backward. Laurence wondered if his wife was still asleep. He was willing to bet a million dollars that she was in bed watching Food Network or some reality show. Cooking shows and reality TV were her favorites, besides the dramatic movies on Lifetime.

Laurence couldn't concentrate any longer. He set the newspaper on the table and stared out the window. He was upset with his sister for calling him in the middle of the night and giving him such bad news. Knowing that the woman who gave birth to him was losing her life really disturbed Laurence. He was affected more than he thought he would be. He still had no intention of visiting his ailing mother, but the thought of her dying was making him angry. He had other situations in his life that needed his immediate attention, like explaining to his wife about his mistress carrying his child.

In his peripheral vision, Laurence saw his wife walk into the spotless kitchen. His heart began to beat faster as he rubbed his fingers together as if they were itching. Being nervous was uncharacteristic of Laurence.

"Good mornin'," his wife said as she walked up to him and kissed his cheek.

"Good mornin'," Laurence replied. He could tell by the worried look on her face that something was bothering her.

"Want some breakfast?" she asked, taking a carton of orange juice from the stainless-steel refrigerator.

"Some eggs, grits, and toast would be nice. That should hold me 'til lunch," Laurence responded while staring at his wife. Something was on her mind. He didn't know exactly what it was, but Laurence could tell that she was nervous about something.

She grabbed the eggs, bread, cheese, and butter from the refrigerator. She set everything on the blue marble countertop before reaching above the sink for a pan and a pot. One of the reasons she watched Food Network was to learn about new meals and desserts that she could create. Cooking was just one of her many hobbies. "My famous cheese omelet smothered in grits comin' right up."

Laurence finished what was left of his coffee. This was the perfect time to tell her about the unborn child. He was nervous, but he knew that this couldn't stay a secret any longer. Each day that went by without her knowing was making the situation worse. Laurence didn't really know how to start such a conversation. "Are you eatin' with me, baby?"

"I'm not hungry," she said. "This glass of juice will be fine for now."

"You havin' breakfast after you work out?"

"I'm not gonna work out today," she said as she moved around the kitchen like an Iron Chef.

Laurence was now sure that something was disturbing his wife. She was skipping her morning workout and breakfast, which were two things she did religiously every morning. "What's wrong, Lynn?" Laurence asked curiously.

"I'm just a little tired. I didn't sleep very well," she said with a half-smile on her face.

"I didn't sleep too good either," Laurence replied. He was staring at his wife as she paced the kitchen in a small pink T-shirt and a pair of gray pajama pants that defined all of her womanly curves. Her hair was pulled back into a ponytail, and her flawless caramel complexion seemed to glow in the morning sun. She had to be the sexiest woman Laurence had ever laid eyes on.

"Who was that calling here late last night?" Lynn asked Laurence. She'd guessed that it was just her brother calling for the umpteenth time, but she wanted to see if Laurence was going to tell her the truth.

Laurence stared at his wife. He didn't want to think or talk about the conversation he'd had with his sister last night. As far as he was concerned, she didn't exist. He wasn't going to tell his wife about his mother's condition, because he already knew what she thought about the situation and what she would tell him to do.

Then he realized she would find out eventually, so he decided to tell her everything. Today was going to be the day that he came clean about everything to his wife. Well, almost everything. Laurence was one who believed that a man should keep a little mystery surrounding himself.

"My damn sista," Laurence finally answered. He could feel himself becoming agitated at the very thought of Renee.

Lynn was shocked by his answer. She stopped whipping the eggs she'd cracked into a glass bowl. Why would his sister call in the middle of the night when she hadn't called the house in years? Renee was the last person on earth she'd have expected to call her house. Laurence was lying, and she knew why he was telling a story. Lynn instantly became upset. "So, my brother did not call here last night?" she asked Laurence with an attitude.

"Why in the hell would yo' brotha call here at that time of the mornin'?" Laurence responded. He was trying not to raise his voice, but he could feel his temper slowly boiling.

"You tell me why Renee of all people would call here at two in the damn morning," Lynn snapped back.

Laurence took a deep breath. He knew arguing with his wife would be futile and a waste of energy. He picked the paper up from the table and stared at the front page. Lynn watched him and waited for his response as he glared at the president's picture on the newspaper. She reminded him of his mother when she used to stand with her hands on her hips, gazing down at him, waiting patiently for him to confess to a lie he'd told her. "Our mother is in the hospital dying from cancer," Laurence said dryly. He put the paper down and looked at his wife.

The kitchen seemed to stand still for a moment. The only noise that could be heard was the animated disc jockey on the soul station running his mouth about a concert the station was staging for Halloween. Lynn was speechless. Even though Laurence wasn't close to his mother anymore, she could still see the pain in his eyes. She wished there were something she could do to make him feel better.

"It's funny. She's dying from lung cancer, and she neva smoked a day in her life," Laurence said. He could feel his stomach turning upside down and his appetite waning.

Lynn ran over to him and gave him a big hug and a kiss. The tears that were forming in her brown eyes began to fall down her face. "You have to go see her," she whispered softly in his ear.

"She don't wanna see me!"

"Why would you say something like that?"

"Believe me, she ain't thinkin' 'bout me."

"She is sick. It just might make her feel better to see your face," Lynn said loudly. She let Laurence go, then walked back to the stove to continue making breakfast.

"Maybe I'll try to go and see her next week. I'm too busy right now," Laurence advised her. He had no intention of ever going to the hospital. He hoped his wife would be satisfied with his response and change the subject.

"Next week!" Lynn yelled. "What if she doesn't make it to next week? You wanna live with that on your conscience? Knowing your mother was sick and you wouldn't even take the time to go and visit her?"

Laurence became irritated. "Her daughter and her fuckin' husband will be right by her side. She really wouldn't notice if I—"

"You selfish bastard, you!" Lynn yelled, cutting his words short. "How heartless can you be? You should be running to that damn hospital to see your mama. If she dies, you're going to hate yourself for not going."

"I told you I was goin'. Not today, though," Laurence said with a frown. He was becoming extremely frustrated and tired of his wife trying to make him feel guilty about the situation. He never should've mentioned his mother having cancer and being in the hospital. Laurence knew how emotional and sympathetic Lynn was at times. "This discussion is over. I don't wanna talk about my mother anymore," Laurence said. The stern tone of his deep voice let Lynn know that the conversation was dead for now.

"Fine!" she replied. Lynn mumbled something under her breath that was unclear to her husband. He hated more than anything else when she did that. Laurence stared at her for a few seconds.

"Why would you think that your brotha called here last night?" Laurence asked her curiously.

"I thought he might have called," she responded. Her voice was barely above a whisper.

"Called for what?" Laurence shot back at her. He could feel his temper steadily rising. His wife was hiding something from him. That was why she was acting strange.

"To see if—"

"Speak up. I can't hear you," Laurence interrupted. He hated when people didn't make eye contact while talking to him. His father always told him that that was a sign of weakness and that the person was probably not telling the truth. Not only was Lynn not looking at him, but her back was turned to Laurence. This infuriated him. He impatiently tapped his fingers on the table, waiting for Lynn to respond.

Lynn turned around to face her husband. His face was as red as a bottle of ketchup. She really wasn't in the mood to discuss anything with him, but he was going to continue asking her questions until he got a response. "My mother called yesterday and told me that my brotha was in jail," she said dryly.

"In jail? What did he do now?"

Lynn turned back around to turn the stove off. She placed the cheese omelet on a plate, then poured the thick and cheesy grits on top of it. The toaster popped, and she spread butter on the brown toast before placing it on the plate. Lynn set the hot black plate down in front of her husband, who was still waiting for her to answer his question. "Enjoy," she said. Lynn walked to the drawer next to the dishwasher and pulled out a shiny fork and knife. She set the silverware on the table next to her husband.

"Thank you," Laurence said, picking up the fork. "Now tell me why yo' brotha is locked up."

Lynn was silent for a moment. She hated talking to her husband about her younger brother because she knew how he despised him. Her brother needed their help now more than ever, so she had to tell Laurence the story that her mother had told her. "Some girl he met in a nightclub accused him of raping her and, um, robbing her of seventy-five hundred dollars," Lynn confessed. She stared directly into Laurence's eyes. She tried hard to hold back a flood of tears.

"Ha, ha, ha!" Laurence laughed sarcastically, taking the fork out of his mouth.

"What the hell are you laughing at?" Lynn said angrily. The tears she'd been holding in began to slowly slide down her face. "What the fuck is so funny?"

Laurence looked at his sobbing wife with a grin on his face. He couldn't believe the story she'd just told him. He took another bite of his meatless omelet, then set the fork down on his half-empty plate. The smirk on his face quickly faded into a sinister frown. "I'll tell you what is so damn funny. Yo' good-for-nothin' brotha is a joke to me. He goes from robbin' people to rapin' women. Fuck him! He needs to spend the rest of his fuckin' life behind bars."

"We don't know if it's true," Lynn cried. Growing up, Lynn and her baby brother were closer than peanut butter and jelly. To lose him in the penal system for more than twenty years would be devastating to her and her mother.

"Are you serious? He's a career criminal, and a bad one at that. I'm willing to bet everything I possess that he raped that woman," Laurence said, shaking his head in disbelief.

"I don't believe one word of that bullshit!" Lynn replied as she wiped the tears from her face.

"You should, because you know he ain't shit!" Laurence responded with a smile. He picked up his fork and ate what was left on his plate.

"I know he didn't rape anyone! I know he didn't do anything like that," Lynn said with passion and conviction. "My brotha is not that type of person."

Laurence smiled and shook his head while he continued eating. He couldn't believe how naive his wife was when it came to her brother. If she saw him snatch an old lady's purse with her own two eyes, she still would say that he didn't do it. She would testify that it was someone who looked like him. *How stupid can she be?* Laurence wondered.

"Why the hell are you still smiling?" Lynn asked curiously. "He's in serious trouble, and we have to help him before he gets convicted of a crime we know he did not commit."

Laurence stated, "Help?" He was completely shocked that she would use that word and her brother in the same sentence. After he failed to pay him back the $2,000 he'd loaned him to stop some loan shark from breaking his neck, he vowed to never help him ever again in life. The only reason Laurence didn't throw him in the middle of Lake Michigan was because he knew how much his wife loved him.

"Yes, he really needs our help. His bail is set at $250,000."

"I wouldn't give a fuck if it were $2.50," Laurence said calmly. He tossed the fork on the empty plate, then stood up.

"You selfish son of a bitch!" Lynn yelled. "What do you have to lose by helpin' someone?"

"I told you I was never dealin' with your brotha again. He already screwed me once. No, we can't help him, so don't ever ask me again. As far as I'm concerned, he's dead," Laurence said with a sinister look on his face.

"Fuck you! We don't need your help!" Lynn screamed at Laurence. She stormed out of the kitchen and ran upstairs. A door slammed shut moments later.

Laurence was about to follow her and ask her why she was slamming doors in the house. That would just make the situation worse, though, so he decided to sit back down and meditate. Laurence was mad at himself because he didn't get a chance to talk to his wife about the baby. He'd wasted his morning talking about her brother of all people. "Damn!" Laurence said with frustration as he banged his hand on the glass table for emphasis.

Laurence merged onto the Dan Ryan Expressway and headed north. He was surprised by how fast he'd gotten dressed and out of the house. In less than ten minutes he had slipped into a pair of black slacks, a matching sweater, and a pair of casual loafers. Laurence grabbed his leather jacket to complete his all-black ensemble, then left the house. He didn't even say goodbye to his wife. He was now driving downtown to his friend's condo. She was at work, so he would have plenty of time to relax and think.

Traffic on the expressway was moving at a snail's pace because of the construction work that was taking place, but Laurence didn't mind. He wasn't in a hurry to get anywhere. This traffic delay gave him more time to think and reflect. Usually Laurence would have the radio or one of his CDs playing, but this bright morning he decided to do without any music or noise. He was oblivious even to the construction workers' loud machines as he daydreamed about his deceased father. Riding downtown always made him reminisce about his father and how he used to take him to poker parties at his buddy's penthouse on Lake Shore Drive.

Laurence tried to think of something more positive, but he couldn't. The day his old man was murdered kept playing in his head like an infomercial on TV late at night. Even though it was twenty years ago, Laurence still remembered the entire incident like it had happened just yesterday.

He rode shotgun in his dad's '76 Cadillac Fleetwood sedan, listening to Al Green on the 8-track player. His dad loved his Fleetwood, but he used to say that the Coupe de Ville was his favorite. "Pretty as ya mama," were his exact words. They cruised through the city in the burgundy sedan, discussing Laurence's future. They passed a pint of Crown Royal back and forth to one another. They'd become drinking partners ever since Laurence graduated high school. His mother didn't like that her husband drank with their son and taught him a lot of bad ways, but she had no control over the situation. One night, they'd had a huge argument about Laurence growing up too fast, and all he could remember was his father telling her that he'd rather his boy drink and have fun with him than with some bums in the streets who didn't give a shit about him.

Laurence could look in his father's face and see that he was high. His eyes were glassy and bloodshot because of the whiskey and the white lines he snorted up his nose.

Al Green sang about how he was "tired of being alone" as Laurence and his dad cruised through the city. After making two sharp left turns, they ended up in an alley and parked behind a stranger's garage. Laurence Sr. put the car in first gear as he explained to his son what they were doing in a dark and deserted alley.

"I gotta go collect my money, son," he told Laurence. He reached over Laurence and pulled a small black revolver out of the glove compartment.

Laurence Sr. cocked the pistol and stuck it inside his coat pocket. He could see the worried look on his boy's face. He patted him on his head and assured him that everything was all right. He would be back in five minutes so they could finish driving around and hanging out. Five minutes or less, he assured Laurence. Laurence Sr. knew that it wouldn't take him longer than that to kill two people. Two thieves owed him thousands of dollars and made no efforts to repay him. He had no choice but to collect on his debt with violence. He jumped out of the Caddy and shut the door quietly behind him.

That was the last time Laurence saw his father alive. He walked into that dark house and was brutally stabbed nine times in the back.

Tears dripped from his face as Laurence realized that he was about to drive past his exit. He quickly merged to the right lane, then jumped off the expressway. Whenever he thought about his dad being murdered, he became extremely sad and full of rage. What really made Laurence's skin crawl was the fact that the person who murdered his dad was never found. He promised himself and his father that he would personally find the killer and make him die a slow and painful death.

Laurence hadn't yet found the killer, nor had the police. He knew that one day he'd get lucky and run across the killer or someone very close to him. Someone was going to pay a huge price for his father dying. That inevitable day was coming. The thought of coming face-to-face with the man who murdered his father put a wicked smile on Laurence's face.

Laurence reached his destination. He gave the valet his car and walked into the high-rise building. The elevator stopped on the twenty-fifth floor. As the doors opened, Laurence stepped off and turned left. He calmly walked to the end of the bright hallway. He stopped in front of apartment 2514. He reached in his pocket and pulled out his keys. The small L.C. initials that hung from his key ring swung back and forth as he stuck the key into the door.

Laurence hung his leather jacket in the closet. He opened the linen closet and grabbed a beige blanket and a pillow. The bedroom door was closed, so he opened it out of curiosity. The bedroom looked just as Laurence expected it to look. There were bras and panties on the floor. The sheets and blanket were falling off the bed, and there were high heels and gym shoes scattered all over the place. Clothes covered the bed and some parts of the cream carpet. *How can this woman live in chaos like this?* Laurence asked himself. He shook his head in disbelief as he closed the door. How could she keep the rest of her apartment spotless and immaculate and then have her bedroom look like a pack of wild dogs had run through it? He laughed as he headed toward the living room.

After pouring a tall glass of vodka with a splash of or-ange-pineapple juice, Laurence sat down on the plush sofa. He grabbed the remote and turned the TV on. *Finally, some peace.* Laurence drank vodka and watched a sports network until he eventually dozed off.

Chapter Five

"Help me," Damien screamed out after hearing footsteps in the dark. The menacing footsteps became louder as they approached Damien. The person coming toward him was either a man with some heavy cowboy boots on or a woman with some six-inch heels on her feet. The thumping sound of the heels hitting the floor became louder and more unsettling to Damien. Whoever or whatever was creeping up on him in the darkness would have to catch him.

He attempted to run, but his efforts were futile. It was like Damien was running on a treadmill, because all he was doing was moving in the same place. Damien tried to scream for help again. No words came out of his dry mouth this time. All he could do was stand there and wait.

The pounding steps moved faster, and they were a lot closer now. Damien looked around in the darkness hoping he would see someone or something. There was nothing. He closed his eyes. There was an eerie silence in the building. The footsteps had suddenly stopped.

Damien kept his eyes shut. He was trembling so violently that you would've thought he had been lying in a tub of ice. His throat was so dry that he couldn't swallow. It burned like hell every time Damien tried. Fear had taken possession of his body. Damien couldn't fight it even if he wanted to. He opened his eyes.

Out of the darkness, a slender hand grabbed him around the neck and lifted his numb body up off the floor. Whatever this was had extremely long fingernails. Damien could feel them gripping his neck. They were as sharp as tiger claws. He looked down through watery eyes, and to his surprise, he could see the face of the person who was about to cut his throat. It was a woman, and she looked angry.

She had thick eyebrows that pointed up at the end of them. Her slanted eyes seemed to be a mixture of red and blue. Her left hand gleamed in the dark, and without hesitation, she viciously scratched Damien across his face. He screamed for help.

"Stop," Damien yelled as he jumped up out of his deep sleep. He looked around the room to see exactly where he was. When he saw Alex eating a personal pizza on the couch next to him, he knew that he was in his parents' home. *Thank God!* He felt his face and his neck to make sure there weren't any cuts or scratches on them. He noticed his brother staring at him.

"What the hell is wrong with you?" Alex asked curiously, taking a huge bite of his hot pizza.

"I just had a bad dream, that's all."

"That's why you screamin' like a girl?" Alex said.

"Shut up. I thought I was being killed."

"That is pretty scary. I had a scary dream too," Alex replied.

"'Bout what?" Damien asked as he stretched and yawned.

"That I was broke!" he answered, then laughed and took another bite of his pizza.

"Let's get ready so we can go to the barbershop," Damien said, getting up.

***

Damien turned the ignition off. He and Alex hopped out of the car. They walked to the front door and noticed a huge sign in the window that read, FREE HAIRCUTS TO-DAY.

Alex opened the glass door, and they walked inside. The first thing they noticed was how crowded the shop was. Women talked among themselves about how beautiful the place was decorated. Kids ate cake and ice cream that the owner had supplied, and the men either played some of the video games that stood against the wall or waited patiently to get their free haircut. Music played while everyone in the shop laughed and talked about current events and sports. Damien knew he was going to have fun working at the shop. Hopefully he could make a lot of money in the process. He was amazed at how the place looked. Money was definitely not a factor when Ken designed and decorated this shop.

The hardwood floors in the shop shone and sparkled so brightly that Damien was almost scared to walk on them. Four twenty-seven-inch flat screens hung in the air while the huge seventy-nine-inch television sat in the back of the shop for everyone to see. The TVs were turned off right now while the customers and workers enjoyed the music. Small surround-sound speakers hung in the air while the actual system sat next to the big-screen TV. The powerful bass that came from the speakers was reminiscent of the sound in a movie theater. A modern-day jukebox sat against the wall next to classic video games such as *Pac-Man, OutRun,* and *Mike Tyson's Punch-Out!!* On the other side of the video games was a fruit juice machine. Ken thought it would be healthier to have a juice machine in the shop rather than a pop machine. Next to the drink machine stood a snack machine that held chips and cookies. There was not a water fountain in the shop.

Damien figured Ken purposely left this out so customers could spend their money buying juice.

"What up, Ken?" Alex asked. He introduced Ken to his older brother.

"I see you feeling a lot betta today, Alex," Ken said.

"Oh, yeah! I'm good now," Alex shot back.

"That's good to hear. You ready to make some money?" Ken asked, looking Damien straight in the face.

"Yes, I am!" Damien answered.

"That's what I wanna hear, some excitement! Let's go in the back to my office and discuss a few things," said Ken. "Alex, make yourself at home. There's food, drinks, and plenty of single women in here."

After a short conversation with Ken, and some hot wings, Damien was back at home in his room. All he wanted to do was lie in bed and go to sleep. Alone in his dark and quiet room was how Damien wanted to spend his night. He was on the verge of depression, and he was drinking more than he ever had. Damien didn't know if he was ever going to get the dark cloud resting above his head to leave.

Whatever his parents were watching on television must've been hilarious, because they were laughing nonstop. The giggling and chatter began to aggravate Damien, so he put his pillow over his head. That didn't work. A loud knock on the door startled Damien, but not enough for him to pull his head up from the pillow.

"Telephone, son," Pops said loudly as he opened the door. He was holding a cordless phone in one hand and a bottle of beer in the other.

Damien pulled his head up and turned around. "You know who this is?" he asked.

"I sure don't. Now here, take the phone so I can get back to my movie," Pops replied. He handed his son the cordless phone, then shut the door.

Damien stared at the phone for a moment, then thought about just hanging up on whoever was on the line. He wasn't feeling good and was in no mood to talk to anyone. What he should've done was tell his parents that if anyone called for him, just take a message. *Too late now.* He cleared his throat and answered the call.

"Yeah, hello," he said dryly.

The soft and sexy voice of a woman was on the line. "How you doin', Damien?" she calmly asked.

Damien pulled the phone away from his face in shock. It was Kenya. She had finally called him after all these months. Why was she calling? What did she want? And why did she leave him? These were all questions that Damien wanted to ask her. He put the phone back to his face. "I'm doing good, and you?" he asked, trying his best to sound convincing.

"I'm fine," she said. "I just wanted to call you and see how you were doin'. I tried callin' your cell phone. Then I called your job, and they told me you were no longer employed there."

"I'm cutting hair in the barbershop now."

"That's real good, baby. Which one?"

"A shop in the suburbs."

"I'll come and take you to lunch one day. We have a lot to talk about."

"We really don't, but okay," Damien said with hesitation.

"I have to go now. Take care of yourself." Kenya hung up the phone before Damien could say another word.

Damien listened to the dial tone. He was confused. Why would she call him after all this time and then hang up after only a minute of conversation? He clicked the

OFF button on the phone. Damien vowed to never speak to her again. And having lunch with her was definitely out of the question. She was the cause of his misery and pain. Their relationship was nothing but a joke to her. Damien was glad she'd called, because he needed some type of closure to their relationship. It was now over.

Little did Damien know this wouldn't be the last conversation between him and Kenya.

Chapter Six

Laurence popped another bottle of champagne. He filled his glass up until the bubbles were running over onto the table. He was slightly buzzed and feeling like a million dollars. The nap he'd taken earlier in the day had a lot to do with his positive energy. After setting the cold bottle down, Laurence took a napkin and wiped the alcohol up from the wooden table. He laughed and sipped on his expensive champagne while watching Harry dance with two female friends of his.

"I need some help!" Harry screamed at Laurence. His long and skinny arms were almost touching the ceiling as they waved side to side.

"You can handle it!" Laurence yelled over the loud music. He picked the bottle of bubbly back up and poured himself another drink. This time he made sure not to spill any on the table. He didn't want the table to be sticky and dirty before the dominoes game started.

"Drink up!" Laurence said, holding his glass in the air.

Harry handed Laurence a Cuban cigar. Then the doorbell rang. "It's about time!" Harry said before running upstairs to open the door.

This time Laurence didn't bother pouring himself another drink. He set his glass down and picked up the bottle that was resting on the table. There was nothing better than cold champagne right out of the bottle. Laurence enjoyed his drink while he watched the girls dance to the house music that was blasting.

Laurence stopped watching the girls when Harry walked back downstairs with the dominoes players.

Laurence and Spoon greeted each other and shook hands. Laurence couldn't believe how gaudy and excessive his jewelry was. He looked like someone straight out of a hip-hop video. The earrings he wore in both ears were as big as ice cubes. Two of his iced-out chains hung down to his crotch, huge diamond rings covered all of his fingers except his thumb and trigger finger, and the platinum watch and bracelets on his wrists were so big that Laurence wondered whether they were real. He already knew the answer, but who was he to question another man's style?

Laurence took one long pull from his cigar, then put it out. He slid the ashtray to the side and grabbed the bottle of champagne. He drank from the bottle like a thirsty kid drinks from a water fountain.

"Dat's why I don't smoke cigars. They stink like a mutha," Spoon blurted out.

Laurence pulled the bottle from his mouth, then turned and gave Spoon a look so cold and evil that he couldn't do anything but turn his head and look the other way. "Bring some more bottles in here. We runnin' low," he said to Harry.

"How you ladies doin' tonight?" Petey asked while watching them browse through the selection of movies.

"We're fine," they both answered in unison.

Harry came to the table with three tall, fancy glasses, two ice-cold bottles of champagne, and the wooden box that held the bones. "Let's get it on, boys!"

"Do you have any Hennessy?" Spoon asked.

"I got whateva you wanna drink. You need some ice and a chaser?"

"Naw, I like it straight up," Spoon replied.

"Cool. I'll bring you the whole bottle back, player. A drunk man can't win in this house," Harry said. He ran off to the bar again.

Petey dumped the bones out of the box and onto the table. He slid the box to the side and began washing the dominos together with his huge hands. Spoon opened one of the bottles of bubbly while Laurence was busy guzzling out of the bottle in his hand.

Laurence slammed the empty bottle on the table. Petey and Spoon looked at him like he was crazy. He was buzzed and feeling great. That was why he loved drinking champagne, because he could drink it all night and still have energy. The hard alcohol didn't do anything but put him to sleep after so much of it. "We need a pen and a piece of paper," he yelled out to Harry.

Harry came back to the table with a gallon of Hennessy and a yellow notepad and pen in his hands. He set the bottle in front of Spoon, then sat down at the end of the table. Laurence was sitting at the other end, while Petey and Spoon were in the middle. "Who wanna keep score?" he asked the table.

"Not me! I cheat too much," Petey answered, laughing.

"Make the rookie keep score," Laurence said.

"Dat's right! You gotta pay dues up in here," Harry said. He pushed the pad and pen over to Spoon, who was sitting to the right of Laurence.

"It's like dat, huh?" Spoon asked while filling his glass with champagne.

"Yes, it is! Now fill up these glasses, rookie!" Petey announced. They all held their glasses in the middle of the table while Spoon poured champagne into them.

The dominoes game was intense. No one was talking anymore. Everyone had their head down studying the board and the bones in their hands. Everyone at the table was just twenty points away from winning. It was Harry's turn to play, and he was taking forever as usual. His concentration was broken by the silence that fell upon the entire room. The music that was playing suddenly stopped. Although he wasn't paying any attention to it, he still needed to hear some type of noise in the room. The dead silence in the basement drove him crazy and made him nervous. Harry couldn't be in the house without the TV or radio turned on. It somehow helped him think and relax at the same time.

"What happened to the music?" he asked the girls. Harry never took his squinting eyes off the bones he was holding.

"We turned it off. We finally found a good movie to watch," the short lady said.

"Well, put somethin' on. It's too damn quiet up in here," Harry replied with frustration.

"Just play! You slowin' the game down," Laurence said. He picked his glass up and took a sip of the expensive champagne. He had a smirk on his face because he just knew that he had the game-winning domino in his hand.

"I wanna see da strippas!" Spoon blurted out. He was filling his glass with Hennessy instead of champagne this time.

Laurence glanced at Spoon for a second with that evil glare. He hated being around people who were wild and couldn't exercise any self-control. He knew that the more this guy drank, the more obnoxious and disrespectful he would become.

Harry slammed his domino on the table so hard that all of the bones lying down jumped up in the air. "Domino," he yelled. He smacked the domino on the table one more time for emphasis.

"Damn," Petey said before refilling his glass with champagne.

"I knew you had that domino," Spoon said, shaking his head in disbelief.

"What took you so damn long to play it? You need me to go get ya glasses?" Laurence yelled from across the table.

"Don't worry about me and how I win. Here, wash 'em, rookie," Harry replied as he pushed all of the bones in front of Spoon.

Seven games later, Laurence was still winless. Harry won the first four games and Spoon somehow managed to win the last three games. He was running his mouth and talking plenty of trash now. Laurence was becoming extremely irritated by his loud mouth and by the fact that he couldn't win a damn game.

"Afta I win dis game, it'll be fo' apiece, Big Harry," Spoon said with confidence. He poured himself another glass of Hennessy. He didn't know how many glasses he had drunk. All Spoon knew was that he was drunk and feeling good. Everyone at the table was intoxicated. They had drunk five bottles of champagne in an hour.

"That was the last game you gon' win tonight," Harry retorted. "We can go to the poker table after this one and play for some big chips."

"I gotta win at least one before I leave," Laurence said aloud. He washed the bones and threw them in the middle of the table. They all grabbed seven apiece, and then the game started.

Spoon was in a zone. He scored a hundred points before anyone else at the table had fifty. He was scoring and running his mouth at the same time while everyone else was quiet trying to figure out what they were doing wrong.

"Afta I win dis one, we can play one-on-one. 'Cause dez cats ain't doing nothin' but taking up space," Spoon shouted to Harry. "They can go sit with the girls and watch a movie or something."

Laurence was sick and tired of hearing Spoon's big mouth. He'd held his tongue all night, but now he had to say something. If he were winning, this motormouth wouldn't even be an issue, but since he hadn't won a single game, every word that Spoon said disturbed him.

Before he could tell Spoon to shut the fuck up, his cell phone rang. Laurence snatched the phone off his hip and flipped it open. He did not recognize the number, so he closed the phone and placed it back on his hip. Laurence stared at his dominos for a few seconds, and then he made a play. He didn't score. Spoon came right behind him and scored fifteen points. Laurence was furious.

"If you po' me anotha glass of Henny, I might let you win da next game," Spoon said to Laurence. He was smiling and rocking his shoulders from side to side as he guzzled the rest of his drink.

Laurence stared at Spoon with malice in his red eyes. He wanted to take those chains that he was wearing and hang him from a tree with them. Not only was he talking trash, but now he was dancing and gloating like he had won the lottery or some type of prize. This really made Laurence uneasy. He was going to knock this guy's teeth out of his mouth if he said one more word to him. His wicked thoughts were interrupted by the ringing of his cell phone again.

Laurence snatched the phone off his hip with so much force that he broke the clip in half. He flipped it open and saw the same unrecognizable number on the blue screen. This time he pressed SEND. "Who the fuck is dis?" he barked at the person on the other end. Laurence became quiet for a moment. Everyone at the table was looking at him. The girls turned to see what was going on.

"When I told you to neva call me anymore, I meant it. I don't wanna talk to you ever again," Laurence said calmly. He hung the phone up after those final words. Maybe now his sister would get the message and leave him alone for good. She had called again to tell him that their mother was dying and that she really wanted to see him before she passed on.

"You a'ight?" Harry asked with concern.

"I'm cool," Laurence replied.

"You sho? 'Cause we can always finish this anotha time if you gotta go," Petey said. "We ain't havin' no luck tonight anyway."

"Let's at least finish this last game," Laurence said. His sister's phone call really disturbed him. He could feel his mood changing by the second. Anger quickly began to take over his body and his emotions.

"The way you been losin' all night, you should wanna quit! Just throw the towel in now and go home!" Spoon shouted. They all could tell that he was drunk by the way he was beginning to slur his words. "Afta I win this shit, you can go finish screamin' on the phone to—"

Before Spoon could say another word, Laurence was already swinging a champagne bottle across his forehead. Glass and blood splattered everywhere as Spoon fell backward in his chair and onto the floor. His eyes were closed as blood gushed from the open wound in his head.

Laurence didn't know or care if he was dead or unconscious. All he knew was that Spoon wasn't running his mouth anymore. Laurence stood over Spoon's still body with only the neck of the bottle left in his hand. He dropped the remains of the champagne bottle on the floor and calmly walked out of the basement like nothing had happened. He could hear the girls screaming in fear as Harry and Petey attempted to wake Spoon up from his unconscious state.

Drunk and exhausted would be two ways to describe how Laurence felt. All he wanted to do was go home and pass out on the couch. This day couldn't end fast enough for him. The things that were going on his life were slowly causing him to revert to his old ways. He hated his reckless behavior, but somehow, he had very little control over it. Laurence was becoming more violent and emotional about small things, and his patience was on the edge of being nonexistent. That was why he couldn't talk to his sister. All she did was cry and make excuses for their mother's actions, and that infuriated Laurence. The reality of the situation was that their mother chose another man over her kids and was now dealing with the consequences of that decision. As badly as Laurence wanted to go see his mother, he just couldn't. He didn't want to talk to her or even look at her.

He hated himself for feeling such animosity toward the woman who gave birth to him. The thought of her dying and being sick made Laurence miserable and depressed. He was actually ashamed of the feelings he harbored toward his family. His father was definitely rolling over in his grave about his attitude toward his sister and mom. Tears began to fall from Laurence's red eyes. The pain that he felt in his heart was inexplicable.

Laurence apologized to his dad for his selfish behavior. He wiped the tears from his face and drove home in complete silence. He was mentally exhausted and on the verge of losing his mind.

Chapter Seven

Damien opened his eyes. He could tell by the loud sounds of the birds chirping and the dark shadow that covered half the room that it was early in the morning. It was definitely too early for him to get out of bed. He didn't have to be at the barbershop until ten. Damien looked at the alarm clock and saw that it was only a few minutes past six. He could sleep for another two hours then wake up and get ready for work. He threw the blanket over his head and closed his eyes. Damien began to drift into a deep sleep while lying comfortably in the fetal position.

No more than three minutes later, he was awakened by soft knocking coming from his closet door. Damien quickly pulled his head from underneath the covers. He glanced around the room to see if anyone was in there with him. No one was there. He stared at the wooden closet door and heard nothing. It was just another weird and crazy dream. Lately he'd been having them quite often. Damien fell back down and closed his eyes. Before he could bury his face into the blanket again, the creepy knocking on the closet door started all over. Startled and nervous, Damien opened his eyes and sat up in bed. The soft tapping on the door continued.

"What the hell?" he whispered. Damien wanted to go open the door and see who or what was in there, but he was too frightened to move.

The eerie knocking on the closet door suddenly stopped. The uncomfortable silence didn't ease Damien's fear because he knew something was in there. The thought of not knowing what was behind the door made his heart thump faster and caused his body to tremble with terror. Damien wanted to open the door and see exactly what was behind it. He stared at the door in shock, wondering if someone was going to jump out of it.

There was a fierce knocking sound coming from the closet door. Damien's jaw dropped, and his eyes grew larger. He didn't know what to do. The knocking became louder and more aggressive. Whoever was in the closet was about to knock the door down.

"Oh, shit!" Damien yelled.

The pounding on the wooden door continued at a rapid pace. Damien could see the knob turning from side to side. He had to hurry and get out of the room before the door opened and . . . Damien really didn't want to think of what could happen. He knew it wouldn't be good. He threw the blanket on the floor and screamed. No words came out of his mouth. Just a loud shrill of fear and horror. Damien looked down and realized that he was lying in a huge pool of blood. The blood was smeared all over his blue pajama pants and gray T-shirt. Damien didn't know who the blood belonged to or where it had come from. All he wanted to do was get out of his room as fast as possible.

Damien jumped up and grabbed the doorknob in hopes of exiting his room. The door wouldn't budge. He pulled the knob so hard that it broke off and fell on the floor. Behind him the closet door continued to tremble. It wouldn't be long before whatever was behind the door came out and showed its face.

Damien kicked the door several times. It still wouldn't open. "Come on, dammit!" he yelled, pounding on the door with his fist. *The door seemed to be glued shut. Damien was somehow trapped in his room.*

"Open this door!" he screamed as he continued to beat his fist against the door. Damien nervously glanced over his shoulder and saw that the closet door was wide open. He stopped banging on the door to see who was in the room with him.

The room was silent and cold. The blood that soaked the sheets began to run down the sides of the mattress. Damien scanned the room as his body trembled with fear. He didn't see anyone or anything, which made him even more terrified because he knew that he wasn't in the bedroom alone. Without hesitating he kneeled down and checked under the bed. The only things he saw were some dusty old shoeboxes and some rap magazines he'd collected in high school. Damien cautiously stepped toward the closet. He kept looking behind him to make sure that no one was following him or trying to attack him while he wasn't paying attention.

The closet door stood ajar as Damien stood in front of the threshold. The bright sun that shone through the window seemed to blind him. Damien turned around and saw nothing but an empty room and a bed covered in blood. He took a deep breath and boldly stepped into his small closet. To his surprise, there was nothing in there, except the obvious: his clothes hanging up on hangers, gym shoes spread across the floor, a basketball and a baseball bat in the corner, and a gym bag and some sweats neatly folded on the top shelf. Damien smiled. Maybe he was hallucinating or just going crazy. He turned around.

Damien tried to scream for help, but no words came out of his mouth. His entire body instantly became as stiff as the Statue of Liberty. The evil woman standing before him almost made his heart explode. She was wearing all black, and her sinister eyes appeared to be the color of fire. Blood dripped from her black fingernails and thick red lips. She looked Damien up and down as if he were on display in the window of a clothing store. The thin woman let out a violent shriek and slashed Damien's face with her long and deadly claws. Blood splattered everywhere as Damien screamed in agony. The crazed woman sliced and mutilated his face over, and over, and over, and . . .

Damien popped open his eyes and jumped up. He was covered in sweat and breathing as if he'd run up a long flight of stairs. He peered down at his T-shirt and pajama pants to see if there was any blood on them. After he realized that nothing but sweat was sticking to his T-shirt, he pulled the covers back to see if the bed was covered in blood. His heart rate slowed down a little when he discovered that there was no blood in his bed. Now all he had to do was check the closet.

Without thinking twice, Damien jumped out of bed and stood in front of the closet door. He gripped the knob with his damp palm and stopped. A cold chill came over his entire body.

"It was only a dream," he said dryly. It hurt his throat to even talk now. Damien glanced over his shoulder just to make sure that he was all alone. The knob on the closet door slowly turned. Damien opened the door and his eyes at the same time.

His closet was still intact. Nothing was out of the ordinary. Damien turned around, expecting to see the woman with the sharp black claws waiting for him. She was nowhere in sight. Damien was joyfully relieved. He checked under his bed just to make sure that the woman with blood dripping from her lips was only in his nightmares. There was nothing but the usual under his bed.

Damien crawled back into bed. He got underneath the blanket, then took a deep sigh of relief. Sleep was the last thing on his mind. He stared at the ceiling fan trying to figure out why he was having nightmares about an evil witch trying to murder him.

Damien swept the hair up from the polished floor as another customer exited the building. The flyers and business cards he'd passed out over the past two weeks were bringing in new customers every day. His clientele had nearly tripled since he'd started working in the shop. Damien was making enough money now to move back out on his own. Instead of renting an apartment, he and Alex decided to buy a home together. They would save their money for six months, then go with their father to look for a house. If they could save $5,000 apiece, then they knew they'd have no problem finding something nice and affordable.

While Damien waited for his next customer to come out of the restroom, he sanitized his clippers and watched sports on the flat-screen TV. He drank some Pepto-Bismol after vomiting up the strawberry oatmeal and toast he'd had for breakfast. The medicine wasn't working at all. It was only mid-afternoon, and Damien was feeling worse than he'd felt when he left the house. He didn't know how much longer he could stand on his feet. Damien's legs were starting to become weak and unstable.

"It's freezing in here," Damien said. He leaned over the chair, trying to gather up some strength from somewhere. He was beginning to feel dizzy and light-headed.

"You don't look so good, man. If you need to go and get some rest, we'll cover fo' you," Damien's coworker suggested.

"I'm cool. My stomach just feels funny," Damien said. He could feel the goose bumps covering his flesh underneath his long black shirt.

But as the afternoon wore on, Damien didn't feel any better. His body temperature was now boiling. Sweat poured from his body as his head began to pound. He was drained. Damien didn't have enough energy to sweep the hair up from the floor. He wanted to go home and dive into bed, but he knew that he was in no shape to get behind the wheel of a car. The outcome of trying to drive in his present condition would probably be fatal. Damien had no choice but to go into the boss's office and lie down. He informed the chubby barber next to him where he was going, then slowly walked into the boss's office.

The wooden door closed behind Damien. The strong and sweet smell of tropical air freshener filled the room. Damien put his hand over his mouth and nose as he walked to the watercooler that sat in the corner. After drinking two cups of water, Damien sat down on the black leather couch. His head was spinning around like a Ferris wheel. Sweat began to pour from his body as though he were sitting in a sauna. Damien pulled his white gym shoes off so he wouldn't get dirt and hair on Ken's furniture. He leaned backward and instantly closed his eyes.

There was jazz music coming from somewhere in the office. Damien opened his watery eyes and noticed a clock radio on Ken's crowded desk. The volume on the radio was so low that he hadn't heard the music when he first stepped into the room. Damien wanted to turn the music off, but he didn't have an ounce of energy left inside him to get up from the sofa. He closed his eyes again and tried to relax while listening to the soft music. Within minutes, Damien was in a deep and dark sleep.

Damien struggled to open his burning eyes. He couldn't recall where he was or how long he'd been asleep. The sound of a saxophone blowing in the background reminded him of exactly where he was. Damien looked around the quiet office in a daze. He was still alone. He tried to sit up, but his head felt heavier than a ton of steel. He felt drugged and heavily sedated. Hopefully a little more sleep would alleviate his throbbing migraine.

The afternoon sun brightly shone through the one window in Ken's office. Damien stared at the white ceiling in a trance as he attempted to fall back into dreamland. He closed his eyes several times and nothing happened. Minutes passed before Damien decided that it was time to get up and go home.

Three more songs played on the radio before Damien finally sat up. He ignored the excruciating pain that was shooting through his head as he put his shoes back on. Sweat no longer escaped his body. Now Damien felt as though he'd been lying in a tub of ice. The cold chills that ran through his body caused him to tremble uncontrollably. Damien knew he was sick. The last time he felt like this, he was in bed for four days straight fighting the flu.

Damien slowly tried to get up off the sofa. The pain that shot down to his stomach was so intense that he almost fell over on his face. He moaned in agony as he clutched his stomach while rocking back and forth.

"Oh . . . ooh, ooh," Damien moaned and groaned. The sharp electric pain running through his stomach was unbearable. He fell back down on the couch as the pain intensified.

Damien sat on the leather couch hunched over with his head between his legs. He was biting his bottom lip, trying to fight the piercing cramps in his gut. The headache he was experiencing was minute compared to the stinging aches that seemed to rip his stomach apart. This pain was ten times worse than the agony his wisdom teeth had caused him.

The pounding pressure in his abdomen knocked Damien off the sofa and onto his knees. He hadn't the slightest idea of what was happening to him. All he knew was that he needed help. There was no way he'd be able to walk out of the office in his present state. Damien wanted to scream for help, but he was in too much pain to do anything but moan. His only chance was to crawl over to the desk and use the phone.

As the seconds went by, the pain in his stomach grew worse. Damien took a deep breath, then counted to three. As soon as he tried to move an inch, the kicking sharp pangs in his gut seemed to wrap around his entire body. The room instantly became blurry. Damien could feel sweat dripping from his face and chest again. His head felt like it weighed a hundred pounds. The pain ripping through Damien's stomach caused his arms to buckle. He fell flat on the carpet. Damien's eyes suddenly shut. There were no more headaches, no more blistering stomach pains, and no more agony, just a sea of deep and looming darkness. Damien was unconscious.

"Try to eat something," the young nurse said to Damien as she pushed a cart of food beside his bed. Red Jell-O, hot chicken broth, and a carton of apple juice were on the tray.

Damien looked at the tube and needle that ran into his left arm. "How long have I been here?" he asked the nurse. His throat was so dry that it hurt to talk.

"This is your second night," the nurse said with a smile. She began to check his IV bag to make sure that he was receiving the right amount of fluids.

"Feels like I been here for months," Damien struggled to say. He noticed how much the nurse resembled the late singer Aaliyah. Damien was convinced that he was dreaming. He closed his eyes and opened them again. The nurse was still there, dressed in her mandatory green scrubs. "Can you bring me a cup of water, please?" he asked.

"Sure. How are you feeling?"

"Better, I guess. The pain is still there, but not like it was."

"That is good to hear, because you looked like you weren't going to make it," the nurse replied. "A few more days of rest in here and you'll be back to normal. I'll be right back with your water."

Damien watched the nurse walk out. He glanced around the dim and quiet room. It felt as though he were the only patient in the entire hospital. This made him uncomfortable and nervous. Damien wondered if his family had come to see him. He stared at the black-and-white movie that played on the small TV while he waited for the nurse to come back.

The nurse entered the room again with a pitcher of water and a plastic cup. She poured Damien a cup, then set the pitcher on his tray. Damien gulped the cold water down. He couldn't remember the last time water tasted so good. He requested a refill from his nurse.

"Try to eat some soup. It'll help you feel better," the nurse suggested, handing Damien another cup of water.

"What was wrong with me?" Damien asked before drinking the water.

"You suffered a severe case of food poisoning," the nurse stated directly.

"Food . . . poisonin'?" Damien responded in shock.

"Yes. But you are going to be just fine," the smiling nurse assured him. "In case you are wondering, these *marks are on your forearm because I had a difficult time finding a vein."*

Damien glanced at the small dark bruises on his forearm. He smiled as he looked up at his nurse. "You not trying to kill me, are you?"

"Now why would I wanna do that?" she said, still brightly smiling. "I have to go down the hall, so eat something and get some rest. I'll be back to check on you. Hit the buzzer if you need anything."

"Yes, ma'am," Damien said with his own smile.

Damien ate a spoonful of Jell-O and drank his apple juice. He didn't even bother with the broth. He had no appetite for food, so he turned the light off. Damien thought about his family. Where were they? It was strange to him that no one called his room to check up on him.

The door to room 409 slowly opened. Damien snapped out of his slumber. He could see the shadow of his nurse in the dark. He glanced at the TV. There was nothing playing. The small, old TV was showing nothing but static and making that annoying sound of fuzz that happens when the TV is on the wrong channel. The hollow sound of heels coming toward him made Damien sit up. He knew for a fact that his nurse had on flat walking shoes. When she'd left the room earlier, she was as quiet as a library on a Sunday night. Now her shoes were making enough noise to wake the entire floor. Something wasn't right.

The nurse stood on the side of Damien's bed. He looked at her and instantly became numb. This wasn't the nice woman who had taken care of him. This was the evil woman from his dreams, wearing all black and standing beside him. He closed his eyes, hoping that when he opened them the scary woman would be gone. When Damien finally opened his eyes, the sinister lady *was looking directly at him with a vicious scowl on her pretty face. She wanted nothing but blood from him.*

"Leave me alone!" Damien pleaded. He couldn't look into the woman's dark eyes any longer. He attempted to get out of bed.

The quiet lady was merciless. She yanked the IV needle out of his arm. As he screamed in pain, she began scraping her long and sharp nails up and down his arms. Blood ran all over the white sheets. Damien's body was too weak to fight back. All he could do was lie there with his hands shielding his face. The unknown visitor was in a rage. She dug her claws into his neck while she used her other hand to slice his face. Damien screeched in anguish. The evil lady flipped the bed over, and Damien fell to the cold floor.

Damien jumped up. He was soaking wet with sweat. He was breathing heavily as he gazed around the office. The radio continued playing, and he was still alone. Damien shut his eyes and looked again to make sure he wasn't in the hospital. He felt his arms to see if there was any blood. There was nothing. Damien rubbed his face and paused. There was a stinging cut on the left side of his face. He wiped the blood from his face and stared at his hand in shock.

Chapter Eight

Laurence stood in front of the mirror with nothing on but a red towel wrapped around his waist. He stared at the new strands of gray hair on his face. He was becoming an old man right before his own eyes. Laurence wasn't ready to be a gray-bearded man. He decided to dye the silver hair on his face back to its original color. And he didn't feel like standing in front of the sink shaving his head or face, so he decided to go out and have it done. Before his afternoon meeting with his accountant, he would find a barbershop that could properly groom him.

Laurence stared at his reflection, thinking about his wife. He was going to tell her about the baby when he woke up this morning, but she was already dressed and on her way out of the house. She told him that she and her girlfriend were going to the gym then a spa to get pampered. Laurence was upset with himself. He should've told her months ago. Tonight, he would sit her down and tell her about the unborn baby. Laurence wasn't going to let anything or anyone get in the way of their talk tonight. He brushed his teeth, then jumped in the shower. Laurence dressed, then stepped out into the breezy winter air.

The barbershop parking lot was fairly empty. It was still early morning. After lunch, the parking lot would be crowded. Laurence pulled his black truck into the lot. He was hesitant because it was a new shop, but he figured, with them being new, he would get excellent customer service. And by the looks of the bare parking lot, he wouldn't have to wait long for service. He could get in and out. Laurence turned off the quiet engine and headed inside the shop.

The life-sized posters of Chicago athletes and the decor of the shop immediately impressed Laurence. He loved the flat screens and the furniture. This place was like walking into someone's basement. The only thing missing was a bar. If he ever thought about going into the hair-cutting business again, this was how his place would look: upscale and classy. People would always patronize a business that was clean with a comfortable and entertaining environment.

"How ya' doin?" one of the barbers said to Laurence. He was sitting on his stool, eating a breakfast sandwich and watching sports on TV.

"I'm good. And you?" Laurence replied. He was still admiring the shop.

"Good," the hungry barber answered, stuffing half the sandwich in his mouth.

Laurence noticed that there were five barbers in the shop, but only two of them were working. The others were sitting in their chairs watching TV and eating, and none of them would touch his head. He didn't have time for anybody to cut his hair and watch TV at the same time. He would go with one of the two guys whose clippers were already hot.

The big, round guy looked like he had just started on his client's head. Half of the guy's head was cut low and the other half was full of thick and long hair that was sticking up like a porcupine. The barber with the cut across his cheek was almost done. He was brushing the loose hair off his client. The young man sitting in the stool had a perfectly trimmed haircut that showcased the sea of waves in his hair. His pencil-thin beard was also trimmed and shaped to perfection. Laurence was sold. He walked in front of the young barber whose name tag read "Damien," and took a seat next to his station.

"Yo, I can take you right here," one of the other barbers yelled out. He was meticulously brushing the front of his hair.

"I'm cool. I have an appointment with Damien right here," Laurence informed the guy. "Thanks anyway."

Damien handed his client his change, then put his money in the pocket of his baggy jeans. The customer walked away while Damien looked at the man sitting down to see if he recognized him. Damien had never seen the well-dressed man before in his life. He wondered why he would wait for him when three other stylists were available. His father didn't raise a fool, though, so he wasn't going to turn down the man's money.

Damien wiped the hair out of his chair. "I'm ready when you are," he said. He grabbed the broom and quickly swept the hair from around the chair.

"Prompt service! That's what I'm talkin' about," Laurence said, jumping up and sitting in the chair.

Damien put the hair in the trash and placed the broom back in the corner. He washed his hands in a small sink and grabbed a paper towel. "Is this your first time here?" he asked.

"Yes, and I'm glad I came in here. It's very clean and nicely decorated," Laurence responded.

"Yeah, it is. We haven't been open dat long," Damien said, grabbing his clippers and spraying them with alcohol.

"Are you the owner?" Laurence asked curiously.

"Not yet. I wanna have my own shop in a year or so, though."

"Now that's the right way of thinkin'. Ownership is one of the keys to controlling your own destiny. All you need is a plan."

"I hear you, though my plans are still under construction," Damien said with a laugh.

"But the vision is there, and that is what's important, young brotha," Laurence explained. "You are fifty steps ahead of everyone else with that way of thinking, trust me."

"What type of business do you own?" Damien inquired. He placed a black cape around Laurence to prevent hair from falling onto his clothes.

"I own Club 38 and some real estate."

All of the barbers in the shop turned around and looked at Laurence. "I went to the one in Atlanta," a bald barber said with excitement. "You own that one too?"

"I own all of them," Laurence stated.

"I went to a Halloween party down there a few years ago. I didn't leave until the next mornin'," Damien said.

"I heard they charge a hundred dollars just to get in da spot," the heavyset barber said.

"You can never put a price on quality," Laurence replied, turning to face the barber.

"Dat's true!" the husky stylist agreed. "I try to tell my customers dat all the time."

Laurence laughed. "In this world you definitely get what you pay for."

Everyone in the shop turned their attention to the TV screen as highlights for the upcoming Bears and Packers game were shown. There was very little chatter among the men as they listened and watched the players discuss Sunday's game.

"How do you want it cut?" Damien asked Laurence.

"You can shave it bald and trim my beard. Can you get rid of these old man gray hairs for me, too?"

"I can do that," Damien answered. He turned his clippers on and began cutting.

Laurence sat in the chair, listening to the humming sound of the clippers slide across his head. He closed his eyes and relaxed. He thought briefly about a business venture that his partner wanted him to invest in. *To open up twenty drive-in theaters on the East Coast would be very risky,* Laurence thought. *If it works, it could be extremely lucrative, but if the venture fails—*

"Do you need any bartenders or any help at the club?" Damien asked, not knowing that he was interrupting Laurence's train of thought.

Laurence opened his eyes. "Well, that all depends."

Damien was quiet for a moment.

"You think you wanna tend bar at night?" Laurence asked.

"Nah, not me. My brotha is a bartender."

"I see. I could actually use some good men in the club. You and your brotha come down tomorrow night, and we'll discuss some business over a bottle of champagne."

"Sounds good to me," Damien said with enthusiasm. "What time should . . . I'm sorry. My name is Damien."

"I know." He chuckled and pointed at Damien's name tag. "It's nice to meet you, Damien, officially. I'm Laurence."

Damien reached over so they could shake hands. He tried not to show it, but he was thrilled to meet such a wealthy and powerful man. He had a feeling that this encounter would change his life forever. Damien grabbed the white jar of shaving cream and began carefully applying it to Laurence's head. Laurence closed his eyes again.

Two customers walked through the door talking loudly as Damien continued to work. One guy, who was short and muscular, was bragging about some sports car that he was going to have by the summertime. He had on a bright red sweater and a matching leather jacket. The red Chicago Bulls hat he wore was turned backward, and the earrings in his ear sparkled brighter than the jewelry that hung around his neck and wrist. This guy's eyes were almost as red as his jacket. He looked as though he'd been up all night partying.

"Who da best barber up in here?" he asked playfully.

The three stylists who were chatting and watching sports all raised their hands.

"I don't care who da best barber is. I jus' gotta get all this hair off my head and my face," the other guy announced. He didn't have on designer clothes or expensive jewelry. He looked as though he'd been living under a rock for months. The black sweatpants he wore were two sizes too big for his thin frame. And his body reeked of alcohol.

Laurence, still relaxing with his eyes closed, had gone back to dreaming about his future business plans. But one of the voices sounded familiar. The loudmouthed guy sounded like his wife's brother. *But that can't be him,* Laurence thought. He was still sitting in a cell because he couldn't raise the bond money that the court requested. Laurence inhaled then slowly exhaled. The thought of his no-good brother-in-law turned his face blood red.

"Come on down here, y'all," the tall barber said to the two men. They walked past Damien and sat in the last two chairs.

"Stop for one second," Laurence instructed Damien. Laurence sat up and glanced to his left. He saw Todd sitting in the chair smiling and laughing. His first instinct was to get up and drag Todd out of the shop. He had to calm down. Laurence took another deep breath. "Todd," he said calmly.

Todd suddenly stopped talking to see who was calling him. He saw Laurence staring directly at him. Todd leaped out of the chair like a frog. "Long time no see," he said, shaking his brother-in-law's hand.

"Yeah, it's been a while," Laurence responded. He noticed how bad Todd looked and smelled.

Todd released Laurence's hand. "Thank you," he said with sincerity. "My situation would be a lot worse if it weren't for you."

Laurence stared at Todd with hatred in his bright eyes. He really didn't have anything to say to him. Anger couldn't describe how Laurence felt. His wife went behind his back and bailed her brother out of jail when he told her to let him rot in there. What she did was equivalent to taking the money and flushing it down the toilet. Laurence would make sure that they both paid severely for stealing his money.

"I'm gonna pay you back this time. I will—"

Laurence interrupted Todd. He didn't want to hear another word. "Don't worry about it. We are family, right?" Laurence asked with a grin. He leaned back and closed his eyes. "We should always take care of one another."

Todd knew something was wrong. Laurence didn't sound right. He sounded like a madman. "Okay. Guess I'll see ya later," he said. Todd stared at Laurence for a moment, trying to think of something else to say. But their conversation was over. He walked back to his chair with a nervous feeling in his stomach.

Laurence was so enraged that he wondered if Damien could see smoke rising from his bald head. He was fighting the urge to jump up and murder Todd right in front of everybody. He had to leave the shop before something terrible happened. Laurence could not sit in the same room as Todd. The sound of his voice made him shiver with rage. Hopefully, Damien would be finished soon.

"That's a wrap," Damien said. He handed Laurence a mirror.

Laurence quickly glanced in the mirror before giving it back to Damien. He had to get out of the shop before he lost his cool. "I appreciate this."

"No problem," Damien replied. He pulled the cape off Laurence and brushed the loose hair from his head and neck.

Laurence was about to jump out of the chair but paused when he heard his ringtone. He grabbed the cell phone off his hip and flipped it open. His wife was on the line asking him about dinner. The sound of her voice made Laurence furious. Evil thoughts floated through his mind as she told him what she was cooking. "Sounds good," Laurence said impatiently. Seconds later, he said goodbye to his wife and closed the phone. He stood up and clipped the cell phone back to his brown leather belt.

"What time tomorrow night?" Damien asked.

"How about nine? Tell them your names at the door, and they'll walk you boys in," Laurence explained. He reached in his pocket and pulled out a stack of bills.

Laurence handed Damien a $100 bill. He shook his hand and swiftly walked out the door. He was gone so fast that Damien didn't even get a chance to thank him. Damien smiled and put the generous tip in the pocket of his jeans. He dialed his brother's phone number to tell him about the meeting tomorrow night. It was sure to change their lives forever.

Laurence stepped in the house and shut the door. Not only was he on the verge of completely losing his temper, but he was also extremely exhausted. The lunch meeting with his accountant lasted well over four hours. Then he went to the office to take care of some paperwork that was waiting on his desk. It was after ten o'clock now, and all Laurence wanted to do was watch a movie and relax. He wanted to be alone. He would deal with his wife to-morrow. Laurence didn't want to hear her voice or see her face at this moment. He was afraid of doing something terrible to her.

The aroma of baked chicken and garlic bread floated throughout the house. Laurence could also smell gravy and vegetables in the air. He kicked his shoes off, then hung his coat up on the silver rack. The smell of the food caused his stomach to growl. He really was in no mood to sit at the table with his wife and have a conversation. That would only lead to what she did for her brother, and then . . . Laurence shook his head. He wanted to grab a plate and eat alone in the basement. The sound of his wife's voice immediately changed his plans.

"Hey, good-looking, I hope you have an appetite," Laurence's wife said while walking slowly toward him. She was wearing a lavender silk bathrobe that was short enough to expose her well-toned thighs and legs.

Laurence didn't respond. He folded his arms as he stared at his wife in disgust. The thought of grabbing her around her neck and squeezing it until she stopped breathing kept flashing in his mind. He tried to think of something more peaceful than death. "What's the special occasion?" he asked angrily.

"Can't a girl give her husband a special treat?" Lynn asked rhetorically. She gave Laurence a gentle kiss on his lips before placing her head on his chest and wrapping her arms around his waist.

Laurence placed his arms around his wife's small waist and squeezed firmly. He closed his eyes as he rested his head on her shoulder. The horrible thought of snapping her neck in half instantly popped back into his head. A wicked grin appeared on Laurence's tired face. There was no doubt in his sick mind that he was going to kill his wife. And it was going to be sometime in the very near future.

"I love you," Lynn stated. She was hugging and holding on to her husband as if he were going away forever.

There was still a deranged smile on Laurence's face. His eyes stayed shut as the vivid images of murder ran across his mind. His wife's words of affection meant absolutely nothing to him now. She was only being nice to cover up for her mistakes. She had a pattern of acting this way, but now she had made a mistake that would cost her severely.

Laurence decided to play along with his wife anyway. "I love you too."

Lynn smiled as she pulled away from her husband's warm chest. "I ran us some water in the Jacuzzi so we can relax and play after we eat."

Laurence stared down into Lynn's beautiful, small eyes. The wicked grin was gone from his freshly shaven face. The idea of drowning her in the Jacuzzi was now floating around in his head. That thought put a smile back on his face. Laurence kissed his wife on her soft purple lips. "Sounds like a lotta fun."

"Well, let's eat. I warmed the food up, so it should be nice and hot," she said. Lynn grabbed Laurence's hand and walked him into the dining room.

The lights in the spacious dining room were dimmed low. Two yellow tapers sat in the middle of the wooden table. Steam floated from the food that was placed on the long table. There were two empty black plates, with sparkling silverware next to them, sitting on top of a yellow tablecloth. A bottle of red wine was the drink of choice for this romantic dinner. Jazz music played quietly to give the dining room the feel of an upscale restaurant. Laurence was almost in shock as he looked around the dining room. He couldn't remember the last time that he and his wife had a romantic dinner at home.

"Everything looks and smells great," Laurence said with sincerity. He sat down at the head of the table, trying to fight the evil thoughts that continued to grow in his head.

"Thank you," Lynn said, pouring wine in the glasses.

Laurence stared at her as she slowly poured the red wine. He couldn't believe that she'd bailed her brother out of jail with his money when he'd specifically told her not to. He was about three seconds away from jumping up and smashing her face on the table.

"Why are you looking at me like that?" Lynn asked with a smile. She set the bottle down on the table and handed her husband a glass.

"No reason."

"Good. Now let's have a toast," Lynn announced. She picked her glass up and held it in the air. "What shall we celebrate?"

Laurence wasn't paying his wife any attention. His mind quickly shifted back to the thought of banging her head on the table until blood covered her pretty little face. He wouldn't be satisfied until she was out of his life forever.

"Laurence Caine!" Lynn shouted. "Are you listening to me?"

Laurence snapped out of his daze. "What did you say?"

"Let's have a toast before we eat," she said.

"And what are we toasting to tonight?" Laurence asked, raising his glass in the air.

"Good love," Lynn said seductively.

The two glasses kissed before Lynn and Laurence tasted the sweet and bitter wine. Lynn kissed her husband on the lips, then proceeded to make him a plate of food. She sat down beside him after making herself a plate of food. Lynn blessed the food, and they began to eat. The soft jazz music playing was the only sound in the room until Lynn decided to break the uncomfortable silence.

"How was your day?" she asked.

Laurence looked up from his plate. He wasn't in any mood to talk. All he wanted to do was eat and go downstairs so he could be alone. Laurence decided to humor his wife with a little conversation so he could keep his mind off killing her. "It was pretty good. And yours?"

"I had a great day."

"My day was too long and too busy. I can barely keep my eyes open."

"My poor husband. I can give you a nice massage," Lynn said. She placed her hand on her husband's thigh and began slowly caressing it.

"You think that'll make me feel better?"

"It will. Then we can make love all night," Lynn said.

Laurence dropped his fork onto his plate. He had run out of patience and was on the verge of snapping Lynn's neck. He grabbed his glass of wine and drank what was left in it. He squeezed the glass and closed his eyes, trying to erase the evil thoughts that continued to swim across his mind.

"What is wrong?" Lynn asked nervously.

Laurence opened his eyes and coldly stared into his wife's face. "You tell me."

"Nothing. Everything is fine. You seem to have something on your mind," Lynn said. She continued to seductively rub Laurence's thigh.

Laurence threw her hand off his thigh as if it were a spider. "What the fuck do you mean everything is fine?" he yelled in anger.

"Why are you yelling and cursing at me?" Lynn asked with a surprised look.

"You know why the . . ." Laurence shouted before stopping himself in the middle of his tirade. He grabbed the bottle of wine and poured another drink. He gulped the wine down and closed his eyes in an attempt to calm down before he exploded.

"What's wrong, baby?" Lynn asked with concern.

Laurence opened his eyes. He was gripping the glass tighter now than he was before. "You gonna sit there and act like you don't know what I'm talkin' about?" he asked calmly.

"I don't know what you—"

"Lynn, just be quiet since you wanna play dumb," Laurence interrupted. "I saw your worthless-ass brother this mornin'. Now do you know why the fuck I'm yelling?" he screamed.

Tears immediately began pouring from Lynn's eyes. She knew she'd made a huge mistake by bailing her brother out of jail, but when she saw how hurt her mother was over it, she had no choice but to help. Her brother promised to give her the money back within two months, so she didn't think that Laurence would ever find out. Lynn knew how naive she could be when it came to her brother. "I had to help him. My mother was worried to death over him. We know he didn't commit this crime, Laurence."

"I thought you were smarter than this. Yo' brother only calls you and yo' mother when he's in trouble. Don't you get it? He likes jail. Why do you think he keeps going back? He's a criminal, and you let him out with my money. What the hell is wrong with you?" Laurence yelled.

"He's going to give us the money back," Lynn cried.

Laurence threw his empty wineglass across the room. The glass crashed into the wall and shattered into a thousand little pieces. "How in the hell is he gonna pay us back?" Laurence shouted.

"Why are you yelling at me?"

In a suddenly calm voice, Laurence said, "I asked you a fuckin' question. How is he gonna give me back my damn money?"

The tears continued to roll down Lynn's face. She dropped her head in disgust to avoid looking into Laurence's eyes. "I don't know."

Lynn's response made Laurence furious. He pushed his plate onto the floor before jumping up from the table. The plate made a loud banging noise as it hit the hardwood floor. Laurence had to get far away from his wife before something terrible happened. He walked out of the dining room and headed downstairs to compose himself.

Lynn didn't try to stop him from walking away. She got up from the table and went upstairs to her bedroom and cried herself to sleep.

Laurence turned the lights on over the wet bar in the dark basement. The blue illumination cast a hazy shadow over the bar. Laurence grabbed a shot glass and a bottle of whiskey. He poured a shot and drank it straight down. After taking a deep breath, he poured another shot. The second shot of whiskey calmed Laurence's raging temper down a few notches. It would take more than a few drinks to calm him down completely.

Laurence sat at the bar and continued to drink shot after shot as the hours passed. The bottle of whiskey was almost empty. He struggled to keep his red eyes open and his head off the bar. Laurence was far past the point of inebriation. He began talking to himself as he grabbed the bottle of alcohol and held it tightly. "I forgive you. I forgive you, baby. You know I love you. I always did. But your brother . . . I'm gonna kill him for you and your mother. He ain't worth the heartache. I love you, baby."

Laurence drank from the bottle with his eyes closed. He talked to himself for a few more seconds before stumbling over to the couch. He fell onto the sofa and slept for the next nine hours.

Chapter Nine

The time on the spotless black stove and microwave read 7:06. Damien sat at the round kitchen table with a bowl of cereal in front of him. After eating two spoonfuls of the sweet and crunchy cereal, he placed the spoon into the red bowl. Damien had completely lost his appetite. For the last thirty minutes, he'd been staring out the window thinking about the nightmare that woke him up out of his sleep three hours ago. The disturbing dreams were happening more often and causing him to lose more and more sleep. At first Damien didn't want to tell his parents about his nightmares, but now he had no choice. They were becoming too crazy.

Damien was mentally exhausted. His red eyes were puffy with dark circles around them from a lack of sleep. He was in a trance as he gazed out the window, trying to recall the eerie dream that woke him up at four in the morning. Bits and pieces of the dream began floating through Damien's head. Damien vaguely remembered sitting in a classroom, taking a test.

All of the students had their heads down, writing while the teacher sat at the desk with a newspaper in front of his face. Damien never saw the teacher's face. All he saw were his brown slacks and his matching shoes, which were propped up on the desk.

Someone was breathing heavily behind Damien. He turned around and screamed as if he'd seen a ghost. No one in the class moved. They continued writing with their heads down, and the teacher never moved the newspaper from in front of his face. The silence in

*the classroom terrified Damien just as much as the evil
woman who was sitting directly behind him. Her long
black hair covered her entire face. Her dark and soul-
less eyes stared into Damien's face with anger. Damien
could feel his legs and hands trembling uncontrollably.
He put his head down on the table and cried.*

*Something was wrong. There was blood all over his
desk. Damien wiped the tears from his face. Blood covered his hand instead of tears. He stared at the blood
on his hand without saying a word. Fear had numbed
his body and glued it to the chair. Blood began pouring
from Damien's eyes and falling onto his lap. He sat in
the chair, unable to move.*

Before the evil lady could kill him, Damien had somehow jumped up out of his nightmare.

The sun was nowhere to be found. It was a dark and
gloomy morning. Rain would soon follow the thunder
and lightning that could be heard and seen. Damien
checked the clock on the stove. It was now 7:32. Damien
wanted to go back to sleep, but he was too afraid that the
dreams would start all over. He wanted to talk to his parents before they left for work. Maybe they had some idea
of what was happening to him in his sleep.

Damien yawned and stretched his arms into the air.
He pushed the bowl of soggy cereal to the side as he laid
his head and arms on the glass table. He closed his burning eyes and drifted awhile into a dark world as the rain
began to fall outside.

"Wake up," Damien's father said as he slapped him
on the shoulder. He set the newspaper he was carrying
down on the table.

Damien slowly lifted his head. He didn't know where
he was or who had hit him across the shoulder. He wiped
his half-open eyes and saw his father standing in front
of the sink filling a silver teakettle full of water. "Good
mornin'."

"Good morning, son," he said, setting the teakettle on the stove. "You must've had a rough night last night."

"I couldn't sleep. I keep having nightmares that wake me up in the middle of the night, every night."

Damien's father paused and bowed his head for a moment in thought. Then he reached into the cabinet and pulled down two black teacups. "You want some tea?"

"No, thanks. I can't really eat or drink anything. I can see that I've lost some weight. I tried eating this cereal, but it almost made me throw up."

Damien's father sat down in the chair beside him. He had a worried expression on his face as he rubbed his gray goatee. "Are these dreams happening every night?" he asked with curiosity.

"Now they are. And it's always the same woman who is after me. I just don't understand what's going on, Pops."

Pops had a scared look on his face. "You said a woman, right?"

"Yes. I came in here so I could talk to you and Mama about it. I know it may sound crazy, but they are really starting to affect me. I'm almost scared to go to sleep at night," Damien said. He turned away from his father and glanced at the clock. It read 8:00 now.

Pops folded his hands on top of his newspaper. "Tell me about these dreams you're having."

Damien began slowly telling his father about the evil lady who wore all black and terrorized him in his nightmares. His mother walked into the kitchen as he began describing one of his dreams in detail. She sat down at the table and listened in shock as her son told them how he woke up with a scratch on his face from the wicked lady in his dreams. There was complete silence at the table for a moment. The teakettle whistled, breaking the scary silence that had fallen over the family.

Damien got up and turned the stove off. "I didn't mean to scare you guys, but this is what I've been dealing with."

"I'm responsible. This cannot be happening," Pops said sadly.

"What's wrong, honey? How are you responsible?" Mama replied.

"I don't know where to begin," Pops said.

"I don't understand," Damien said with a nervous look on his tired face. He sat back down at the table. "You know why I keep having these crazy dreams?"

Pops glanced at Damien before looking at his wife. He could feel tears beginning to well. He hung his head in shame as Alex walked into the quiet kitchen.

"Good morn. Y'all havin' a family meeting without me?" Alex asked, opening up the refrigerator.

"Good morning, son," his mother replied.

"Come and have a seat," his father said, fighting back his tears.

"Is everything all right, Pops?" Alex asked with concern. He could see the worried look on his father's face.

"You all right?" Mom asked as she grabbed her husband's hand and squeezed it tightly.

Pops didn't say a word. The tears began slowly rolling down his face.

Alex didn't bother pouring himself a glass of orange juice. He sat down at the table across from his brother. Watching Pops cry almost brought tears to his own eyes. This was only the second time in his life that he'd seen his father cry.

"There is something I have to tell y'all. I'm so sorry. I should have told you this years ago, but I was too scared," Pops said as he wiped the tears from his face.

"What is it?" his wife asked with authority. "You are scaring me."

Pops looked around the table at his family. He could see the fear in all of their faces. There was no easy way to begin his story. He took a deep breath and gathered his thoughts.

"Bob, are you sick?" his wife asked. She didn't recognize how badly her hands were shaking.

"No."

Everyone at the table breathed a sigh of relief. That was good news, at least.

He added, "Just listen to what I have to say."

They stared into his eyes as he began to tell his story.

In 1916, Pops's great-grandmother was pregnant with her sixth child. She was 30 years old and married to a man nineteen years her senior. Besides working as a maid, she was also responsible for cooking and making sure that the house was always clean. Her husband of thirteen years worked as a farmer in the daytime and as a small-time bootlegger at night. Many of his nights were spent in dirty saloons and brothels. On rare occasions, when he was sober, he was a kind and generous man. But when he drank, he turned into a different individual. He became an evil and violent man who abused and terrorized everyone he knew.

It was on a hot and humid night in July that the life of Pops's great-grandmother would change forever. She put all of her children to bed except her oldest. Her oldest daughter loved sitting in the kitchen with her and watching her cook. Every night her mother would cook eggs, grits, and ham for her husband so when he came home drunk, he'd have a hot meal to eat. If he didn't have a hot plate when he came home from the saloon, he would yell and curse and beat his wife. On this night, Pops's great-grandmother was behind the stove, happily cooking for her husband and talking to her daughter, when she began experiencing terrible pains in her stomach. At first she thought it was the baby kicking, but the pain was too severe. She dropped the hot pot filled with grits on the floor and fell into a wooden chair.

As Pops was told, the stinging pain in his great-grandmother's stomach was too intense for her to stand on her feet. When she tried to get up, with the help of her daughter, she fell right back down into the chair, screaming and hollering. The drunken husband walked through the front door as his wife continued to cry and scream in agony.

Pops's tall and thin great-grandfather, whose name was Rayford, stormed into the kitchen expecting to see a hot meal on the table. He immediately lost his temper when he saw the pot of grits all over the floor and his wife moaning and crying in agony. Rayford cursed and threatened his wife, telling her to get up and make him dinner, while his daughter watched in terror. He warned her that she would receive the beating of her life if she didn't get up from the chair. The great-grandmother cried as she tried to describe to her husband the pain in her stomach that seemed to be ripping her insides apart. Rayford became furious with her excuses. The liquor that he'd drunk was turning him into a demon. He smacked her across the face so hard that she fell out of the wooden chair and onto the floor. She screamed in pain as her daughter yelled out.

Rayford grabbed his screaming wife and violently lifted her up off the ground. He continued to curse and berate her as he threw her across the kitchen. Her head viciously collided with a stack of logs before she hit the ground. Rayford furiously knocked another pot off the stove as he stomped out of the kitchen in a rage. He went into his room to sleep off the alcohol that had taken control of his mind and body. Rayford didn't know that that would be the last time he'd ever see his wife and daughter.

Pops's great-grandmother was unconscious. A large amount of blood poured out of the open wound from the back of her head. The impact of being brutally shaken and slamming into the floor caused her to hemorrhage internally and externally from her womb. The oldest daughter screamed and panicked as she tried to wake her mother up. After a few more failed attempts to revive her mother, the daughter rested her head on her chest. She cried hysterically before jumping up and running outside to find some help for her dying mother.

Minutes later the daughter came back in the house with the old woman from two houses down. The daughter had spotted her sitting in her rocking chair staring blankly at the sky. The old woman listened carefully as the girl quickly told her the story of what her father had done. The quiet old lady, whose name was Mrs. Wick, was known to the kids as Mrs. Witch. She grabbed her walking cane and slowly stood. She followed the crying daughter as she continued to stare up at the dark sky.

Mrs. Wick walked into the hot kitchen with the daughter. Blood was smeared all over the floor. Pops's great-grandmother was turned over with her face lying in a pool of blood. The young girl screamed as she ran to turn her mother back over on her back. Mrs. Wick, who was ten years older than a century, stood in silence as she gazed around the kitchen. Her bronze skin turned red as she began mouthing words to herself. She stepped over to the bleeding woman and placed her cane on her chest. There was no heartbeat. The woman was dead, and from the large amounts of blood pouring from her womb, so was her unborn baby.

"She is dead for now," Mrs. Wick said to the little girl.

The daughter cried and screamed hysterically as she held on to her mother. The old woman told her to go and sit with her brothers and sisters while she took care of her mother. The little girl didn't move. Mrs. Wick poked her with her cane and demanded that the girl leave the kitchen. The daughter angrily got up and left the room, but then she crept back and peeked around the door. Mrs. Wick, who had long silver hair and dark gray eyes, knelt down next to the dead woman.

Pops was told that Mrs. Wick rubbed her wrinkled hands slowly up and down his great-grandmother's cold face. She closed her eyes and silently mumbled strange words to herself. Her small hands began rubbing the face of the woman more rapidly the faster she spoke. Mrs. Wick grabbed the woman's bloody hand and squeezed it before rubbing the hand across her face. She continued to speak unknown words as she bent over and began whispering into the woman's ear. Mrs. Wick suddenly let go of the hand and began shaking the corpse while continuing to speak into her ear. Moments later the old lady rose to her feet. She stared at the body with her demonic eyes as if she were looking through it. She continued to speak words to herself as she slowly walked out the back door. She was never seen again in the town of North Hill after that night. The daughter ran off to hide in her bed.

The next morning, the little girl sprang up out of her sleep. The once-dark house was now filled with the sun's orange and yellow glow. The girl was hoping that last night's incident in the kitchen was all a bad dream. She ran into the kitchen and realized that everything she saw was real. The kitchen floor was covered with blood, but her mother was gone. She ran through the house screaming her mother's name and looking for her. Her mother's body was not in the house. The little girl opened her parents' bedroom door.

The shrill that came from the little girl's mouth woke the rest of the children. She continued to scream as she stared at her father's naked and bloody body. There was no skin on his neck, and the skin that was left on his face looked as if it were burned. The little girl could also see that her father's eyes were gone and that his hands and genitals had been severed from his body. After vomiting, the little girl ran out of the house crying and screaming in shock. Her father was mutilated, and her mother's body had somehow vanished from the house.

As Pops continued to talk, he could sense how uneasy and uncomfortable the story was making everyone at the table. They were staring at him in disbelief with their mouths wide open. No one said a word. They all just sat in shock. Pops was reluctant to tell the remainder of the story, but he knew he had to tell it all so they'd understand.

The body of Rayford's wife was never found. The person who murdered him was never captured. Mrs. Wick was found dead miles away floating in a creek. All of the great-grandmother's children went to live with her sister.

The death of Rayford's wife began to haunt and terrorize her children one by one. They all had similar stories of their dead mother trying to kill them in their dreams. She would appear in most of their nightmares holding an infant in one arm and a butcher knife in the other. The horrifying dreams continued until all of the children were dead. None of Rayford's children lived to see their fiftieth birthday, which was the age he would've turned a week before he was brutally murdered.

Louise, the youngest daughter of Rayford and his wife, allowed the nightmares and the visions of her mother drive her insane. One night in October she hysterically leaped out of bed, screaming and shouting at her mother. Blood ran from deep cuts that covered her face and neck. Louise stood in the middle of the bedroom violently pulling her long hair from her head and scratching the skin off her face with her sharp fingernails. Her husband tried to grab her and calm her down, but it was too late. Louise had already run toward the closed window and jumped out of it. Glass shattered everywhere as she fell from the two-story home onto the concrete. Louise died instantly from a broken neck.

Pops stopped talking for a moment. He gazed around the table to see everyone's reaction to what they were hearing. His wife stared at him with tears in her eyes, and his boys had their heads down in disbelief. Pops knew that he should've told his wife his family story thirty years ago when he met her, but he knew that she would've left him as soon as she heard the bizarre tale. Pops could see the betrayed and hurt look in his wife's eyes. He knew that their relationship would never be the same after this conversation.

"I'm so sorry," Pops said to everyone.

No one at the table said a word. His wife had a stunned expression on her face. She couldn't believe that her husband would hide a family nightmare from her through all the years of marriage. No words could express the anger and fear that she was feeling. Damien's mother began to cry as she continued to stare at her husband.

"We are the only family members left," Pops said, tears rolling down his face.

"Pops, have you had nightmares?" Alex asked.

"I never had one nightmare about my great-grandmother. But my brother used to have them all the time, like Damien," Pops replied.

"Why don't you say her name?" Damien asked nervously.

"I was told never to say my great-grandmother's name unless I wanted her to come visit me," Pops said.

There was complete silence at the kitchen table. Thunder roared loudly outside, and rain continued to hit the pavement at a ferocious pace. Paranoia and fear were in the eyes of everyone. Something evil was coming for all of them, and they had no control over it.

Chapter Ten

Laurence was feeling great and having a very good morning. He dressed and headed to the gym. He ran three miles around the indoor track before working his chiseled arms and back on the machines. He left the crowded gym after sitting in the sauna for thirty minutes. Exercising always increased his appetite. Breakfast would be the next stop of the day.

Laurence sat in a restaurant sipping his juice while watching people eating and having a good time with their families. He saw a young mother feeding her child eggs and bacon and instantly thought of his own mother. Laurence wondered how she was doing and if she would ever come home. He thought about visiting the hospital and surprising her. Maybe it was time to reconcile with his mother and sister, he thought.

After watching the mother happily feed her son, Laurence was convinced that it was time to make peace with his family. He decided that it was time for all of them to put the past behind them and start all over. Laurence didn't realize how much he missed his mother and sister until this very moment. The family atmosphere in the diner was something that had been missing in his life for too many years. Laurence made plans to visit his mother in the hospital later in the day.

Laurence sat at the table daydreaming about his mother. He hoped that she would embrace him and not give him the cold shoulder. He planned on apologizing for his stubborn behavior and letting her know how much he loved her. Laurence knew that he was wrong for not wanting his mother to move forward after his dad died and have a life of her own. He prayed that his mother would accept his apology and forgive him for his insane behavior.

Laurence ate his breakfast, tipped the waitress $100, and walked out of the diner with his mother on his mind. The thought of visiting her made him nervous.

Chapter Eleven

Laurence stood alone in the elevator of his mistress's apartment building. He was expecting someone to come running onto the elevator at the last minute, but to his surprise the door closed. He pushed the number 25 on the panel, then stepped back against the wall as the elevator began to ascend to its destination. Laurence looked around the glass-covered elevator. Although he was having a great day, he didn't like the person staring back at him through the mirrors. That person was slowly losing his mind and becoming insane.

The elevator came to a halt. The silver door opened, and Laurence stepped off onto the top floor of the building. He walked down the dim and quiet hallway. Laurence quickly turned around and looked down the corridor. He thought he heard someone walking behind him, but no one was there. A strange feeling of paranoia suddenly came over Laurence. He pulled his keys from his jacket pocket and checked down the hall one more time. He was still alone. Laurence opened the door to the apartment. He walked inside and shut the door.

Laurence placed his keys on the sparkling dining room table. He could see his reflection clearly in the glass table. This was a reflection he was beginning to despise. He grabbed his cell phone and turned it off before setting it next to his keys. Laurence planned on relaxing without any interruptions for the next few hours. Later in the day he would pay a visit to the hospital where his mother was

staying. Laurence walked over to the entertainment system and turned on the stereo. Within seconds, jazz music
could be heard throughout the lake-view condo.

Laurence brushed his teeth, then rinsed his mouth
with blue mouthwash. He undressed and stepped in the
shower. He stood in the hot water for over thirty minutes,
thinking about his mother and sister. Laurence thought
about hugging his mother and telling her how much he
loved her. He also had to apologize to his sister for acting
like an asshole toward her. He realized that she was only
trying to keep the family together. Laurence planned on
stopping at the floral shop and buying the most expensive bouquets of flowers for his sister and mother. This
was definitely going to be one of the best days of his life.

Laurence tried closing his eyes several times, but nothing happened. He couldn't sleep. He felt like an anxious
kid on Christmas Eve waiting in bed all night for the sun
to rise. Laurence stared at the ceiling with his eyes wide
open thinking about his mother and sister. He thought
about the times when he and his sister would argue and
his mother would intervene and make both of them hug
and kiss one another. Laurence laughed when he thought
about the times when he'd rip the heads off of his sister's
Barbie dolls. They would argue all day and then watch a
movie together at night. Laurence really missed his sister.
His eyes began to water as he tried to fall asleep.

Laurence's smile wouldn't disappear as he daydreamed
about his childhood. Then all of a sudden, a thought ran
across his mind. Calling his sister was the only thought
on Laurence's mind at the moment. Something in the
back of his consciousness kept telling him to pick up
the phone and call Renee. He wanted to wait and surprise her with his visit to the hospital, but a voice inside
his head kept telling him to dial her number. Laurence
decided to trust his instincts. Maybe they could have

lunch before they went to the hospital to visit their mother.

Laurence stood up from the couch. He was wearing black sweatpants and a blue Chicago Cubs T-shirt that was a size too small for him. He walked into the kitchen and grabbed the cordless phone off the marble counter. Laurence sat down on the couch again and stared at the TV. The animated announcer on the screen moved his hands side to side as he talked about football. Laurence smiled as he looked at the phone. He knew in his heart that he was doing the right thing, but all of a sudden, he had a funny feeling in his stomach. What if Renee and his mother didn't want him back in their lives? Then an image of his mother dying of cancer flashed in his eyes. There was no time to think about what if and why not. Laurence hit the TALK button on the phone.

The humming sound of the phone begging for someone to dial a number began to annoy Laurence. As hard as he tried, he couldn't seem to remember Renee's phone number. The numbers scrambled in his head as he attempted to recall them. He had no luck remembering Renee's number, so he hung the phone up in frustration. Laurence shook his head in disgust as he thought about how long it had been since he'd actually picked up the phone and called his only sibling. He tossed the phone to the side and thought about his cell phone. Renee's number was stored in there.

Laurence grabbed his phone and thought about pouring himself another cocktail. He decided to wait until he spoke with his sister. He turned the phone on while watching the muted television. There was a beer commercial showing a German shepherd drinking his owner's beer while the man ran to the kitchen to grab a bag of chips. Laurence immediately took his attention away from the commercial when he heard his phone beeping. There were new voicemails he needed to check.

Laurence decided to check his messages later. Right now, he was going to call his sister and make peace with her. He found her name in his contact list. Laurence paused before making the call. He was trying to remember when and why he stored Renee's number in his phone. The only reason he could think of was his wife. She more than likely put Renee's number in his phone in hopes of him calling her one day. Well, this would be that one day. Laurence stopped stalling and finally pushed the SEND button on his phone.

The phone rang. Renee's voicemail finally came on, advising the caller to leave a message because she was unavailable at the moment. Laurence closed his phone and tossed it on the table. He thought about calling her back and leaving her a voicemail. There was no need, though, because he was going to see her later in the day. Laurence quickly changed his mind. He picked his phone back up from the table, but before he could redial his sister's number, she was already returning his call.

"Hello," Laurence said, and he cleared his throat.

"Laurence, it's me, Renee," she said as she sniffled. Her strong and confident voice was now replaced by a fragile and sorrowful tone.

Laurence could hear the pain in Renee's voice. Something was wrong. She sounded like she'd been crying. "Renee, is something wrong?"

There was a short pause on the other end of the phone. It felt like hours to Laurence, though. The silence was followed by Renee bursting into tears. "Mama's . . . gone," she cried loudly.

Renee's words sent chills throughout Laurence's body. The entire world seemed to stop for a moment. He was trying to comprehend what his sister had just said. Maybe he didn't hear her right. "What?" he blurted out as his hands trembled.

"She died this morning. I've been trying to call you," Renee said as she continued to sob and mourn the loss of their mother.

Laurence dropped the phone on the floor. He didn't need to hear anything else. His eyes began to water as images of his mother lying in a casket began to flash across his mind. Laurence closed his eyes and tried to picture something other than his mother resting in a casket with a white dress on. He couldn't get the morbid, graphic images out of his head.

Laurence felt sick. He didn't know if he was going to vomit or black out first. How could his mother die before they made peace with one another? he angrily questioned. His plans of making a surprise visit to the hospital were thrown out the window. His mother was dead, and there was nothing Laurence could do to bring her back. Laurence became infuriated. He could feel his blood simmering underneath his skin. The sick feeling was suddenly gone. There was nothing inside Laurence but rage now.

Laurence stared at the ceiling with his hands folded behind his neck. The tears in his eyes dried as he continued to think about his mother. He could clearly see a casket, covered in bright pink and yellow flowers, being lowered into the ground. The strange thing about this mental picture was that there were no people standing around the coffin. The graveyard was empty.

Laurence's daydream was disturbed by the music of his ringtone. He didn't bother looking at his phone. At this point he couldn't care less who was calling him and what the call was about. Laurence needed something to calm him down before his boiling temper pushed him into the world of insanity. He sprang from the couch and grabbed a bottle of clear tequila from the kitchen's minibar.

The more tequila Laurence drank, the angrier he became. He drank the hard liquor straight out of the bottle as if he were a cowboy in an old Western. Laurence was upset with himself and with his mother for dying on him. He was drunk and blaming himself for his mother's death. His pain transformed into rage as he continued to turn the bottle of alcohol upside down. Someone was going to pay a huge price for his mother's death. Laurence would make sure of that. She died because of her husband's bad habits. Laurence smiled as he thought about another surprise visit that he could make later on in the day.

Day faded into night as the birds stopped chirping and the sun shifted to the west. The cold breeze blowing throughout the city blew the bare trees back and forth like a seesaw. A full moon glowed in the dark sky as a shiny black truck turned onto Lakewood Street. The Escalade parked right in front of the house on the corner whose address read 5916. There were no lights on in the home. The house was completely empty.

Laurence put his truck in park and turned the ignition off. He sat in silence as he patiently waited for his mother's husband to return home. Until then he would drink tequila out of his silver flask and wait. Laurence glanced around the quiet neighborhood. *So much for a good day,* he thought. His day had turned into a nightmare. Laurence could hear the wind howling as he began to drift into a world of darkness.

A red coupe speeding down the street with its music blasting startled Laurence. He jerked in his seat as he

opened his burning eyes. For a moment he couldn't recall where he was and what he was doing. He took a swig
from his flask and looked at his mother's house. There
was a light on. The old man was home. Laurence drank
the rest of his alcohol, then threw the flask on the passenger seat. Revenge was the only thought on his mind.
He snatched his keys from the ignition and grabbed two
plastic bags off the passenger seat. The bags contained
beer and sandwiches. Laurence opened the car door and
stepped out.

Laurence walked up to the porch and rang the bell
twice. The wooden door opened after several moments.
The old man had a surprised expression on his face when
he saw Laurence standing on his porch.

"I brought you some beer and sandwiches," Laurence
said as he shivered from the cold and blustery wind. He
even managed to fake a smile as he stared at the old man
with hate in his eyes.

"Well, come on in outta that cold," the husband suggested. He opened the screen door and let Laurence into
the warm house. The husband still had a surprised look
on his face as he shut and locked the front door.

Laurence stepped into the dim house and handed the
husband the two plastic bags. He could instantly smell
the strong stench of cigarette smoke in the air. "I thought
you might like a beer and something to eat," Laurence
said as he stared at the husband with disdain.

"Thanks! I'll put this in the fridge. Have a seat, and I'll
get you something to drink," the husband said.

The sound of this man's voice angered Laurence in a
way that was beyond rage. He wouldn't be satisfied until
he was dead. Laurence walked toward the living room
smiling and whistling.

The living room was immaculate. Laurence looked
around hoping that his mother would walk in and ask

him if he wanted something to eat or drink. He sat down and continued to stare at all of the family portraits that were placed throughout the room. The photos of his mother and her husband disgusted Laurence. His mother was gone, and this bastard was still living. Laurence wanted to get up and knock all of the pictures off the wall, but he decided against such out-of-control behavior. He noticed a cigarette burning in an ashtray on the sparkling glass coffee table. A bottle of whiskey sat beside the ashtray. Laurence thought about taking the cigarette and sticking it into the eyes of the old man.

"Hear you go," the husband said to Laurence, giving him a beer. He took a seat in the brown recliner right next to the sofa.

"Thank you," Laurence replied. He never bothered to look at the old man. His eyes were glued to the basketball game that was showing on the flat-screen TV.

"I miss your mother already," the burly and bearded husband said. He poured himself and Laurence small glasses of whiskey. "I don't know what I'm gonna do without her."

Laurence watched the husband drink the glass of whiskey down before pouring himself another one. Everything about this man disgusted him: his voice, his looks, his walk, and especially his arrogant attitude. "I was going to surprise her and visit her today. Guess I was too late, though," Laurence said sadly.

"She would have really loved to see you," the husband responded. He grabbed his cigarette from the ashtray and relit it.

Laurence watched with contempt in his red eyes as his mother's second husband puffed on his cigarette. He was losing his patience and didn't know how long he was going to be able to sit and talk with this man. "I know she would've," Laurence said quietly before taking a drink of whiskey.

"What am I gonna do without my wife?" the old man asked. He began to weep as he continued to blow smoke into the warm air. "She was all I had."

Laurence was not affected by the husband's crying. He was the sole reason his mother was lying in a morgue. If she had never met him, she would still be alive. The lung cancer that killed her was caused by his excessive smoking.

Laurence was ready to leave. His face turned blood red as he furiously watched the husband blow smoke into the air. "Excuse me. I have to use the bathroom," he said as he stood up from the brown leather sofa.

Laurence walked through the dark dining room and into the hallway. He stood in front of the bathroom door thinking of his mother. He would never get his chance to apologize to her and tell her how much he loved her. This thought drove him insane. He grabbed the stainless-steel .32 Magnum from the small of his back. Revenge was the only thought on his mind at the moment.

Laurence cocked the hammer back on the pistol and calmly walked back into the living room. He could hear the husband weeping as he stepped behind his chair and placed the gun to the back of his neck. Without hesitating, Laurence pulled the trigger. The husband instantly fell forward into the coffee table, causing it to shatter. Laurence smiled. Blood began to run onto the cream carpet. He was dead.

Chapter Twelve

Damien and his brother sat outside of Club 38 waiting for the valet to park Damien's truck. They could hear the roaring wind howling as they waited.

The valet took Damien's truck, and they walked past the long line to the front door of the club.

"We have an appointment with Mr. Laurence," Damien said with confidence. "He told us to be here at nine."

The doormen looked at each other for a second. They were already forewarned by the boss that the boys were coming and that they were to treat them like royalty. They were also told to not let them in if they were one minute late. Laurence knew that he wouldn't be able to trust them if they couldn't make it on time to their first meeting with him.

"What are your names?" asked a bouncer wearing an ostentatious pinky ring.

"I'm Damien, and this is my brotha, Alex."

The menacing-looking guard pulled his phone off his hip and chirped the boss to let him know that his guests were at the door. The boss chirped him right back to let him know that he was taking care of something, but he wanted him to escort them to his office, where they could sit and have a drink while they waited for him. The guard put his phone back on his hip before unhooking the black rope from the silver pole. "Come on in, guys."

"Have a seat and make yourselves at home. Mr. C should be here shortly," the muscular bouncer said to them as he was walking out the door. He stepped out of the office and didn't bother to shut the door behind him.

Damien looked around the immaculate and spacious office. "So, this is how the rich live."

"Yes, it is," Alex replied. He noticed that the other end of the office had a bar, a flat-screen TV that covered the entire wall, and a black leather sectional sofa. "This guy is a neat freak just like you," Alex said to his brother. He noticed how the polished hardwood floors shone just as bright as the dark desk.

"He might be worse than me. This place is spotless. I'm almost scared to walk on the floors."

There was a soft knock on the open door that startled Damien and Alex. A tall, thin man wearing a black tuxedo and bow tie entered the office. He was carrying a silver tray holding two bottles of champagne and two sparkling glasses.

"How are you gentlemen doing tonight?" the host with the pencil-thin mustache asked.

"Good, and yourself?" Damien asked.

"Just great. And thanks for asking. I have some fine champagne for you two, courtesy of the club," the host said with a smile.

"Thank you," Alex said. "I will take it." He jumped up and grabbed the tray from the host.

"I'm Joseph," the host said to Alex, extending his hand to him. Joseph introduced himself to Damien. After making sure that the brothers were comfortable, Joseph left the room and headed back downstairs to continue greeting and serving customers.

The first bottle of champagne was history. The brothers were working on the second bottle as they continued to wait for the boss to arrive in his office. Now, ten minutes had gone by without them saying a single word to one another. They sat and drank in silence. The thumping bass from the speakers was the only sound that could be heard in the warm office.

Laurence seemed to appear out of nowhere. The boys were shocked when they saw him standing by the door and smiling at them. They rose from the plush leather couch, holding their glasses. "How you doing, Laurence?" Damien asked.

"I'm doing great." Laurence said, shaking Damien's hand. "This must be your brother."

"I'm Alex." They shook hands as Damien introduced them to one another. "Very nice to meet you," Alex added.

"Likewise," Laurence replied. "Let me take those hats and coats."

Moments later, Laurence reappeared with three bottles of ice-cold champagne in his hands. "Now we don't have to share," he said, handing the brothers a bottle apiece. He walked to the door and closed it before taking a seat behind his desk. "You boys smoke cigars?"

"I do," Alex blurted.

Damien glanced at his brother and grinned. He knew Alex could probably count on one hand the number of cigars he'd smoked in his life. "I don't. I got sick after smoking one before," Damien said.

"A good cigar will never make you sick or nauseated. I got something good for both of you boys," Laurence said. He reached inside his bottom drawer and pulled out a box of stogies. Laurence grabbed three cigars from the full box, then placed the box back in the drawer. "These are only for kings," he said, admiring the cigars.

Laurence reached back into his bottom drawer where he kept his cigars and pulled out two black marble ashtrays. There was an orange lighter inside each round ashtray. "Here you go," he said as he pushed one of the small ashtrays toward Alex.

Damien grabbed the lighter and lit the thick brown cigar that he was holding in his mouth. He closed his eyes as he slowly blew smoke from his mouth. "I like the way this tastes."

"These are the finest-tasting cigars in the world," Laurence stated. He put some fire on the end of his stogie and began taking soft pulls from it.

Alex lit his cigar. He took a hard pull and began to cough. The thick smoke shot from his mouth as he leaned over and continued to cough and hack.

"Rookie!" Damien laughed.

Laurence smiled. "Are you boys hungry? We have some of the best chefs in town."

"I don't really have an appetite," Damien said as he puffed slowly on his cigar.

"I'm good right now," Alex said before taking another drink to stop his throat from burning.

"Well, maybe later we'll get something," Laurence said. He took a deep, hard pull from his long stogie and calmly blew the smoke from his mouth. "Let's talk a li'l business, shall we?"

Damien and Alex sat straight up in their seats like two students eagerly waiting for the teacher to speak. They drank from their bottles of champagne as they carefully listened to every word that the boss had to say.

"Do you boys want to be rich?" Laurence asked the brothers, looking directly at them.

"Yes, we do!" Alex said with enthusiasm.

Damien nodded in agreement with his brother as he continued to take light pulls from the long cigar.

"Good. I need people around me who think big and want the best out of life. If you boys are committed to hard work, then the amount of money you can make is infinite in this business. I'm spending entirely too much time in here, so eventually I want you two to run it for me.

Are you up for the challenge?" Laurence asked. He took a long drink from the cold bottle that was resting between his legs.

"Definitely!" Damien said.

"I can see the hunger and passion in your faces. I need that in here. Some boys who will work hard and expand on what we're doing. There will be weekly meetings with me and very long hours, so you will have to give up the barbershop."

"Not a problem," said Damien.

"You boys will travel often to the other clubs to see how everything operates. How does it sound so far?" Laurence asked.

"It sounds great to me," Alex answered. He smiled as he drank champagne out of the bottle.

"I'm ready to start now!" Damien said.

"I want you boys to learn every aspect of this operation. I will make the two of you assistant managers once you do that. In a few years, you boys will be able to run the entire club."

"When do we start?" Damien asked anxiously. He put the burning cigar into the ashtray, then picked up his bottle of champagne from the floor.

"In the morning. I want you boys to see the business when it is closed so I can explain to you in detail how we operate. You will work the kitchen, the door, the bar, the DJ booth, the entertainment room, and the promotions department for the next six months. That way you'll be well versed in all departments. Then I will personally teach you how the nightclub game functions and prospers," Laurence stated.

"We will be here," Damien said.

Laurence stood up and walked around to the front of his immaculate desk. He blew smoke into the warm air after taking a deep pull from his cigar. "Let me say this

before we go any further. I take my business very serious-
ly, and I will not tolerate any disrespect, dishonesty, or
disloyalty. This is a multimillion-dollar operation, and I
will not jeopardize it for anyone. The punishment for vio-
lating my code of ethics will not only be termination, but
I will personally . . ." Laurence smiled, figuring his point
was well-taken. "Do we have a deal, or do you boys need
some time to think about everything?"

"We have a deal. There is nothing to think about," Alex
said.

"We definitely have a deal," Damien echoed.

"Then it's time to celebrate," Laurence stated as he
extended his hand to the boys to officially seal the deal.
"We need more champagne. I'll be right back," he said,
disappearing into the back of the office.

"I can't believe this is happenin'," Damien said with
excitement.

"Now we can make some real money. Five years from
now we'll be rich and the owners of our own club," Alex
said, smiling.

Damien stared at his brother with sudden concern. He
didn't say what he was really thinking. He didn't know if
he would be here five years from now.

Laurence grabbed his sweet stogie and relit it. He
closed his eyes and deeply inhaled. As the smoke slowly
floated from his mouth, an idea suddenly came to mind.
"I have a job for you boys. Early tomorrow morning, the
two of you will pick up fifty thousand dollars in cash for
me. You will count every dollar to make sure all of it is
there. If it is one dollar short, I'll need you to call me
and let me know. A car will pick you boys up at six in the
morning, so be ready to go. He'll drive you to a rental car,
which you'll take into Michigan. Is everything clear so
far?"

Damien and Alex nodded.

"A few more things before we go downstairs," Laurence said. "The directions to your exact destination will be given to you in the morning, as well as the name of the man who will give you the cash. No one rides in the vehicle but you two. And no one knows about this but you. I expect you to be in my office by noon tomorrow with the money. I don't wanna tell you boys what will happen to you if my money comes up missing or short."

Damien and Alex looked worried, but they knew this was a chance to prove themselves to the boss. They would drive to Michigan despite their concerns about what exactly would happen once they got there.

"For your time and effort, I will pay each of you seventy-five hundred dollars in cash," Laurence stated. "It should be the easiest money you boys will ever make. All you're doing is driving a few hours and counting a couple of dollars."

The boys smiled as they thought about the money they were going to make. The fear and doubt in their minds evaporated as soon as the boss said he was paying them $7,500 apiece.

"Ask me right now if you have any concerns or questions," Laurence said, staring directly into the boys' eyes.

"We'll take care of everything tomorrow," Alex stated.

Damien, Alex, and the boss sat in the office for hours drinking and laughing. They didn't leave the club until early the next morning.

Chapter Thirteen

Laurence opened his eyes. His foggy vision cleared up after he rubbed his red eyes with the palm of his hand. His head throbbed from all the champagne and tequila he'd drunk in the club. All Laurence needed was some cold water and a lot more sleep to make his headache subside. He lay on the leather couch trying to recall how he got downstairs in the basement. He vaguely remembered pulling into the garage. Everything after that was a complete blank.

Laurence yawned and stretched out his arms while looking around the quiet and dark basement. The absence of the sun, and the gray clouds hovering above the city, gave the basement a dull and gloomy look. Laurence noticed that the radio and TV were turned off. He couldn't remember a time when he came into the basement and didn't turn on either the TV or the radio. Maybe his wife came down and turned everything off, he thought. He continued glancing around the room and noticed a bottle of whiskey sitting on the floor beside him. Laurence grabbed the bottle and stared at it. The bottle of dark alcohol was almost empty. "When did I drink that?" he whispered to himself.

The pounding headache seemed to escalate as Laurence struggled to remember what he did once he pulled into the garage. Everything was dark and blank from that point on. He grabbed the whiskey bottle, hoping it would somehow help him with his sudden case of amnesia. That didn't help either. Laurence let go of the bottle, but what he noticed sent chills through his body.

Laurence closed his eyes and took a deep breath. When he reopened them, he was hoping that the blood on the sleeve of his shirt would be gone. To his disappointment it was still there. He checked the sleeve on his left arm and noticed there was blood there too. Laurence was confused. Whose blood was on his shirt and why? He raised both arms in the air and stared at them for a moment. There were two long cuts on each of his hands. "What the hell happened last night?" Laurence asked.

Something strange happened last night and Laurence couldn't remember anything. All he knew was that he woke up in his basement with a bottle of whiskey beside him and blood on his white shirt. Not to mention the long lacerations on his hands. Laurence sat up on the sofa. He grabbed the whiskey and finished what was left of it.

The strong alcohol made Laurence's headache instantly go away. He set the empty bottle on the coffee table next to his keys, cell phone, and jewelry. He took a closer look at his jewelry. There was blood smeared all over his watch and diamond ring. There was no blood on his cell phone and keys. Laurence stared around the room to see if anything was different or abnormal. Everything seemed normal and in place. He fell back on the sofa trying to remember. As Laurence stared at the blood on his sleeve, violent and graphic images began to appear in his mind. He closed his red eyes and sank into a deep and dark place that took him back to earlier events.

Laurence could vividly see himself walking into his spacious kitchen from the garage. The kitchen was dark, as was the rest of the house. He grabbed a bottle of water from the refrigerator and drank it down within seconds. After throwing the plastic bottle in the garbage, Laurence headed upstairs to kiss his wife.

Laurence walked up the spiral staircase and into his room. He noticed that the bathroom light was on, and he could hear his wife talking. Laurence stepped in front of the bathroom door and stopped. Who the hell was she talking to at five in the morning? After listening to his wife's conversation for a few minutes, he realized that she was on the phone with her mother. Laurence was about to turn around and go in the basement until he heard his wife say that she would give her brother the money for his legal fees. Laurence became furious. His wife finished by telling her mother not to worry about anything because she would make sure that everything was taken care of.

Laurence wanted to kick the door down and throw his wife out the window. He had to take a deep breath and compose himself. The longer he stood behind the door, the more aggravated he became. He finally decided to open the bathroom door and talk to his wife. As Laurence stepped inside the bathroom, he stared at his wife soaking in a bubble bath while casually talking on the phone.

"Hey, baby," Lynn said as she stared up into her husband's bloodshot eyes. "I'll call you in the morning, Mama." She turned the phone off and set it on the side of the Jacuzzi.

"Why are you in the tub this late?" Laurence calmly asked. He was trying his best to mask his anger and frustration.

"You mean this early. I couldn't sleep, so I decided to soak in the tub and wait for you. Now take your clothes off, and get in here with me," Lynn said with a smile.

"You decided to call your mom and wake her up at five in the mornin'?"

"No, she called me a while ago. Said she couldn't sleep from worrying and stressing over my brother."

Laurence could feel his face turning red. He had to leave the room while he was still calm. "I'm going downstairs."

"Come get in here with me, and then we'll go to sleep," his wife suggested again, as she rubbed bubbles across her neck.

"I'm too tired and drunk. I gotta lie down before I pass out," Laurence replied. He gave his wife a fake smile, then walked out of the bathroom.

"I'll be in here relaxing if you change your mind," she said softly. She could tell by the tired look on Laurence's face that he wasn't coming back.

Laurence walked down to the dark basement. He didn't bother turning any lights on. He took his leather coat off and tossed it across one of the barstools. He did the same thing with his black suede jacket before walking over to the sofa. Laurence set his keys and cell phone on the marble table before falling across the couch. For some reason his wife's conversation with her mother began playing over and over in his head. The more Laurence thought of their conversation, the angrier he became. She would continue to financially support her criminal-minded brother if he didn't put a stop to it. Today was the day that it would stop for good.

Laurence jumped up. As he slowly walked upstairs, he could feel his sanity slipping away from him. His wife and her brother were not the only cause of his rage. The bottled-up anger he felt toward his mother and her deceased husband was also the reason why Laurence was beginning to lose his mind. Something terrible was going to happen if he went back into the master bathroom. Laurence kept telling himself to go back downstairs and go to sleep, but his legs continued to climb.

Laurence reached the top of the stairs and stopped. The words of his wife talking to her mother seemed to be on repeat in his head. The thought of her loving her brother more than she loved him drove him mad. He was the one taking care of her and making sure that she had all of the luxuries in life. His wife had betrayed him, and that was something that Laurence could not tolerate. Now she would suffer the consequences.

"I hoped you would come back," his wife said as Laurence stepped back into the steamy bathroom. She immediately noticed the evil look on his face and how his hands trembled uncontrollably.

"You still giving my money to yo' worthless-ass brother, huh?" Laurence asked, moving toward the Jacuzzi.

"What are you talking about, Laurence?" Lynn asked nervously.

Laurence stood in front of the Jacuzzi and stared down at his wife. "I heard you tell your mama that you would handle all his legal fees."

"I told her I would loan him the money for a lawyer. She's going to help him pay us all of the money back," Lynn said calmly. The red in her husband's eyes had a demonic look to them that was beginning to frighten her.

"I thought I told you before not to give your brotha another dime of my money," Laurence said. "You love that son of a bitch more than you love me?"

Laurence's wife sat up in the Jacuzzi. "Are you drunk? Why would you think I love him more than you?"

Laurence wanted to walk out of the bathroom and go downstairs, but his anger wouldn't allow him to leave. "I'm tired of you and your fuckin' family!" he said, almost whispering.

"You *are* drunk. Please go and get some sleep, baby," Lynn pleaded with Laurence. He was starting to resemble a madman with his bulging red eyes.

Laurence didn't say another word. He reached down into the steamy water and grabbed his wife by the throat.

She screamed and kicked as he violently squeezed her thin neck. She scratched his face and hands several times with her long, sharp nails. Despite the blood from the deep scratches, Laurence continued to choke his wife. Out of fear for her life, she grabbed one of her shaving razors from the side of the tub and sliced both of her husband's hands. Warm blood flowed from his hands into the hot water as he yelled in agony. Laurence released his hands from his wife's bruised neck.

She dropped the razor into the water. He let her go just in time, because she was about to run the sharp razor across his eyes. She gasped and fought for air while holding her sore neck. Laurence stared at the blood pouring from his hands as the rage inside him continued to boil.

"H . . . help me, Laur . . ." his wife struggled to say. She still was coughing and gasping for air.

Laurence palmed his wife's face with his burning hand as he viciously pushed her head underneath the piping-hot water. Her legs and arms jerked wildly as he held her head under the bubbling water. Water splashed everywhere as she fought for her life. Laurence pressed down harder and harder until his wife's head was touching the bottom of the Jacuzzi. Moments later the kicking and the splashing of the water stopped. She was dead.

Laurence stood up and stared at his wife's dead body. Her eyes and mouth were wide open as she floated in the bloody water. He smiled while looking down at her. Laurence turned the lights out and closed the bathroom door.

Chapter Fourteen

A brown Toyota sped down a dark highway. There was no moon. No lights shone on the empty road. It was so dark that even the silhouette of trees in the woods could not be seen. Nothing else seemed to exist on this road but the speeding sedan and the darkness that surrounded it.

Damien drove with both hands on the steering wheel. He turned his bright lights on so he could see farther ahead, but that didn't work. The only thing in front of him was total darkness. It seemed as though they were driving into another world.

Damien became terrified when he realized that they were all alone on the abandoned highway. Something was wrong. Damien slapped his brother across the chest in a futile attempt to wake him up. Alex lay back in the passenger seat with his head leaning against the window. Damien couldn't hear him breathing, so he hit his chest again. Alex didn't move or make any noise. Damien became frightened.

"Wake up, wake up!" Damien shouted, hitting his brother with his fist as hard as he possibly could. He took his eyes off the road and glared at his brother for a second. Alex seemed lifeless. The Corolla swerved to the right, causing Damien to grab the wheel before they ran off the road into a ditch.

There was a scary silence inside the Corolla. All Damien could hear was his own heavy breathing. He began to panic and fear for his life. He thought that turning the radio on would help him calm down. Damien powered up the stereo, but all he could hear was static. All of the radio stations were out. Damien turned the stereo off and glanced at his brother. Alex looked like a corpse.

Damien could feel his eyelids closing. He immediately opened them and sat up in the leather seat. He had to pull over before he ran the car into the woods. Damien glanced at the fuel gauge. His worst nightmares were slowly becoming true. The orange low-fuel light shone brightly. He didn't have much time left.

Sweat ran down Damien's face. The thought of running out of gas in the middle of nowhere made his legs tremble nervously. He could feel his heart pumping faster. Damien needed a drink of water to help calm his erratic breathing. He turned around to see if there was a bottle of water on the back seat. The only things Damien saw in the back were four large piles of money. Where did the money come from? Damien immediately knew the answer to his question. He and his brother had stolen the money from their new boss. Now they were driving as far as they could to get away from him.

"You are not dead!" Damien said as he reached over and touched his brother's face. It felt like a piece of frozen meat. Damien quickly pulled his hand back.

The brown Toyota came to a screeching halt. Damien had been driving so fast that he drove right by an exit ramp. He quickly put the car in reverse and stepped on the gas pedal. He couldn't get off the murky highway fast enough.

As Damien drove off the curving ramp, he noticed a filling station to the right of the road. He also noticed that there weren't any streetlights. The entire town was pitch-black except for a dim light coming from the gas station. Damien's hopes of finding some help for Alex faded as he carefully looked around the deserted road of this small town. He cautiously pulled into the small gas station.

It was ancient. There were large black bugs and spiderwebs all over the gas pumps. The station looked as though it had closed down decades ago. There was rusted orange paint all over the building and pumps that were decaying and falling apart. Dead grass and weeds covered the area. Damien had a terrible feeling that someone or something was hiding in the tall grass. He wanted to drive off and look for another gas station, but he knew that he wouldn't get far.

The quiet and abandoned area petrified Damien. Anything could be out there. He kept turning around to make sure that he was alone. He stepped to the front door. He grabbed the handle and quickly turned because he thought he heard someone standing behind him. No one was there. Damien opened the loud, creaking door and walked inside.

A strong and lingering smell of cigar smoke floated throughout the air. The thick smoke that Damien inhaled caused him to cough and gasp for air. He glanced around the filthy store while struggling to catch his breath. "Hello," he yelled, and he cleared his throat. There was no answer. "Is anybody here?" he asked. It was so quiet in the station that Damien could hear the buzzing from a light that was on the verge of falling from the ceiling. There was also an echo in the room. The haunting sound of his own voice made Damien pause. He had a strange feeling that he wasn't alone.

There was an old green phone sitting on the dusty counter. It was covered with spiderwebs and insects. Damien didn't think the phone would work, but something in his mind told him to try it anyway. What did he have to lose? Before grabbing the phone, Damien jumped back and almost tripped over one of the holes in the floor. He was staring at a ghost.

Damien stared at Laurence as he puffed on his cigar and blew smoke out of his nose. Laurence was smiling and shaking his head while staring back at Damien.

Damien tried to run out of the store, but his legs wouldn't move. It felt like bricks were strapped to his ankles. "We have yo' money in the car," he said, trying to catch his breath.

Laurence didn't respond. He continued puffing his cigar and laughing at Damien. His laughter grew louder while he stared into Damien's frightened eyes.

"All of the money is in the back seat," Damien said, looking up at the open ceiling. He didn't know if he saw rats in the ceiling or if his imagination was just playing tricks. Laurence was laughing harder and harder. Damien didn't understand what was so funny. "I'll go get the money right now," he said with hesitation.

The more Damien talked, the louder Laurence's laughter seemed to get. He watched Damien very carefully but never responded to anything he said. He just casually smoked his cigar and laughed as if Damien weren't in the room.

Damien could feel something hot and wet running down his leg. He had somehow lost control of his bladder. He looked down at the small puddle of urine forming by his foot. A humiliating feeling of shame came over Damien. Laurence's psychotic laughter put so much fear in him that he'd lost control of himself. Everything would be all right once he gave the boss his money back. "I'll be right back with the money," Damien said as he ran out of the store. All he could hear behind him was Laurence's loud and demented laughter.

Damien dove into the car and slammed the door. All he wanted to do was give the boss his money and drive as far away from the gas station as possible. He turned toward Alex to try to wake him up again. Alex was not in the passenger seat. Damien stared at the empty seat in disbelief. Where could Alex have gone? Damien turned around to see if he was sleeping in the back seat. Nothing was on the back seat either. The money was gone and so was Alex.

Tears poured from Damien's eyes. He was all alone in a world that was lifeless. Damien glanced at the store and noticed that the lights were out. He opened the car door. A hand suddenly grabbed him by the neck.

The hand that was tightly wrapped around Damien's neck loosened its grip and threw him on the ground. He grabbed his bloody neck as he turned around and stared at the dark shadow. The evil lady had on the same black dress that she always wore in Damien's dreams. Her long, dark hair covered her face, but Damien could see her cold and sinister eyes staring down at him. Blood dripped from her lips. Damien closed his eyes, hoping that the lady would somehow vanish into the silent night. Seconds later he could feel sharp, piercing teeth sink deep into his neck. Damien tried opening his eyes, but they were shut tight. He tried screaming, but nothing came out of his mouth but hot air. The furious woman began clawing her knifelike nails across Damien's face in a fit of rage.

Damien tried to open his eyes again and break free from the woman who was slicing his face. A hand was covering his face and holding him hostage in his own bed. Something powerful was stopping him from waking up from yet another nightmare. Damien began to panic. His arms and legs began to kick wildly. He knew that if he didn't wake up soon, the outraged lady was going to kill him. Damien tried to open his eyes, and to his surprise they opened.

He jerked out of his sleep and sprang from the bed as if rats were crawling all over the sheets. After a few moments, he got back into bed and stared up at the dark ceiling. For some strange reason his new boss frightened him just as much as the wicked lady in his nightmares. There was something dark and sinister about the man. Damien had a bad feeling about him. His latest nightmare convinced him that the boss was a madman.

The short trip to Michigan was supposed to have been the easiest money that Damien and Alex ever made. All they'd had to do was pick up the money, count it, and bring it back to the boss. It was a simple and harmless assignment. Somehow things just hadn't gone as planned. Damien stared at the ceiling, worried about what the boss was going to do when he found out that things hadn't gone like he'd wanted them to.

Damien closed his eyes. He wanted to replay the entire trip back in his mind. He didn't know exactly when things went wrong, but he did know who to blame. An eerie image of Laurence smoking his cigar and laughing wildly came across Damien's mind. He blocked the demented vision from his mind and tried to focus on the events of yesterday morning.

A black Hummer with dark-tinted windows pulled up in front of Damien's house. The driver of the SUV honked the horn several times before Alex and Damien slowly walked out of the house. They both were hungover and dead tired. Neither of them had gotten more than one hour of sleep. They jumped in the back seat and shut the door as the driver drove off.

"Good mornin', boys," the driver cheerfully said between sips of his hot coffee. The boys could see that he was a very large man by the way his round stomach rested on the steering wheel.

"Mornin'," Damien said sluggishly. His red eyes burned from a lack of sleep, and his stomach turned from the cigars he'd inhaled.

"You boys look exhausted. That must've been one helluva party last night. How 'bout some breakfast before you hit the highway?" he asked, turning the volume on the radio up.

"I'm too tired to eat," Damien replied. His eyes were closed now, and all he could see was a world of darkness. He smiled when he heard the music that the driver (who never told them his name) was listening to. It was some country-and-western song.

Alex didn't respond. He was snoring and already in a deep slumber. The driver glanced in his rearview mirror and saw that both boys were knocked out. He turned his music up louder and sang his country songs as he drove east on the Bishop Ford Expressway.

"Wake up, boys," the round driver shouted. He clapped his large hands several times to get their attention. "Let's go, wake up!"

Damien and Alex opened their burning eyes and looked around the Hummer in a daze. They didn't know exactly where they were. Damien looked out the window and realized that they were in a gas station parked beside a Toyota Corolla.

"Have a safe trip, and I'll see you boys back here at noon," the driver said. He handed them the car keys, a gas card, and a piece of paper with all the instructions that they would need. "If there are any problems, call the boss ASAP. Now get out. My woman is making me a special breakfast this morn," the driver said with a sly grin on his round and bearded face.

As soon as the boys jumped out of the SUV the driver pulled off. Damien and Alex stared at one another with half-open eyes. Neither one of them had enough energy to get behind the wheel and drive. "You drive there, and I'll bring us back home," Damien suggested as he leaned on the trunk of the car.

"I can't keep my eyes open, and my head is bangin'. You drive there and I'll drive back," Alex suggested.

Damien said, "Let's just flip for it." He reached into his pocket and pulled out a shiny quarter. "Call it in the air."

"Tails!" Alex said, watching the quarter fall.

Damien grabbed it and smacked it on the back of his hand. He looked at it and smiled. "Guess you get to sleep first."

Alex was snoring before Damien made it to the expressway. Damien didn't know how he was going to stay awake for the two-hour drive. He yawned and rubbed his red eyes as he entered highway 94.

Damien glanced at his brother. He was still snoring softly with his head leaning against the passenger window. The time quickly passed. Damien had found a burst of energy from somewhere, because to his surprise he wasn't as tired as he was when he first got behind the wheel. The money that he was going to make was probably the reason he was feeling refreshed and energized. After the radio station went out, Damien's thoughts were entirely occupied by that money. He spent the entire two-hour trip daydreaming about how rich he was going to be.

Damien exited the expressway and entered a town called Stoneville. He followed the directions on the paper. After slowly driving through the small town for fifteen minutes or so, Damien pulled into a gated community. A guard wearing thick glasses and a dark blue baseball cap asked his name before making a phone call. After getting the okay from the homeowner, the slender guard let Damien and his sleeping brother through.

Damien drove around a circle of mansions before finding the home he was looking for. He drove up a long U-shaped driveway before parking the sedan in front of the double doors. "Wake up," he said as he pushed Alex.

Damien got out of the car and looked around in amazement. This house was beautiful. There was a marble water fountain in the middle of the yard that matched the cream-colored brick of the three-story home. The meticulous landscaping of the home let Damien know that the owner was detailed and artistic. There were stone statues of women and other abstract statues that stood out in front.

Damien stepped on the welcome mat and rang the bell. A few moments later, a tall, lean man answered the door. "You must be Damien," he said.

"I am. Are you Mr. Blake?" Damien asked.

"Yes," he said. Mr. Blake was wearing silk green pajamas with a matching robe. He looked to be in his early forties only because there were sprinkles of gray throughout his neatly trimmed beard. He shook Damien's hand before telling him to pull into the garage.

Damien walked back to the sedan and got in. This is really living, he thought as he continued to admire Mr. Blake's home. The garage door opened, and a shiny white Bentley coupe slowly pulled out of it. As Damien stared at the luxury car, he didn't realize that Alex was opening his eyes.

Alex thought he was dreaming as he watched the owner get out of the coupe and direct Damien to pull into the three-car garage. "We here already?" Alex asked as Damien eased the Corolla in.

"I see you finally woke up outta yo' coma," Damien said. He put the car in park, then shut the engine off. "I thought you was dead over there. I don't care how tired you are, you drivin' back. Now let's go," Damien said. They got out of the car as the garage door closed.

Damien and Alex looked to their right and noticed a black Mercedes truck and a navy blue Cadillac Escalade gleaming in the dark garage. Mr. Blake got their attention by telling them to follow him.

The boys followed Mr. Blake into the house and down a winding wooden staircase. They walked past a long bar and stopped in front of a pool table. "You boys want something to drink?" Mr. Blake asked.

"Water is fine," Alex said.

"I'll take any kinda pop you have," Damien said.

"Water and a Pepsi," Mr. Blake said when he handed the bottles to Damien and Alex.

"Thanks," they both said together.

"No problem," Mr. Blake replied. "Now let's take care of this so you boys can get back on the road. I know time is money." He opened up a black leather briefcase that was sitting on the pool table.

Damien and Alex couldn't believe all the money sitting right in front of them. They had never seen fifty grand at one time. They both stared at the money with their mouths wide open.

Mr. Blake sipped his yellow cocktail before saying, "Count it, and make sure all of it is there. Should be fifty thousand."

Damien counted stacks of $1,000 while Alex and Mr. Blake engaged in a little small talk.

"What's the name of that movie?" Alex asked, looking up at the life-sized screen.

"That is Midnite Terror, *one of my favorites."*

"All fifty is here," Damien said with excitement.

"Good, now you count it just to verify that everything is everything," Mr. Blake said to Alex.

After Alex counted the money for a second and third time, Mr. Blake shut the briefcase and handed it to Damien. He shook their hands and escorted them back up the stairs to the garage. Before the boys pulled out, Mr. Blake let them know that he was going to call the boss and remind him to pick up his own money next time.

Damien was in a deep and dreamless sleep by the time Alex pulled into the driveway of a local fast-food restaurant. To curb his outrageous appetite, Alex ordered two double cheeseburgers, one large fry, a barbecue chicken sandwich, and an extra-large Sprite to wash all of the grease down. He slowly ate his food as he drove back to Chicago, blasting 2Pac's third CD. While Damien slept off last night's liquor, Alex daydreamed about the briefcase full of money that was in the trunk.

It was five minutes past noon when Alex pulled into the gas station behind the black Hummer that had dropped them off. He wondered how long the Hummer had been waiting for them.

"Wake up!" Alex said to Damien as he hit him across the chest.

Damien sat up and wiped his red eyes. His vision was still blurry and cloudy from the deep sleep that had taken control of him a few hours ago. He recognized where he was, then slowly exited the Corolla. Alex was already out taking the briefcase out of the trunk. They hopped in the back of the Hummer, then Alex slammed the door shut.

"You boys have a good trip?" the driver asked with a smile.

"Yes, we did," Alex proclaimed.

"I'll take that case from you. The boss says he'll see you two tomorrow at noon," the driver said as he drove off onto the highway.

Alex gave the oversized driver the case full of $100 bills. Before they knew it, Damien and Alex were being awakened by the driver. They were back at home.

"You boys take it easy, and get some rest," the naviga-
tor of the Hummer said while chewing on a candy bar.

Alex and Damien slowly climbed out of the SUV. The
burly driver cranked up the volume on his country mu-
sic and drove off into the cold and bright day.

Damien walked into the house behind Alex, feeling ex-
cited about the money that they'd just made. They drove
out of town dead tired and exhausted, but the pay they
were receiving for it was well worth it. Damien went
into his room and fell across the bed. All he wanted to do
was sleep. Hopefully there would be no dreams.

As Damien began drifting into a deep sleep, Alex
opened his door. "Check this out," he said with a big grin.
He closed the door, then pulled out five stacks of money
from his back pockets. He threw the money on the bed
next to his brother.

"What the hell is this?" Damien asked with a puzzled
look.

"It's five extra thousand for us to split."

"Where did you get it from? Don't tell me you—"
Damien began yelling.

"No, listen. I counted fifty-five grand, not fifty. So, I
figured we'd split the extra that wasn't accounted for,"
Alex said, trying to convince Damien.

"You did what?" Damien yelled. "You stole five grand
from this man? You wanna get us killed? Are you stupid
or what?"

"What! Nobody will eva find out."

Damien was livid. "Alex, I counted fifty thousand
dollars. If you counted anything more than that, then it
was a trap, and you fell right into it."

Alex replied, "You miscounted the money. I'm tellin'
you, there was fifty-five grand in that case. These rich
guys won't miss five grand that they neva knew was
missing anyway."

"Why would you take five grand when he paying us seventy-five hundred? Take this money and get the fuck outta my room. And tomorrow you givin' back every dollar you took," Damien yelled as Alex walked out.

Damien glanced at the clock. It was now 4:09. The sun would be setting soon. He closed his eyes again and rolled over. The lunchtime meeting he and his brother had with the boss consumed his thoughts. He knew that the boss wouldn't be laughing when he found out what Alex had done.

Chapter Fifteen

Laurence sat in his immaculate office thinking about his mother. Miles Davis played over the sound system as he drank shots of tequila and puffed on his imported cigar. He was patiently waiting for noon to arrive so he could meet with the boys and give them their pay for the job they'd completed. Laurence also planned to meet with his brother-in-law and have a discussion with him.

After the two meetings, Laurence would be leaving town for a couple of weeks. He had some business to take care of in California and Atlanta. He really needed to get out of Chicago and clear his mind anyway. He was becoming a madman driven by his anger and emotions. Instead of thinking rationally before he reacted, like he always did, Laurence was acting on impulse and his own bottled-up rage. Two weeks away from home would do his mind and body some good. He would have a chance to relax and think about everything that had been going on in his life lately. If he continued to lose his temper and let his rage get the best of him, things would definitely get worse.

Laurence's thoughts were interrupted by a knock on the door. He glanced at his diamond watch. "Come on in," he said, pouring another shot of tequila.

One of the club's massive bouncers opened the door and stepped inside the office. His wife's brother was standing right behind him. "Todd is here to see you," the bouncer said in his deep baritone.

"Let him in," Laurence said. He drank the shot of alcohol down and slammed the glass on his desk.

The bouncer stepped aside and let Todd into the plush office. "The driver will be here soon, boss," he informed Laurence.

"Cool. I'll be down there."

The muscular bouncer, who looked as though he were a professional bodybuilder, nodded before walking out of the office. He quietly shut the door behind him.

Laurence stood up and shook Todd's hand. He could smell the alcohol coming out of his pores. The glazed and hazy look in his eyes let him know that Todd had been drinking and smoking cannabis already. Laurence instantly became upset. "Have a seat," he snapped, pointing to the leather couch.

Todd sat down and looked around. The room seemed to be moving in a slow, circular motion. This was his first time in Laurence's office, and little did he know that it would be his last. "This is real nice, you know," Todd said slowly as he stared at the photos on the wall.

Laurence didn't respond. He was too upset to say anything. How dare he come to a meeting with him smelling like booze and looking like a drunk? And not only did Todd reek of cheap liquor, but he looked terrible. His face and neck were full of long, thick hair, and his oversized jeans and sweatshirt were filthy. Laurence thought about throwing Todd out the window and into the trash where he belonged. He could feel himself slipping and losing control of his temper. Laurence took a deep pull from his cigar and exhaled.

Todd rubbed his hands through his matted hair and smiled. He was drunk and high. "I tried callin' my sista a few times but ain't get no answer. You know where she is?"

Laurence smiled. He was not about to engage in small talk with Todd. "She's resting."

"I'll call her again when I leave—"

Laurence cut Todd off in the middle of his sentence. "Stop bullshitting and playin' games with me. You know why I told you to come down here. Now when are you going to have my money?" he asked impatiently.

Todd sat up on the couch. He knew that there was no way he could repay Laurence anytime soon. He had no intention of paying him back anyway. "Can I have a shot of that?"

"You look and smell like you had enough. After I'm done talking, you can leave and go drown yourself in a bottle of whiskey. You have two weeks to give me back all of my money," Laurence demanded.

"How am I gonna get that type of money in two weeks?" Todd asked with a slight grin.

"At this point I don't give a fuck how you get it. When I get back here in two weeks, you better be sittin' in that seat with all of my money," Laurence said before drinking back his shot of liquor. The silly grin on Todd's face began to infuriate him.

Todd replied jokingly, "What if I don't get the money?"

Laurence stood up from his chair. "You must think I'm playing with you!"

"Just calm down, man. I know you ain't jokin'. Let me try to borrow the loot from my homeboy or my mama," Todd said. The grin was completely gone.

Laurence was too angry to sit back down. He was also upset with himself for asking Todd to come down to his office and talk. He knew that Todd was a petty criminal who wanted nothing out of life. There was no way he'd ever get his money back, and he knew that. Todd was just going to come back to his office in two weeks with another dumb excuse, so Laurence decided to give him a pass. The money was crumbs to him anyway. It was just the principle of the matter. Todd would eventually be right back in prison, or someone was going to kill him. "Don't worry about the money. I don't want you to give me a dime."

"Now you jokin', right?" Todd asked.

"I'm dead serious. And I don't ever want to see you again, because if I do . . . You're a fucking disgrace to your mother and sister. Just look at you," Laurence said.

Todd replied, "Man, fuck you too. Ain't nothing wrong with me!"

"I didn't hear you. Say that again?" Laurence asked as he grabbed the thick bottle of tequila. He could clearly picture himself breaking the bottle over Todd's head.

"You heard me. Ain't nobody scared of you. What you gonna do?" Todd boldly asked. The alcohol and drugs gave him false courage, and he began to slur his words.

Laurence smiled as he sat back down in his chair. Todd was drunk, so it didn't make sense for him to argue and go back and forth with him. Laurence was tired of smelling and looking at his pathetic brother-in-law anyway. In a few seconds he'd have him escorted out of the club. Laurence poured himself another shot of tequila, then set the bottle underneath his desk. If he didn't see the bottle, then he wouldn't be so tempted to smash it across Todd's head.

"You don't believe me, but I'ma get you . . . I'ma get you yo' money. All of it. Just give me a couple more months," Todd said.

Laurence did not say a word. He was done talking to Todd. He drank his shot down, then put the glass in his bottom drawer. He was about to call security to escort Todd out of the building, but the knock on the door made him lose his train of thought. Laurence was a little tipsy from the nine shots of tequila he'd drunk. "Come in!"

The muscular bouncer opened the door and escorted Damien and Alex into the office. He immediately left without saying a word. He left so fast that Laurence didn't get a chance to tell him to take Todd out with him. It wasn't a big deal, because everyone would be leaving the office soon anyway.

Laurence greeted Damien and Alex and told them to have a seat next to Todd. He told them who Todd was as he looked at his watch. "You boys are five minutes late. I'm deducting that from your pay," the boss said. He had a stern look on his face.

Damien and Alex looked at one another. They were late because the bouncer was on the phone and wouldn't bring them up until he finished his conversation. Damien was about to explain the situation to the boss but decided against it. That was minor compared to the situation that he wanted to discuss with him.

"Sorry, boss, it won't happen again," Alex said.

"You boys are too serious. You gotta learn to relax and have fun," Laurence said.

"Don't let this man intimidate you!" Todd blurted out.

Laurence stared at Todd for a second with evil in his eyes, then turned his attention back to the boys. He informed them that he had to fly out of town for a couple of weeks. He let them know that as soon as he got back, they'd start training and working in the club. Laurence also told them that they did a good job on their first assignment. Damien and Alex gave each other a nervous glance. They didn't know if the boss was serious or if he was being sarcastic.

Damien wanted to tell the boss about the situation with Alex and the money, but he just didn't know how to start the conversation. The boss had specifically told them to call him if there was a problem, and they didn't. He was definitely going to be upset and probably disappointed. There was no excuse for Alex's behavior, and Damien knew that they both were to blame for his greed

and stupidity. Damien had only two options: either tell
the boss about the extra money and deal with whatever
consequences that followed, or never say anything about
the money. The last option seemed more sensible to him,
although Damien had a bad feeling that the boss already
knew about the missing money.

"Well, I got things to do, so let me take care of you
boys," Laurence said. "Todd, I need you to step out into
the hallway."

"I ain't leavin' until we finish talkin'," Todd replied de-
fiantly.

Laurence shook his head. He was becoming very frustrated with Todd and his disrespectful behavior. "Look, I
know you drunk and high off something, but if you don't
get outta here right now, I'm going to throw you outta
that window!" Laurence said harshly as he pointed at the
window to his left.

Damien and Alex were extremely uncomfortable. The
conversation between the boss and his brother-in-law
was getting out of hand. They both stared at the pictures
on the wall as they listened.

"Big and bad Mr. C. How you gon' be tough when you
jealous of yo' own wife?" Todd yelled out. The alcohol
was really beginning to get the best of him now.

Laurence smiled. "What?"

For some strange reason Todd was trying to see just
how angry he could make Laurence. The liquor gave him
courage that he'd never possess if he were sober. Todd
continued to run his mouth and provoke Laurence. "My
mama always said you was jealous of they relationship
'cause you and yo' mama didn't have one."

Damien and Alex both turned and looked at Todd.
Why would he say something like that when the boss's
mother just passed away? They knew that it was time to
go before things got worse.

Laurence didn't say a word. He just stared at Todd. Todd was smiling, but he could see in Laurence's dark eyes that he wasn't playing. He'd crossed the line, but he really didn't care. He was drunk and feeling good. And he would say whatever was on his mind whether Laurence liked it or not.

The boss glanced at his gleaming watch. It was almost time for him to head to the airport. "Let me take care of you boys so we all can get outta here," he said as he stood up from his chair. "I'll be right back." Laurence walked into the back of the office.

"You two punks work for my brother-in-law, huh?" Todd asked.

"Yup! You gotta problem with it?" Alex shot back.

"I see you gotta smart mouth on you," Todd replied.

"Whateva problem you got, take it up with the boss," Damien said.

"I'm takin' it up with you two, you two punks! And I'ma take whateva he payin' y'all," Todd threatened.

Alex was becoming annoyed with Todd. He turned and looked him in the face. "You ain't takin' nothing from no-body. Shut yo' drunk ass up and leave us the fuck alone!"

"I got something for both of y'all when we get outside," Todd said loudly. He pointed two fingers at both brothers and made a shooting gesture.

Alex was about to respond to Todd's threat but was stopped when his brother slapped him across the chest with his hand. "Don't say another word to that drunk. He really ain't worth it," Damien demanded.

"I knew you boys were smart," Laurence said as he stepped in front of his desk. He had two bottles of champagne in one hand and two small brown packages in the other. "Never argue with a fool."

"Fuck all of y'all!" Todd yelled out.

Laurence smiled. "This is for a job well done," he said as he handed each brother a bottle of champagne. "And here is your money. I put a li'l extra in there for you boys, too," he said, handing them both a package.

"Thank you!" Damien and Alex said.

"You don't have to—"

Laurence was cut off by his brother-in-law. "Why won't you let me work and make some money? I'm family. My sista always said you was a selfish bastard," Todd blurted out.

Laurence gave Todd a cold and menacing stare. Then he turned his attention back to the boys. "Like I was saying before I was rudely interrupted, don't thank me. You boys earned every dollar. Now go out and have some fun. Take your girlfriends out to dinner or something. Life can be short, so go out and enjoy it."

"We are definitely gonna have some fun," Alex said, smiling.

Damien was smiling, but he wasn't thinking about his money in the brown package. His thoughts were on the cash that was back at home. Now that the boss trusted them, how was he going to explain the stolen money? Damien figured if the boss knew about the money, he would've said something, so the only thing for them to do was to keep it between themselves. They would have to act like it never happened.

"I'll call you boys when I get back here in two weeks. So, enjoy yourselves, and don't spend all that money in one place," Laurence suggested.

Damien and Alex were about to get up and walk out of the office when the boss stopped them. "Wait a second. We'll all leave together," he said.

"I ain't moving until you tell me why you won't give me a job," Todd said as he rubbed the long hairs on his chin.

"I didn't say you were going anywhere," Laurence replied with a smirk. He glanced at his watch again, then pulled a handgun, known as the Black Widow, from his waist.

Damien and Alex were terrified. They didn't know if the boss was going to shoot all of them or just Todd. They both trembled nervously as they sat frozen on the couch.

Before Todd could say another word, Laurence had already cocked the hammer on the gun and fired a shot into his abdomen. He quickly cocked the Black Widow again and fired another shot into Todd's chest. Todd screamed in agony as he bent over and fell to the floor. Blood began to pour from the two wounds onto the floor.

Damien and Alex stared at Todd in disbelief. This was the first time they'd seen anyone get shot and killed. It was more horrific and gruesome than what they'd seen in the movies.

Laurence tucked the revolver back on the side of his waist and underneath his black suede jacket. He stood over Todd and stared down at him. Todd moaned and cried out for help from Laurence. Laurence was unaffected by Todd's plea and the blood that continued to pour from his wounds. He wanted his brother-in-law to die a slow and painful death.

"Let's get out of here now," he said to Damien and Alex. Then to Todd, he said, "I'm putting you out of your misery. Now your mother will have some peace."

Laurence turned the sound system off with a remote control before walking to the door. He turned the lights out as he and the brothers exited the office. They could hear Todd screaming and pleading in agony for them to come back and help him. It was too late. He would suffer and bleed until his time ran out.

Chapter Sixteen

Damien sat in the barber chair and watched the morning news. It was eight in the morning, and he was in the shop by himself. His first client would arrive in forty-five minutes, so he had enough time to relax and watch TV. The last two weeks or so had been stressful and busy for Damien. He was working twelve hours or better every day, and then he would go home and just lie in bed. Damien was too afraid and paranoid to sleep. He stayed up all night thinking and listening to the radio. His thoughts were consumed by his nightmares and by the incident at the boss's office. Damien's body would eventually shut down on him and force him to get an hour or two of sleep. Then he'd wake up and head to the barbershop. This had been Damien's routine for the past two and a half weeks. Not only was he working all day and not getting any sleep at night, but he wasn't eating much either. Damien would eat a candy bar or two while he was working, but that was all. He was beginning to lose more weight and look unhealthy.

Damien stared at the woman reporting the news, but he wasn't listening to anything she said. He had a lot of things on his mind, and one of them was his brother. Alex had been drinking and partying like a wild man lately. He had been spending money like it grew in their backyard, too. He had a lot of new shoes, new jewelry, a new car, and plenty of high-priced clothes. Alex was having fun living carefree. Damien didn't understand how he could be so comfortable spending the stolen money when he knew what type of man the boss was. He told Alex not to spend it just in case the boss found out about it and wanted it back. Alex wouldn't listen. He kept telling Damien to have some fun. That statement was funny to Damien, because it was exactly what the boss had told him to do.

The local news anchors continued to report the top stories of the day as Damien swiveled in his chair and faced the mirror. He wondered if he was becoming too paranoid over his bad dreams and the stolen money. No one seemed to be as worried as he was. His parents never mentioned the family curse again, and they acted as though it didn't exist. Damien assumed it was their way of dealing with an uncontrollable situation. Just ignore it and deal with whatever happens. That was probably the only way to live life with some sense of peace and happiness. Damien had to adopt that same attitude if he ever wanted to have a normal life. Overcoming his fear of sleeping and his horrible nightmares was not going to be an easy task. But if he didn't, Damien was positive that the evil lady in his dreams would kill him. The thought of her and her long, deadly fingernails made Damien's skin crawl.

Two and a half weeks had gone by, and Damien hadn't heard a word from his new boss. If he knew about the money that Alex had stolen, he would have called and said something by now, Damien thought. After watching the boss kill his own brother-in-law in his office, there was no way that they could tell him about the stolen money. Damien was sure of that now. He was hoping that the boss wouldn't call him when he got back to town. The thought of working for such a ruthless and insane person terrified him. The image of the boss smoking his thick cigar and laughing hysterically flashed across Damien's mind. He had a bad feeling that the boss would be calling him very soon.

Todd lying in a pool of his own blood and begging for help was another vivid image that Damien couldn't clear from his mind. He could clearly hear Todd moaning and screaming in agony as he choked on his own blood. Every time he thought about the bloody shooting, he would cringe with fear. Instead of Todd dying in a pool of his own blood, Damien would sometimes see himself and Alex lying in blood with their eyes closed. The graphic and morbid picture would fade away as Laurence aimed his gun at them and squeezed the trigger.

Damien closed his tired eyes as he sank deeper into the black leather chair. He could hear the weatherman saying that light snow was in the forecast for the evening.

"I thought you were dead," Damien said curiously to Todd.

Todd glanced at his brother-in-law, and then he stared at Damien for a moment. He erupted into loud, hysterical laughter. His laughter must've been contagious, because Laurence began to laugh hysterically as well. Damien didn't get the joke or see the humor in anything he'd asked Todd. He became nervous as Laurence and Todd continued to laugh obnoxiously at him. Damien grabbed his drink and drank it down as fast as he could, then slammed the glass on the bar.

Laurence was laughing so hard that his eyes began to water. He suddenly stopped and wiped the tears from his eyes. "Do you have the money that you and your brother stole from me?" he asked, looking directly at Damien.

Damien didn't know what to say or do. He glanced at Todd, who was still laughing uncontrollably. Then he turned his attention back to the boss, who was no lon-

ger laughing. "No, I don't. It's at home," Damien finally answered.

Laurence burst into loud laughter again. His laughter sounded more demented and psychotic than it ever had to Damien. He wanted to leave the bar but was afraid of what was on the other side of the door.

All of a sudden, the laughter and the music came to a sudden halt. The bartender was silent, and so was the boss. Damien noticed the boss reaching behind his back and pulling out a long Smith & Wesson. His heart seemed to skip a thousand beats as he realized that the gun was pointed at his abdomen.

"You got one last chance. Do you have my money or what?" the boss sternly asked Damien. He grabbed his drink and swallowed it down before throwing the glass into one of the dark corners of the lounge. When the thick glass shattered all over the wall and concrete floor, Laurence could see Damien almost jump out of his chair.

Laurence fired two shots into Damien's stomach without blinking an eye. He began to laugh outrageously as Damien looked down at the blood that was pouring from his abdomen. He wasn't in any pain, but he was losing a large amount of blood. Damien could hear Todd laughing so loud and hard that he was on the verge of choking. How could they laugh when he was bleeding to death? Damien held his head up and glanced at the boss. He wanted to ask him to help him before it was too late. Before one word came out of Damien's bloody mouth, the boss was already firing more shots at him. The loud and piercing shots sounded like thunder to Damien. He closed his eyes as the boss continued to laugh wildly and squeeze the trigger.

The sound of someone knocking on the glass door caused Damien to open his eyes. He glared around the empty barbershop in a daze, thinking that the boss was still shooting at him. The pounding on the door continued as Damien realized that he wasn't dreaming anymore and that there was no blood pouring from his stomach. He looked at his watch. It was now 8:53. The person banging on the door must be his first client of the day. Damien jumped up from his chair to let the customer inside. He didn't recall falling asleep, and he definitely didn't realize that he'd been asleep for almost an hour.

Damien's cell phone rang. His heart skipped a beat. The last person he wanted to receive a call from was on the line. Damien listened closely as the boss told him to meet him downtown immediately for breakfast. He said that he had a few things he wanted to discuss in private with him and only him. Damien knew that something was wrong when the boss told him to meet him in a high-rise building instead of a restaurant. The boss gave him the address and apartment number where he was and told him to be there in thirty minutes. Laurence quickly hung up the phone. Damien didn't even get a chance to let Laurence know that he was in the barbershop. He slowly set his phone back on the counter and stared at the floor. Damien had a pretty good idea of what the boss wanted to discuss in private with him.

Damien decided to call Alex and tell him where he was going and why. He called Alex several times but got nothing but his voicemail with loud music playing in the background. He was probably still asleep and recovering from a long night of partying in the club. Damien tried calling home, but there was no answer. The phone seemed to ring more than ten times before he could hear his mother's soft voice on the answering machine. He closed his phone and slid it inside his jeans.

Damien was paranoid. Chills went up and down his spine as he closed his eyes and tried to gather his thoughts. He didn't want to have breakfast with the boss, but if he didn't show up, it would make him seem suspicious of something. Maybe all the boss wanted to do was eat and have a conversation about business with him. He did say that he would call when he arrived back in town, and now he was back. But why was it so urgent that they have breakfast? And why did the boss insist that he come alone?

"Is everything okay?" the client asked.

"Not really. I have an emergency. I have to leave for a little while," Damien replied. He was still staring at the floor trying to decide if he should go. The image of Todd lying in a pool of blood appeared in his head. Damien knew that he had no choice but to meet with him.

"Something I can do to help?" the customer asked with concern as he turned the chair around to face Damien.

"I wish you could," Damien said, grabbing his keys off the counter. "Here comes Hill. He can cut yo' hair. I gotta go!"

Damien made it downtown in less than thirty minutes. He tried several more times to reach his brother, but once again there was no answer. All he got was his noisy voicemail again and again.

Damien pulled up to the front door of the high-rise building and stepped out of the truck. He exchanged greetings with the elderly valet attendant, tipped him $5, then proceeded to walk inside of the luxurious building.

The immaculate building was quiet and empty. Damien looked around to see if there was a security guard or front desk clerk on duty. He had a feeling that he was being watched on a monitor in some secret security room in the building. That made him feel safe and a little less paranoid. Damien slowly walked toward the elevator and pushed the button with the arrow pointed upward. The elevator door immediately opened. Damien stepped inside and watched as the door closed in front of him.

After Damien pressed the number 25 button, the elevator began its ascension. He finally realized while staring in the mirror how tired and stressed he was beginning to look. Damien's red eyes had heavy bags and black circles underneath them. And the weight he was steadily losing made him look sick. Damien didn't want to admit it to himself, but he was slowly withering away. His frail reflection was physical proof that something was wrong. Something powerful and evil had taken control of Damien's mind and body, and there wasn't anything that he could do to stop it.

The bell rang as the elevator door slowly opened. Damien looked up and saw that he had arrived on the twenty-fifth floor. His heart began to pound faster as he continued to stare at his reflection. He was nervous and extremely worried about meeting with the boss. Damien stepped off the elevator and paused. The door closed silently behind him as he looked down the long hallway. He remembered the boss telling him to turn left once he got off the elevator. Damien walked as slowly as possible down the hallway. He thought about turning around and going home, but he knew that would only make the situation worse.

The walk down the hallway didn't take Damien as long as he wanted it to. He stopped in front of apartment 25-14. Damien took several deep breaths and closed his eyes as he gently tapped on the door.

Moments later the door opened. "Come on in. I've been waiting for you," Laurence said with a smile.

Damien stepped inside the quarter-million-dollar condo without saying a word. The nerves and feelings of terror that he thought he left in the hallway were still running through his body. He handed the boss his coat after they greeted one another with a handshake. Damien glanced around the spotless condo while the boss disappeared into the back with his coat.

The smell of eggs, bacon, and toast lingered in the air. The last thing on Damien's mind was food. All he wanted to do was get this conversation over and go back to the barbershop.

"Come over here and have a seat," Laurence said as he reappeared from the back of the apartment.

Damien walked over to the beige sofa and sat down. He looked around at the colorful abstract art that decorated the walls. He also noticed several plants neatly scattered throughout the place, as well as scented candles organized all around the room. The pink flowers that sat on the coffee table convinced Damien that the condo he was in wasn't Laurence's, or at least not only his. A woman lived here.

"I tried to wait, but I couldn't," Laurence said. "My stomach was rumbling, so I had to hurry up and eat. You hungry?"

"Not right now. I don't have an appetite," Damien replied as he continued to survey the apartment.

Laurence sat on the couch and turned the channel to the sports network before tossing the remote on the table. "Well, let's discuss why I asked you over this early in the morning," he said, looking directly into Damien's face.

Damien became even more paranoid. He had a bad feeling that the boss was about to mention the money that Alex had taken. He didn't know what to say, so he didn't say anything.

"I need a drink. You want one?" Laurence asked as he got up from the sofa.

"I'm fine."

"Well, I'm not. I need a drink."

Damien watched the anchors on the screen debate about drugs in sports as he waited for the boss to return.

He was wondering if he should tell Laurence about the stolen money. That would at least allow him to clear his conscience.

"Now let's talk, shall we?" Laurence said. He sat back down on the couch with an ice-cold bottle of vodka and a glass. He placed the bottle and sparkling glass on the table. "How did you think you'd get away with stealing from me?" he calmly asked Damien while filling his glass with vodka.

Damien was speechless. He didn't have any response because he didn't know how to answer such a question. He could feel his heart pounding violently and his hands shaking.

"You and your brother stole five grand from me and you have nothing to say?" Laurence asked. He took a sip from his glass and smiled. "I trusted you, and this is how you repay me."

"I didn't know anything about the money, not until we got home. I would never steal from you or anybody else!" Damien said, looking directly at the boss.

Laurence took another drink of vodka. "First you steal from me, then you look me in my face and lie to me."

"I'm not lying to you. My brother foolishly stole the money. I knew nothing about it until we got back here. I just didn't know how to tell you," Damien replied.

"So, you knew weeks ago and never said a word? You are just as guilty as your brother," the boss said. "Ya know, I used to be a very good judge of character."

"I'm sorry! I should've said something to you," Damien said. "I just didn't know—"

"Don't be sorry. You two knew exactly what you were doing," Laurence calmly said as he interrupted Damien. "It don't make sense why you would take five when I was paying y'all seventy-five hundred."

"Alex was being greedy."

Laurence drank his vodka straight down before slamming the glass on the table. His peripheral vision allowed him to see Damien almost jump off the couch when the glass banged against the table. "It was a careless and juvenile mistake. Now your whole family will pay for his actions. I told you never to steal from me."

"It was all my fault. Let me deal with the consequences," Damien said, looking at the floor.

Laurence grinned. "Too late! Your mother and father will never make it home from work today, and your brother . . . let's just say he will never steal from anyone ever again!"

Tears fell from Damien's eyes. At this point he didn't care what Laurence did to him.

"Don't cry now. You and your greedy brother brought this upon yourselves. All you had to do was listen to me. This really is my fault . . . for trusting you. Now I have to correct my error," the boss said as he stared at Damien.

"You don't have to hurt my parents. They didn't do anything to you," Damien pleaded. He began wiping the tears from his face. The thought of his parents being killed made him livid.

"I told you, everyone in your family will pay for your and your brother's stupid mistake. What's done is done. Maybe next lifetime you'll make better decisions," Laurence said with a sick smile on his face. "We gotta go soon. But before we leave, I want to introduce you to a very special friend of mine," he said.

Damien didn't know what to expect. He thought about running out the door, but he was too afraid that Laurence would shoot him in the back. He had a weird feeling that someone was going to come from the back of the condo and attack him. Fear overcame Damien as he watched the boss pour another drink.

"Come on out here, baby," Laurence yelled. He sipped his vodka while watching Damien look around the room.

He thought he was going to make a move for the door. To his surprise Damien didn't. "Bring my friend with you, too!"

Damien looked in surprise as a tall and gorgeous woman stepped into the living room. Her womanly curves could clearly be seen in the short pink robe that she wore. Her smooth and well-toned legs were on display, as well as her cleavage. The woman stared at Damien and spoke. "Hello, Damien!"

Damien couldn't believe his eyes. He thought he was dreaming. "What are you doing here, Kenya?" he asked. It was obvious why she was there, but those were the only words that came to Damien.

"I live here," she responded. She stared at her ex-boyfriend. He looked very tired and a lot thinner since she'd last seen him.

"Where is she?" Laurence asked Kenya.

"Right here, baby!" she said as she pulled the Black Widow from behind her back. She handed Laurence the gun while Damien continued to stare at her.

"Good girl! Now go get dressed so we can get out of here," the boss said.

"I'll be right back. Don't leave me," Kenya said. Before she left the room, she walked over to Damien and kissed him on the lips. "Goodbye," she whispered in his ear. She walked into the back and disappeared as Damien followed her with his eyes.

"Now that is a woman!" Laurence said, massaging the Black Widow. "I'm sorry I had to take her from you."

Damien couldn't say a word. He just knew that he was having one of his many nightmares. The evil lady from his dreams put a curse on him that was never coming off.

"You still in love with her?" Laurence asked Damien.

Damien hesitated. "No, I'm not."

"I was trying to do you a favor since I took her away from you. I was giving you a chance to make a whole lot of money, so much money that you wouldn't have a clue what to do with it. But you blew it. You not only embarrassed that woman in there, but you embarrassed me," the boss said sternly. "She only wanted to help you."

"She told you about me, and you felt sympathy for me?" Damien asked.

"She told me you were a good guy, so I said I'd help you get over her by putting a lot of money in your pocket. But you screwed me!"

"Tell her I said thanks for nothing," Damien said. He thought about grabbing the gun from Laurence and shooting his way out of the condo. But he knew what the outcome of that would be. The image of Todd lying face down in his own blood flashed across Damien's mind.

Laurence stood up and pointed the gun at Damien's head. "That's all you have to say after we went out of our way to help you?"

Tears began to fall down Damien's face again. He knew his time was up. There was nothing left to say. The old lady in his nightmares was calling him to join her. The family curse had finally caught up to him.

"I was gonna make Kenya kill you since she insisted that I help you, but why turn her into a demon?"

Damien closed his eyes. He could clearly see his family sitting at the dinner table eating and laughing with one another. The tears steadily rolled down his face as he saw his mother and father smiling and laughing. He saw a quick glimpse of him and Alex playing basketball at the park together. The sun was shining bright, and the sky was blue. Then there was a dark image in his mind. The old lady from his nightmares was pulling his dead body out of a river. She dragged his body into a field of dead bodies.

Damien's visions stopped when he heard the clicking sound of the Black Widow. The gun sounded like thunder as it was fired at him. He fell onto the floor from the impact of the bullet. Damien closed his eyes and never opened them again.

Laurence stood over Damien's lifeless body and stared at him. He took a long swig from the bottle of vodka after he threw the gun on the couch. Kenya walked into the room and stared at him. They gave each other an uncomfortable smile. It was time to get on the jet and start life over somewhere else. They walked out of the apartment and slammed the door shut. The couple held hands as they walked down the silent hallway and stepped onto the elevator.

Part 2

Chapter Seventeen

Two and a Half Weeks Ago

Laurence stuck his key into the door and turned the knob. He walked into apartment 25-14 with a black briefcase full of money. The money was the daily earnings from the club, which Laurence would deposit into the bank tomorrow morning. He took his loafers off at the door and stared around the dimly lit room. Burning candles were placed all around the room as soft romantic music played. It was almost four in the morning, and Laurence was exhausted. All he wanted to do was have a glass of wine and go to bed. It was obvious that Kenya had other plans.

"There is my handsome man!" Kenya said as she walked into the living room. She was wearing a black tank top, which was too small for her breasts, and matching lace panties.

Laurence smiled as he stared at Kenya with desire in his eyes. "And what is all of this?" he asked playfully.

Kenya walked up to her man and passionately kissed him. "Did you miss me?" she asked, kissing his neck.

"Yes!"

"I missed you too, and I'm going to give you a nice, relaxing massage. After that you can do whatever you want to do with me," Kenya said seductively.

"Only a fool would turn that down. I just need to sit down for a moment and clear my head," Laurence said before kissing Kenya on her lips.

"I'll go pour us some red wine."

"Sounds good," Laurence replied before walking to the sofa and falling down. He set his briefcase down beside him and his keys on top of it.

Kenya made her way into the kitchen and grabbed two wineglasses from the cabinet. She pulled a bottle of Colgin Red Cariad 2009 off the wine rack, and then she grabbed the electric corkscrew. "You look tired, baby. Busy night at the club?"

"Very busy. I have something I have to tell you," Laurence said as he loosened his black tie from his neck.

"What is it?"

"Your ex-boyfriend finished the job that I gave him today, but he stole some of the money out of the briefcase," Laurence explained.

Kenya stopped pouring. "What!"

"I'm surprised too because he seemed like a good kid. But money changes many of us, especially when it is right in front of your face."

Kenya began filling the glasses again. "Damien is not a thief. And I know he wouldn't blow this opportunity by stealing anything from you."

Laurence was trying not to let this small situation irritate him. "The amount of money that was in the briefcase when Damien received it was different from the amount that was in it when he gave it to me."

Kenya walked out of the kitchen with the two full glasses in her hands. "That doesn't sound like Damien, but . . ."

"We all have fallen victim to temptation at one time or another in our lives," Laurence said as he stared at Kenya's body.

Kenya handed Laurence a glass before sitting down on top of him. "Have you brought this matter to his attention?"

"Thank you," Laurence said, and he took a sip. "No."

Kenya drank from her glass until it was almost empty. "How are you going to handle this?"

Laurence drank his wine straight down. "I'm going to kill him."

A chill and goose bumps crawled on top of Kenya's flesh. Her heart pounded as she stared at the menacing glare in Laurence's eyes. "Why do you have to kill him?" she asked nervously.

"Because he stole from me."

"How much did he take?" Kenya inquired.

"That is irrelevant at this point. What is important is how I handle this minor situation," Laurence replied with anger in his voice.

"Can you give him a pass, for me?"

Laurence smiled. "No. But what I will do is put a bullet in his head and one in his brother's head."

Kenya was afraid of Laurence and turned on by his power. "You don't want to do something that you'll regret later on. Please think about this."

"I have thought about this. If I let him live, what does that say about me and my character? He stole money that I've sweated and bled for. Death is coming to your friend, and there is nothing that you or he can say to stop it!" Laurence explained with fury.

Laurence was ruthless and dangerous, and Kenya knew that the first time she laid eyes on him. There was nothing she could say or do to convince him otherwise about Damien. Kenya left the subject alone. She wanted Laurence now more than ever before. Kenya grabbed his empty wineglass and set it on the floor along with hers. She slowly pulled her black tank top off and tossed it aside. Laurence grabbed Kenya's face and passionately kissed her as the soft music played and the candles burned.

Present Day

Damien's eyes were wide open as his dead body lay in a puddle of warm blood. There was a dark shadow standing above him. The lady in black caressed her long, thick hair as she stared down at Damien's lifeless body. It was not wise to interfere with a witch and her family business. The woman with the black fingernails was very possessive of her own. Anyone who foolishly took the lives of her loved ones would suffer pain that they couldn't comprehend. Her job was to come back and bring them home when she was ready and only when she was ready.

The lady in black was seething with rage at the person who'd interfered with her family business. The only reason he wasn't floating in a lake right now, with his eyes missing from his face, was that he didn't know who he'd killed. But that didn't excuse him or the bitch who'd watched it happen. Their lives were in her hands now.

She closed her burning eyes and took a deep breath. The lady was furious. Her red lips opened wide as she let out a painful screech. She would make sure that the remaining days of Laurence Caine and Kenya Snow were full of misery, pain, and grief. Oh, yes! These two murderers were going to pay a deadly price for what they did to Damien and his family. There was no need to rush with them though. She would let them get comfortable and settle into their new life. She wanted them to suffer and feel her wrath before she slowly killed them. Days would go by. Seasons would change.

The lady in the black dress that scraped the floor kneeled down beside Damien. She closed his terrified eyes before gently kissing him on his forehead. The witch placed her hand in the pool of blood. She closed her dark eyes as she wiped the blood all over her beautiful face, tasting and drinking it.

Thunder rumbled outside as the lady whispered into Damien's ear and rubbed his stiff face. Heavy raindrops poured. The dull and dark gray sky cast an eerie black shadow inside the apartment. After whispering unknown words into Damien's ear, just as another witch had once done to her, the lady in black stood back up on her high heels.

"You can join us now!" she said as she stared at the body.

Moments later, Damien's body was gone. Only a puddle of blood on the carpet remained.

The dark, menacing eyes of the woman in black glanced around the quiet room. She noticed a bottle of liquor on the table and the gun that Damien was murdered with. The foolish man who had killed one of her family would be back soon for his weapon, she was certain of that. The lady picked up the bottle of alcohol and blew her breath inside of it. She smiled a wicked smile as she set the bottle back down. Just as she was sure that the killer would come back for his gun, she was positive that he would drink what was left in the bottle.

The elevator door closed slowly. For Kenya, the door and everything around her seemed to be moving in slow motion. She squeezed Laurence's hand and closed her watery eyes. Laurence stared at Kenya through the spar-

kling glass that covered the elevator walls. How beautiful and sexy this woman was. Her dark skinny jeans put
her curves on display, and the cleavage that poked out
of her tight gray sweater made Laurence bite his bottom
lip. He couldn't wait to get to wherever they were going.

Laurence pulled Kenya to his chest and began passionately kissing her. She was surprised at first but quickly
fell into rhythm. They kissed, groped, and pulled on one
another as if they were never going to see each other
again. As Laurence slammed Kenya into the mirror, the
elevator began jerking up and down before it suddenly
stopped. They both stumbled and fell to the ground from
the thunderous vibration. Then the lights went out. Kenya screamed as she looked around and saw nothing but
darkness. Laurence grabbed her and pulled her to her
feet. An invisible motor hummed, and the lights were
back on. The elevator continued its smooth descent to
the main floor. The door slid open and broke the silence
between the soon-to-be newlyweds. They both breathed
a sigh of relief as they stepped off the elevator.

Laurence paused before he and Kenya walked out of
the building's revolving door. Something was missing.
He glanced around the quiet lobby trying to think about
what he'd forgotten. The Black Widow was still upstairs
in the apartment. That old gun had sentimental value to
Laurence, and he was not going anywhere without it.

"Wait right here, baby! I forgot something upstairs,"
Laurence said.

Kenya was still nervous and shaken up from watching Damien get shot. "What did you forget?" she asked,
frightened.

"My revolver!"

Although the lobby was empty, Kenya still felt the need
to whisper. "Please don't go back up there. Let's just get
out of here. I'm scared."

Laurence kissed Kenya on her forehead. "Everything is all right. Now wait right here while I run upstairs. I'll be back in a few minutes."

Laurence didn't give Kenya a chance to respond.

Back on the twenty-fifth floor, he felt uneasy as he glanced around the quiet hallway. No one was there, but it felt as though a presence loomed over him.

In the apartment, he walked into the living room and saw his gun still sitting on the couch. There was a puddle of blood on the floor, but there was no body. Damien was gone.

"What the hell!" Laurence whispered to himself. He closed his eyes. Maybe he was hallucinating. When he opened them, the scene was exactly the same, just a pool of blood on the floor. Damien was dead. Laurence was positive of that. So how could his body mysteriously disappear?

The lady in black watched Laurence with curiosity. He was tall and extremely handsome, but a murderer, nonetheless. There was a nervous look on Laurence's face as he glanced around the room. He couldn't see the evil lady, but he could definitely feel her presence. Laurence didn't know how close he was to having his eyes ripped out of his face and being thrown off the balcony to his demise.

Laurence grabbed the bottle of vodka just as the evil lady had suspected he would. He took a long swig from the bottle and set it back down. The poison that was mixed with the alcohol would damage Laurence's stomach for his remaining days. Laurence picked up the gun and cocked it back as if he were about to shoot someone. He was paranoid and frightened as he suspiciously glared around the apartment, trying to figure out what happened to Damien's body.

The lady in black watched him angrily. She decided to give him something to think about before he left the quiet apartment.

"Your life is mine," she whispered.

Laurence froze for a moment. He thought he heard a voice, but how could he have when he was in the condo all alone? Something was wrong. First Damien's body mysteriously disappeared, and now voices could be heard in the apartment. Laurence was noticeably disturbed.

Kenya would be worried if he didn't hurry up and get back downstairs. Laurence walked backward to the door. He opened it and stepped back out into the eerie hallway.

The evil woman watched Laurence walk out the door. She smiled as she thought about the pain and agony that she was going to bestow upon him. The lady walked to the balcony and watched the rain fall. Thunder rocked and lightning struck with a vengeance.

The booming thunder seemed to vibrate the building as Laurence quickly made his way to the elevator. As the elevator door slid open, Kenya's worried eyes were staring Laurence directly in the face. He took a deep breath and tried to forget about the missing body.

"What took you so long?" Kenya asked anxiously.

Laurence hesitated before responding, "I just had to use the bathroom."

"You look like you seen a ghost. You all right?"

"Yeah, I'm good. Now let's get the hell out of here."

Laurence grabbed Kenya's arm and quickly escorted her out of the building. He looked back one last time to make sure that no one was following him.

Chapter Eighteen

A year had passed since Kenya had become Mrs. Laurence Caine. Neither one of them wanted a big, extravagant wedding, so they'd flown to Las Vegas and had Elvis perform the ceremony. For five straight nights the newlyweds had partied like they were college students. They danced in the clubs, gambled away thousands of dollars, and had wild sex wherever and whenever they felt the desire. Laurence and his wife didn't shy away from the bar either. They drank fruity mixed drinks and shots of tequila until they damned near passed out in the casino. The Caines were having the time of their life, and Laurence didn't want the fun to end. He couldn't remember laughing and smiling so much. Kenya was definitely the one. If only his parents were still living to see how happy he was.

After their long and exhausting nights in Sin City, the newlyweds had travelled to the Bahamas. Laurence knew that a serene island, with a beautiful view, would give him and his bride a chance to relax and talk about their future together. They sat in the hot sand, looking out at the sky blue water for hours. Laurence and Kenya talked about having kids right away. She wanted three or four, while he only wanted one. Laurence felt that he was too old to start having a bunch of kids. And he was afraid of his evil ways being passed down to his children.

Laurence and Kenya had spent two relaxing weeks in the hot and humid Bahamas. When they weren't playing in the water and lying out in the sand, they were in their villa making love. When the honeymoon was over, Laurence had told his wife that he owned a piece of property in southern Illinois where they would relocate and raise their children. A new wife! A new city! A new attitude! Laurence was overly excited about starting anew and changing his life.

Kenya's bright smile and joy quickly turned sour when she heard the name of the city they were moving to. She had terrible, terrible memories of this place as a kid.

The small town of Redgrass was located 281 miles south of Chicago. The town was covered with tall trees, dirt roads, and small businesses that were built during the early 1950s. There was one liquor store, one grocery store, and one small hospital in the entire town.

Laurence used to visit Redgrass as a kid with his father. Every summer they would drive down in his Cadillac and hang out for the weekend with one of his friends. Big Moses was his name. He seemed like a giant to Laurence back then. He had five boys and a house big enough for all of them to have their own room.

Laurence and the boys played outside in the humid air from early morning until late at night. They rode dirt bikes and four-wheelers, played basketball and football on the gravel and dirt, and swam in the town lake. The boys also ran through the woods shooting at rabbits and squirrels, and anything else that was moving, with their slingshots and BB guns. Laurence fell in love with the quiet town of Redgrass as a kid. That was why he decided to move there with his new bride. He needed to rebuild his life in a town where nobody knew him.

Now, a year after they'd married, the Midwest was coming out of one of the worst winters on record. Over a hundred inches of snow had fallen throughout the frigid season. Laurence had plowed and shoveled three or four times a day most of the winter. Then the temperature in Redgrass had gone from one extreme to the other. The mountains of snow were now gone. The below-zero temperatures and biting windchill were over. Now it was raining. It drizzled for three days before it began to pour.

Laurence sat up in his king-size bed, flipping through an exotic car magazine. He was also watching the Final Four basketball tournament playing on the screen that hung on the wall. Kenya was in the bathroom, soaking in a hot bubble bath. Lightning continued to brighten the dark sky. The roaring thunder rocked the atmosphere as the heavy downpour collapsed on top of the roof.

Laurence was disturbed by a frightening scream. It was his wife. He dropped his magazine and jumped out of bed. When Laurence burst through the bathroom door, he saw his wife sitting in a tub full of blood. He couldn't stop her from screaming.

Chapter Nineteen

Laurence first saw Kenya standing in line at the movie theater. He was at the late-night show by himself to watch the sequel to one of his favorite action movies. She was there with her boyfriend buying tickets to a horror film called *Bloody Basement*.

Kenya was gorgeous. Her big brown eyes sparkled, and her beautiful smile made Laurence stare with lust in his eyes. Her tight blue jeans and blouse showcased her womanly curves. And the high heels that Kenya wore made her as tall and stunning as a runway model. Passion and desire consumed Laurence. He had to meet this woman and talk to her.

Laurence followed closely behind Kenya and her boyfriend as they entered the crowded theater with popcorn and drinks in their hands. Her sexy switch and the way she walked was driving him crazy. Laurence sat a few rows back from the seemingly happy couple. As the previews began to play, he stared at the lovebirds as they kissed and whispered in each other's ears.

Bloody Basement was your typical slasher flick. It was full of blood, gore, and violence. Laurence continued to switch his attention from Kenya to the screen as the audience screamed and jumped during each scene. And then finally, just as Laurence knew she would, Kenya stood up and headed out of the dark theater.

There was a sly grin on Laurence's face as he strolled out of the theater. He watched Kenya walk into the ladies' room, so he decided to boldly wait outside the door for her.

Kenya smiled when she walked out. She noticed Laurence staring at her and shaking his head in delight.

"How are you doing?" Laurence asked.

Kenya paused and turned around. "I'm doing pretty good, and yourself?"

Laurence walked up to Kenya so that they were face-to-face. Her brown skin was flawless. The sweet perfume that she wore smelled divine. "I'm good now. Can I take you out to dinner tomorrow?"

"Charming, handsome, and aggressive. I like that in a man," Kenya replied.

"So, I will pick you up tomorrow night at seven."

"I saw you staring at me in the ticket line, and then you follow me to the restroom. You're not a stalker, are you?" Kenya asked with a smile.

"No. I just go after what I want," Laurence replied as he looked Kenya up and down.

Kenya grabbed Laurence's face and whispered her phone number into his ear. Her soft lips grazed his ear and sent chills throughout his body. She then turned around and walked back to the movie theater.

A few months later, Kenya was calling her boyfriend and telling him that their relationship was over.

Chapter Twenty

Present Day

Dr. Halmer's office smelled of fresh cinnamon as usual. His multiple degrees, certificates, and accolades hung on the bright green wall opposite a beautiful painting of the Chicago skyline sitting under a full moon. Everything on the doctor's desk was meticulously and carefully arranged. The stacks of papers, the pen holder, and a few books all seemed to be neatly placed in order. Kenya sat nervously in the leather chair, staring up at the ceiling. Laurence was studying a black-and-white photo of Dr. Halmer and his wife. He assumed it was their wedding picture because of how they were dressed.

The silence in the warm office was broken by a soft-spoken voice. "Good morning to you all," Dr. Halmer cheerfully said.

"Good morning, Doctor," Laurence replied. He stood up to shake his hand.

"Same to you," Kenya said dryly.

The elderly, thin doctor sat down at his desk in a brown leather chair. He picked up his candy dish and offered them a piece of peppermint or butterscotch. They both declined. He pulled his square corrective lenses off and stared directly at Kenya. "Well, let's discuss the tests I ran on you."

Kenya's heart began to pound faster. She grabbed her husband's hand and squeezed it as if she were trying to break it.

"The blood and hormone tests were fine. The structural exam came back without any issues as well. There is still no scarring or damage to the uterus or to any other of your reproductive organs."

Tears fell down Kenya's face. She smiled as she looked at her husband.

Dr. Halmer placed his thick frames on the desk. "You are a healthy young woman who is more than capable of carrying a child. But there seem to be some inexplicable complications at the moment. Because this is your third consecutive miscarriage, there is reason for concern."

"But nothing is physically wrong with me?" Kenya asked.

"The female body is a complex organism. The test results say one thing, but your body is not responding to a new life, so the answer to that question is yes and no," the doctor said matter-of-factly.

"I understand," Kenya replied, wiping tears from her face.

"Depression is common with such an unexpected loss as this one. Mrs. Caine, I recommend you give your body and mind time to heal and rest."

"How much time?" Laurence asked.

"That depends on your wife. You want to make sure she is strong enough to handle being pregnant again when it happens. You kids can also take some time to consider alternatives to childbirth. Some options are—"

Kenya interrupted him. "No, thank you. If I can't have my own kids, I don't want none!"

"Point well taken," Dr. Halmer replied.

Laurence stood up. "Thank you for everything, Doctor. We'll see you soon."

"My pleasure, my pleasure. You kids take care and remember to make sure you get plenty of rest, Mrs. Caine."

"I will. Thanks again for everything."

The old doctor, who had a thick gray mustache that fell
to his chin, walked the disappointed couple out of his office. He expected to see them again in four to six months.
What Dr. Halmer didn't know was that he would never
see Mr. or Mrs. Caine ever again.

After leaving the doctor's office, Laurence stopped at
one of the local diners. He suddenly had the appetite of
a wild beast. He ordered two of the largest steaks in the
restaurant to go along with butter rolls, brown rice, and
French fries. Kenya only ordered a chicken salad. Food
was the last thing on her mind at the moment.

"Are you going to eat all of that food?"

"I think so. My stomach is rumbling."

"I'm scared, Laurence. I want to have a baby so bad.
Something is wrong. I can feel it," Kenya said while fighting hard to hold back tears.

"Nothing is wrong. We both have been tested and
checked over and over. We just have to be patient."

Kenya didn't respond. Laurence knew that he was trying to convince himself as well as his wife that everything
was going to be all right. Deep down inside he felt the
exact opposite though.

The food finally arrived. Laurence's mouth watered,
and his eyes widened as the gum-chewing waitress set
the hot plates on the table. He thanked the red-haired
lady and began devouring his lunch. Kenya picked over
her salad until she just gave up. She set her fork down
and stared around the small diner. If Laurence only knew
how much she hated this town . . .

*There was no moon. No stars shone in the black sky.
Nothing but darkness surrounded Laurence as he ran.*

His breathing became heavier as the footsteps behind him got closer and closer. Laurence wanted to turn around to see what was behind him, but he didn't dare. As he sprinted anxiously into a sea of blackness, something began to wrap around his neck and choke him. Warm and scaly skin continued to entangle Laurence's neck until he couldn't breathe. He stopped running as he started to gag. He knew that a snake was trying to kill him. From the darkness, Laurence could see the bright green eyes of a king cobra staring viciously at him. What really made his skin crawl and his heart thump erratically was the smirk on the snake's brown face. The creature seemed to be laughing at Laurence. The snake's smile quickly vanished as Laurence reached for his head. He opened his mouth wide and lunged toward his victim.

"Wake up, wake up, wake up," Kenya said as she shook her husband.

Laurence opened his eyes and saw his wife staring down at him in surprise. His arms were stretched out in the air, and his right fist was clenched so tight that it began to tremble.

"You were having a nightmare?" Kenya asked, pushing Laurence's arms down back by his sides.

"I guess so. My hand is still shaking."

"You were screaming and trying to grab something in your sleep. What was the dream about?"

Laurence rubbed his hazy eyes. "I remember a long snake wrapping around my neck and—"

"Stop it! Stop it! I hate snakes," Kenya announced.

"I thought you wanted to hear about my dream."

"I did until . . . Snakes scare the hell out of me. I cannot look at them, and I don't talk about them. Period!" Kenya confessed as chills and goose bumps began to travel down her back.

"Why? What happened to you?" Laurence asked with concern.

"I don't want to talk about it. Snakes horrify me! Now can we go back to sleep?"

Laurence didn't respond. He just grabbed his wife and pulled her on top of him. They lay in silence as the sun began to rise. Moments later they both were sound asleep.

Chapter Twenty-one

Kenya kissed her husband on the lips and watched him walk out of the bright room. He was going out to run some errands and to shop for a new toy, as he put it. Laurence wanted Kenya to ride with him, but she declined his offer. She preferred to stay in the house and lie in bed, watching TV and sleeping. Kenya had no desire and no energy to do anything. The visit to Dr. Halmer's office had drained all the life out of her. Kenya's healthy appetite was becoming a fading memory. She thought about taking some medication for the pounding headache that was blurring her vision.

The blazing sun shone through the windows of the master bedroom. Kenya grabbed the remote control and flipped through the many TV channels. Nothing was on that she was interested in watching. Reruns of her favorite reality shows were playing, so Kenya left the TV on the movie channel. She slowly crawled out of bed and went to close some of the curtains in the room. Every step that Kenya took on the wooden floors seemed to make her headache increase. The room was dim now. Kenya hoped that a nap would alleviate her throbbing headache and make her feel better. She had something important to do before she went to sleep. Kenya walked into her walk-in closet and unzipped her brown purse, which was sitting on a bench. She grabbed an unopened envelope and walked back out of the closet.

Kenya sat up in bed staring nervously at the wrinkled white envelope. In it was a letter written to her by Damien over a year ago. Kenya had refused to open the envelope because of all the feelings it would bring back. But right now, a million emotions were running through her rattled mind as she stared at it. Kenya was sad and hurt as she thought about how her ex-boyfriend's life ended. The guilt that she felt inside knowing that she was partly responsible for his death was slowly driving her insane. Kenya's eyes watered and her hands trembled as she took her time opening the envelope.

Kenya took the letter out and threw them both onto the bed. She couldn't get the horrible thought of Damien being shot in the head out of her mind. Kenya put her head into her hands and began sobbing uncontrollably. Guilt made her heart hurt, and it caused the tears to flow like a waterfall.

Minutes later, Kenya tried to compose herself by taking several deep breaths. She wiped the tears from her red eyes as she picked the letter up off the bed. Her headache was still an issue as she began to read.

> *Dear Kenya,*
> *I really don't know how to start this letter, but let me just say that I miss you very much. I never thought that we wouldn't be together. I mean, I always thought that we would get married one day and have kids. But I see now that that will never happen. I understand that life changes and people change every day. But when you called me and told me that it was over, I was devastated, to put it mildly. Things were already going bad for me, and then you called and told me you were moving on. I can't describe how terrible I feel, so I won't bother trying. I thought I had closure after we talked*

again, and I told myself that would be the last time we talked. But then something happened I feel I have to tell you about. You are the only person I can trust and who will believe what is happening to me.

To make a long story short, my family is cursed. I know that sounds weird or crazy, but it's true. Without getting into details, there has been a curse on my family for generations. My father said that one of our dead family members is coming back to bring us all "home." Because of the strange things that have been going on with me, I have no choice but to believe him. A woman has been trying to kill me in my dreams. When I wake up, I can still feel her presence in the room. I'm scared to death of what is happening. I'm actually terrified to write about this because I don't know what she will do to me.

This lady has been trying to kill me with her sharp fingernails. Every time I go to sleep, she is waiting for me. Believe me, I wouldn't tell you this if it weren't true. Eventually this evil lady is going to take me "home." I had to tell someone this story because my entire family may be dead very soon. There is a lot more to this story that I'm not sharing, but if anything happens to me and my family, it is the curse.

Although I'm scared of the future, I know that life goes on, so I'm trying to do my best to live. Just know that I will always love you, and I wish you the best.

Maybe I was wrong when I vowed to myself that we'd never talk again. I hope I was.

Sincerely,
Damien

Tears fell on the letter as Kenya read it again. The fact that Damien was gone hurt like hell, and there was nothing she could do about it. After reading Damien's words for the third time, Kenya folded the letter and put it back into the wrinkled envelope. *Did he really believe that his family was cursed?*

Kenya was confused and upset by Damien's letter. If he had called her and told her what was going on in his life, maybe she could've helped him. It was too late to do anything now. Damien was dead and gone. Kenya took the envelope back into her closet. She wanted to rip it up and throw it in the garbage, but her aching heart wouldn't allow her to. She tucked the morbid letter away in her purse just in case she ever wanted to read it again.

The humidity and the temperature continued to rise outside. Kenya stared out her bedroom window at the birds in the trees, replaying Damien's every written word in her head. And then the horrific image of Laurence shooting him in the head began playing in her mind. Kenya couldn't take any more pain. She walked back to bed and cried and cried until she eventually fell asleep.

Chapter Twenty-two

Laurence stuck his key in the ignition, started the engine, and slowly pulled his black truck down the long driveway. A piercing and burning sensation shot through his stomach and caused him to suddenly smash on the brakes. Laurence clutched his stomach and fell over to the passenger seat. The excruciating pain that seemed to be ripping his abdomen apart was almost unbearable. Laurence bit down hard on his bottom lip and closed his eyes, hoping that the burning pain would quickly subside.

Moments later the agonizing pain was gone. Laurence sat up and looked in the rearview mirror. Something strange was happening. He just didn't know what it was. He took his foot off the brake and stepped on the accelerator. Laurence made a right turn out of his driveway, then headed toward Highway 9.

Laurence drove in silence down the deserted highway. He would usually have his loud music blasting while behind the wheel, but not this time. It was just him, his thoughts, and the empty road.

Laurence thought about his mother, whom he'd last seen more than a year ago resting peacefully in her bronze-colored casket. Even in death she'd been beautiful. There'd even seemed to be a slight smile on her stiff face. Laurence had held his mother's lifeless hand as he stared into her face for hours. There was so much pain and regret built up inside him. Everything he wished he could've said over the past years came out right there in front of the casket. Laurence talked and cried until he could talk no more. He'd walked out of the morbid funeral home feeling like a huge weight was lifted from his shoulders. He could now move forward with his life, and his mother could truly rest in peace after finally spending time with her only son.

Laurence continued to drive as thoughts of his parents flooded his mind. Although he hadn't gone to the actual funeral service, his dad would be proud of him for visiting with his mother before she was buried in the ground. He definitely wouldn't be proud of him for refusing to speak to his sister. Laurence could see him scornfully shaking his head and telling him and Renee to "make it right, right now," as he always did when they argued and fought as kids. Laurence had to smile as he thought about his father scolding them. Things were different now. He had no intention of having a relationship with his younger sister, and he felt no regret about it.

The sun shone brightly as the temperature continued to soar. It wasn't even twelve o'clock yet, and it was already ninety degrees outside. Laurence was forced to let his tinted windows up and turn the air on. Thoughts of his family continued to consume him. Now that his father and mother were deceased, he had no family left. Laurence felt alone. This was a feeling he hadn't felt since his dad passed away. Now it was just him and his wife. No kids. No kids in the future. Just him, her, and a big house. Laurence felt that a curse was put on him for the way he'd treated his mother over the years, and the punishment for his behavior was that he wouldn't get a chance to raise kids of his own.

Laurence didn't want to admit that he was cursed, but he knew something was wrong. Every chance he had of becoming a father was stopped by unknown circumstances. Last year Laurence was excited and full of pride because he was finally having the son he always wanted. When he got to the delivery room, the doctor said that Kenya was having internal complications that were causing the baby tremendous stress. Laurence Jr. had to be cut out of her. He was stillborn, and Kenya nearly lost her life because of a severe loss of blood. Laurence walked slowly out of the hospital, dejected and angry at the world. He remembered drowning his pain in a bottle of—

"In 1.1 miles, take the Watertrail/158a East exit," directed the voice coming from the GPS. Laurence made a sharp right turn on Watertrail and proceeded to his destination.

While Laurence was exiting, Kenya was back at home trying to wake up from a horrifying nightmare. Every time she tried to open her eyes and lift her head from the damp pillow, she was stopped by someone yanking her ponytail and pulling her down back onto the bed. Kenya tried to scream for help, but no words came out. She was trapped inside of a bad dream, and no one was around to wake her up.

Kenya ran as fast as she could through the quiet woods. She looked up at the dull gray sky and around the wooded area, but she didn't dare look behind her. Someone or something was chasing her, and Kenya could sense danger. What terrified her more than anything was that she couldn't hear any footsteps or anyone breathing behind her. There was an eerie silence in the woods. Kenya realized that as hard as she was running and as heavy as she was breathing, she could hear nothing. She was so scared that she closed her eyes and ran, and ran, and ran.

The thought of running into something and falling down forced Kenya to open her eyes. If she fell, she'd be at the mercy of whatever was pursuing her. A piercing chill ripped through her body as she considered turning around to see what was chasing her. Kenya looked up at the dull gray sky and around the thick green forest again. She took a deep breath and looked over her shoulder without breaking her stride. There was a black shadow directly behind her. Kenya gasped for air. She turned around and closed her eyes again, but it was too late.

Run! Run! *Kenya screamed to herself. She suddenly felt a cold hand grab and squeeze her neck. She stopped running and yelled in agony as sharp claws dug in. Those same nails began brutally ripping at Kenya's neck as if they were trying to detach her head. The black shadow threw her on the ground and grabbed her hair.*

Kenya jumped up out of her sleep screaming hysterically. She sat in bed shaking uncontrollably as she tried to figure out exactly where she was. When she finally stopped screaming, she glanced around the room and realized that she was at home and not in the woods. Kenya took a deep breath. Thankfully, the nightmare was over.

She was drenched in sweat, as were the beige sheets and pillow. She climbed out of the bed and walked into the bathroom. Laurence was gone, but for some strange reason Kenya didn't feel alone. She quickly shut the bathroom door and locked it.

The pain in Kenya's neck travelled up to her head. She needed some medication now to alleviate the tremendous pain and throbbing. She found some aspirin in the medicine cabinet. After swallowing five pills, Kenya took off her wet shorts and T-shirt. As she stared in the mirror at her naked body, sweat continued to pour from her neck. When Kenya wiped her neck, she realized that the liquid on her hand was too thick to be sweat. The blood in the palm of her hand dripped onto the ceramic floor. Fear paralyzed Kenya for a moment. She couldn't breathe, move, or stop staring at the blood.

Kenya snapped out of her trance. She nervously looked around the spacious bathroom and checked the lock on the door again. She was still alone, and no one could get in. Kenya turned the hot water on and stepped into the shower. She closed her eyes and thought about the creepy letter she'd read from Damien. It was disturbing and unreal. Kenya didn't know what to believe, and of course she couldn't call Damien to ask him about it. Kenya did know that Laurence could never find out about the eerie letter. Tears fell from her eyes as she again saw a bloody image of Damien being murdered by her husband.

Chapter Twenty-three

Laurence turned into the customer parking lot of Jim's and parked his truck. He grabbed his keys and put on his designer sunglasses before exiting the SUV. The sweltering heat and humidity outside was suffocating. It was damn near unbearable, Laurence thought as his brown V-neck T-shirt clung to his skin.

The colorful banner that sat on top of the brick building read JIM'S EXOTIC MOTORCYCLES & SPORTS CARS. The blazing sun shone brightly on him as he walked toward the glass double doors and stepped inside.

The cold air circulating throughout the showroom floor was very much appreciated. Laurence pulled his white baseball cap off and wiped the sweat from his forehead. He put his hat back on his bald head and began to pace. Laurence kept his sunglasses on as he casually looked at the colorful motorcycles and fancy sports cars. He was there to buy a sports car, so he paid little attention to the suicide and dirt bikes on display.

As he walked around the immaculate showroom, he noticed that he was alone. There were no patrons or workers to be found. Music played in the background, maybe a soft or classic rock station. Laurence didn't really care what music was playing or who was singing. He was there for one specific purpose. His patience was slipping and growing thinner as the seconds went by.

Laurence had many pet peeves, but bad customer service was definitely number one on his list. There had been numerous occasions when he'd experienced terrible customer service that forced him to take his business elsewhere, like when he was looking to purchase a home in Arizona, and he walked out on the real estate agent. The real estate agent, who was very nice and friendly, was showing Laurence a beautiful home when her phone started ringing. Instead of turning her phone off or telling the person on the line that she was conducting business, this woman decided to hold a conversation while showing the home. Laurence couldn't believe it. How rude of her to talk on her cell phone and try to describe the house to him at the same time. He was so pissed off that he just walked out of the mansion without saying a word. That real estate agent had cost herself a huge commission. Laurence hired another real estate agent and purchased the home for over $3 million.

After ten minutes of him pacing the showroom floor and browsing the car selection, still not one representative of Jim's had come to greet Laurence or ask him if he needed help. He was about to walk out, but then something beautiful caught his eye.

A sparkling fire red Ferrari sat in the corner all alone. Laurence walked slowly around the Italian-made car, admiring it as if it were a beautiful woman. The 458 Spider sat on twenty-one-inch chrome rims that were so clean they looked like they were made of glass. The interior was black with red piping on the seats to match the fire red exterior. Laurence was sold. He didn't have to think twice about buying this Ferrari.

"Can I help you, sir?" a loud voice asked Laurence.

Laurence ignored it. He suddenly became irritated again. *Now they want to greet me after I've spent 10 minutes walking around this fucking place without any service?*

A short, thin man stepped in front of Laurence with a big smile on his face. "I'm Robert," he said, extending his right hand to Laurence.

Laurence stared at Robert's hand for a few seconds, then reluctantly shook it. *This asshole has some nerve.* Still no words came out of his mouth.

As a salesman, Robert had the pleasure of dealing with all types of customers with various personalities. In his twenty-two years in the business, there was nothing that he hadn't seen, so dealing with Laurence and his attitude didn't change his approach to selling. "You see anything that interests you?" Robert asked with a bright smile on his clean-shaven face.

Laurence couldn't hold his tongue any longer. He pulled his dark sunglasses off and stared Robert directly in the face. "You assumed, because of how I'm dressed, that I couldn't afford anything in here. You figured I'd browse around, dream about owning one of these cars one day, then leave."

Robert continued smiling. He was convinced that Laurence was there to window shop. This guy had on army fatigue shorts, a brown V-neck T-shirt, and a pair of crisp white Stan Smiths with no socks. Robert knew that he was wasting his time but decided to humor the customer anyway. "Our policy is not to discriminate against anyone who walks through those doors. I'm here alone on Tuesdays and—"

Laurence cut off the bald salesman in the middle of his explanation. "There is no excuse for bad customer service. I wanna buy this Ferrari and get outta here before I change my mind."

"Well, how is your credit, sir?" Robert asked.

Laurence was steaming now. "I said I wanna purchase this car, not finance it." The anger was beginning to come through his voice.

"You know, this baby here, she costs over a quarter of a million dollars," Robert said sarcastically.

Laurence smiled. He could feel himself slipping into a dark place. "Go in your office and write this sale up before I make a phone call and have this fucking place shut down," he said harshly.

The bright smile quickly faded from Robert's face. He didn't know who the man standing in front of him was. Or who he knew. He did know that he looked very serious. Robert could in no way jeopardize the family business, so he proceeded to his office.

In less than an hour, Laurence was the owner of the fire red Ferrari 458. He managed to purchase the sports car for $10,000 less than the asking price, and Robert agreed to ship his truck back home to him for free. Although Laurence was happy about the final sales price, he was still very upset with the smiling salesman. Before he drove off in his new toy, Robert thanked him again for his business and attempted to shake his hand. Laurence said, "Fuck you!" Then he pushed the red engine start button. The exhaust screamed loudly as he stepped on the accelerator. As Laurence pulled out of Jim's parking lot, he noticed an all-black Mercedes-Benz slowly pull in past him.

Chapter Twenty-four

The terrible pain in Laurence's stomach resurfaced as soon as he made a left turn onto Highway 9. The burning and intense cramping forced him to exit the highway and pull over at a deserted rest area. Laurence felt nauseated and lightheaded when he placed the sports car in park. He quickly opened the door and vomited. The blazing sun caused beads of sweat to drip from Laurence's face as he continued to spew onto the burning ground.

Laurence wiped his mouth when he was sure that there was nothing left in his stomach to throw up. When he shut the car door, he noticed that there was also blood on the back of his hand. Laurence closed his eyes and took a deep breath. The vomiting didn't make his stomach feel any better. There was still piercing cramps and torturous flames pulsating in his gut. Laurence needed some cold water and antacid. He turned the engine off and slowly stepped out of the car.

When Laurence opened the door to the rest area, a cold burst of air hit him in the face. He glanced around the small, empty room. There was an information desk, two vending machines, and a water fountain in the clean lobby. Laurence saw the sign that read MEN'S ROOM and followed it.

Cold water splashed onto Laurence's face and into his eyes. The cold water was refreshing as he rinsed the blood and vomit from his mouth. He instinctively jumped when he saw a dark shadow walk behind him in the mirror.

Laurence quickly turned around and looked around the quiet bathroom. He didn't hear anyone come through the door, but he checked the two stalls anyway. Both stalls were empty. Laurence wasn't going crazy or seeing things. There was definitely a dark figure that walked behind him. He rinsed his face and mouth one last time before walking out of the restroom with his back facing the door.

An ice-cold lemon-lime pop made a thumping sound as it fell to the bottom of the vending machine. Laurence bent down to grab the generic soda when he heard a whisper echo throughout the desolate rest area. He dropped the can of pop and jumped up.

Laurence nervously scanned the cold room. He definitely heard a whisper, and he thought he heard what the eerie voice said. This was the same creepy whisper that Laurence heard over a year ago in the apartment. He grabbed his can of pop out of the vending machine and walked back to his Ferrari, once again with his back facing the front door.

The inside of the Ferrari felt like an oven as the blazing sun shone directly on top of it. Laurence hit the start button and turned the air conditioner up another notch. He opened the can of lemon-lime pop and poured it down his dry throat. The carbonation from the soda eased some of the burning and trembling in Laurence's stomach. He closed his eyes and waited for the soda to finish working in his abdomen. Seconds later Laurence was asleep and snoring lightly.

"The test results came back, honey. The doctors couldn't find anything wrong with your stomach," Laurence's mother said with joy.

"That's right, son. You probably just need to change your diet and get more rest," Laurence's father suggested.

Laurence lay back on the inclined hospital bed, staring at his parents in shock. He couldn't believe that they had come to the hospital to visit him. Laurence looked at the tubes protruding from his arm. He hoped that his parents were going to take him home, because he hated everything about hospitals.

"Mom, I can't stay in here. Are you taking me home?" Laurence asked anxiously.

Laurence's mom rubbed his bald head. "Not today. The doctors want you to stay a few more days so they can monitor you."

"We'll be back tomorrow to check on you. Now relax and get some rest. You look worried for no reason," Laurence's father said.

There was a knock on the door, and then two nurses wearing navy blue scrubs entered. "Can you excuse us for about ten minutes?" one of the nurses asked with a smile.

"We were about to leave anyway," Laurence's mother said before kissing her only son goodbye.

Laurence's father followed his wife and kissed his son on the cheek. "See you in the morning."

When Laurence's parents walked out of the cramped hospital room, one of the nurses shut the door and locked it.

"Why are you locking the door?" Laurence asked curiously.

The short nurse put her finger to her mouth. "Shhh," she whispered.

Laurence's heart began to beat faster as the two nurses walked up to his bed with evil and malice in their dark eyes. He tried to get up from the bed, but he was immobile. Laurence was at the mercy of the two nurses.

"Kill him slowly," a voice whispered from the back of the room.

Laurence took his eyes off the nurses and noticed a dark shadow standing in the back of the cold room. His eyes grew bigger and bigger as both young ladies turned around.

"Yes, ma'am," both nurses said in unison.

The taller, heavier nurse pulled out a syringe as long as her forearm. "I'm going to drain all of the blood from your body with this," she said in a voice just above a whisper.

The other nurse reached into her back pocket and showed Laurence a sharp scalpel. "And I'm going to cut off those hands with this here," she said with a grin.

Laurence screamed in agony as the nurse stabbed him in the stomach with the deadly needle. Then she laughed wildly as she yanked the needle out. Blood splattered everywhere as the deranged nurse shoved the syringe back inside of her patient. Laurence screamed and screamed until he finally opened his eyes.

Laurence looked side to side hoping to see his parents. They weren't there, and neither were the psychotic nurses or the dark figure. Laurence set his empty soda can in the cup holder. He put the Ferrari in reverse and drove away from the vacant rest area.

Chapter Twenty-five

Kenya stood under the steaming shower with her eyes closed. The pain pills that she took were finally starting to work. The pain in her neck wasn't as intense as before, but it still was burning and stinging from the deep cuts and gashes. Kenya was beginning to feel drowsy and lightheaded. She needed some rest, but she couldn't stop thinking about that damn nightmare. Kenya was convinced that someone else put those gashes on the back of her neck, not her. Ever since she was a kid, she'd had thousands of nightmares and had never once woken up bleeding or with scars on her body. This town of Redgrass was haunted with evil spirits. Kenya knew that if she stayed in the small town, things would get worse.

Kenya washed the melon-scented body wash from her bronze skin. She planned on eating her favorite snack, which was cheese popcorn, and watching the Cooking Channel once she got out of the shower. The pain pills would have her in a deep sleep before the first commercial break, Kenya was sure of that. She grabbed a pink razor and began slowly shaving. As she began to shave under her right arm, something suddenly happened.

Kenya screamed as something unknown gripped her hand and forced her to cut and dig into her underarm with the pink razor. She tried to drop the razor, but the pressure around her bloody hand was too intense. Kenya hollered hysterically and cried out in agony as her hand continued to brutally run the sharp razor up and down her armpit. The hot water from the shower washed pieces of her skin and blood down the drain.

The bloody razor fell into the tub. Kenya was shaking and yelling so frantically she didn't realize that nothing was in her throbbing hand anymore. She finally put her arm down. Her armpit felt like a fire was being lit inside of it. Kenya stared at her bloody hand for a moment. Terror consumed her. She was too afraid to walk out of the bathroom. Kenya sat down in the tub and screamed out for help, but she was all alone. The pain pills had finally taken effect. Kenya sat back and closed her crying eyes. The hot water ran on her naked body as she slept.

Chapter Twenty-six

The sun shone brightly through the windshield of the Ferrari as Laurence slowly drove it up the driveway of his home. There was a sly grin on his face as he turned the engine off. Laurence had driven well over a hundred miles per hour all the way home without seeing one police car on Highway 9. He had to look in the rearview mirror as he thought about his sudden urge for sports cars and speed. *Yes!* Laurence was having a midlife crisis and enjoying the beginning stages of it. He stared in the mirror at a man who was at peace and truly happy for the first time in his adult life.

Laurence stepped out of his new car and into the sweltering heat. He didn't bother parking in the garage because he planned on taking his wife out for a joyride after he took a long, cold shower. Laurence casually walked around his new toy, admiring it as if it were an ancient sculpture. Moments later he was opening the front door of his home as beads of sweat dripped from his face.

Laurence closed the front door and paused. He immediately knew that something was wrong. The house was too quiet, which was weird because Kenya always had music or the TV playing in the kitchen. Laurence pulled his sunglasses off and glanced around the living room as he wiped the sweat from his face.

"Kenya! I'm home," he yelled out.

There was no answer, just complete silence. She was probably soaking in the tub with the door closed or running on the treadmill with her headphones on. Laurence knew she wasn't doing either one, but that was the only rational explanation he could think of at the moment.

Laurence took a deep breath. He walked to the stairs and up to the master bedroom. Every step he took on the immaculate hardwood floors sounded as if Bigfoot were walking across them. Laurence's imagination and the creepy silence in the house were beginning to disturb him.

Laurence stepped in the massive bedroom and stopped. The first thing he noticed was the flat-screen TV on the wall. There was a woman standing in the middle of the desert, wearing an all-black sleeveless dress and a shiny black mask. Her red lips and dark eyes were not covered by the frightening mask. A long, thick yellow python was wrapped around her neck as if it were a piece of jewelry. The squirming snake was much longer than the lady's beautiful black hair, which fell to her waistline. Laurence watched as the woman opened a dirty chest full of the same type of snake that was dangling from her neck. She began throwing the snakes into a blazing firepit one at a time. No sound came from the flat screen. Laurence shook his head. *Why would Kenya watch a show like this when she's petrified of snakes?* He walked toward the bed to get the remote control to turn this mess off.

The remote control was not on the bed or on either nightstand. What Laurence did find on the bed were sheets with blood on them. Looking at the blood made him nervous now. He was trying not to think of the worst-case scenario, but it was beginning to become a reality.

"Kenya, where are . . ." Laurence stopped. He was wasting his breath. The silence in the room allowed him to hear the shower running.

As Laurence turned around to head into Kenya's bathroom, he heard a crunching sound. He looked down and realized that he was stepping on the remote. Laurence bent down and grabbed it, but when he looked at the flat screen again, the lady with the Python around her neck was gone. There was a cartoon on with a bunch of kids riding their bikes with helmets on and chasing the ice-cream truck. Laurence threw the damn remote on the bed. Something strange was happening. He had no idea what it was though.

Laurence turned the knob on the bathroom door. It was locked. He beat on the door like a maniac and yelled out his wife's name. There was no answer. *My wife is dead,* was the only thought that kept popping into Laurence's mind. He stepped back and kicked the door in. The door fell off the hinges on Laurence's first attempt.

Laurence pushed the falling door to the side, then quickly scanned the tan floor. There was nothing on the floor but her clothes. He ran to the shower, and his worst fears suddenly became true. When Laurence pushed the brown shower curtain back, he saw his wife lying in the tub with her eyes closed. Blood flowed down her body into the drain as the steaming water sprayed on top of her. *My wife committed suicide, and I wasn't here to stop her,* flashed through Laurence's mind as he turned the shower off. He picked Kenya up from the tub and carried her into the bedroom, then laid her across the bed.

Laurence checked Kenya's neck for a pulse. *Thank God!* She was still alive. He slapped her on the face in an attempt to wake her up. She didn't respond. Laurence noticed the bottles of pills on the bathroom sink. He had no idea how many pills she'd swallowed. Blood continued to pour down Kenya's right side. Laurence lifted her arm and saw that her armpit looked like someone had been digging a butcher knife through it.

"What the fuck!" he said, surprised. Laurence ran to the bathroom to grab a towel so he could dry his wife off and stop the bleeding from the huge hole in her armpit.

Laurence quickly dried his wife's wet body. As he began to stop the bleeding from her armpit, she jumped up screaming and crying hysterically. Laurence tried to hug her and calm her down, but it didn't work. Kenya continued to holler and shake dramatically like someone was torturing her. Laurence just held her tightly until she finished.

"What did you do?" he asked as Kenya began to calm down.

"Something is trying to kill me," Kenya whispered. She couldn't stop her arms and legs from trembling.

"How many of those damn pills did you take?"

Kenya ignored the question. "She's trying to kill me, Laurence. Do you hear me? She's going to kill me!" she yelled out.

Laurence stared at his wife. He could see the fear in her eyes. Depression was causing her to be paranoid and have anxiety attacks. And now she was beginning to mutilate her own body. Laurence had to get her help immediately before things got worse.

"This doesn't look good. I'm taking you to the hospital," Laurence said while staring, puzzled, at the hole in his wife's underarm.

"We have to hurry before she comes." Kenya was too terrified to think of what would happen if the black shadow from her nightmare returned.

Laurence jumped up from the bed and went into the bathroom to get a bandage for his wife's underarm. He dumped the two bottles of pills into the toilet and flushed them. He was convinced that they were driving her crazy and causing her to hallucinate. Dr. Halmer warned him of dangerous depression symptoms like the ones Kenya was experiencing.

The bandage that was tightly wrapped over Kenya's wound didn't stop the bleeding completely, but it did slow it down a lot. Kenya knew that if she hadn't taken the five pills earlier, the pain from the hole in her armpit would be unbearable. She stepped outside into the burning heat, wearing purple sweatpants and a matching T-shirt. Laurence and his wife climbed into the Ferrari and headed to Redgrass Community Hospital.

Chapter Twenty-seven

Kenya began talking as soon as Laurence pulled out of the driveway. She told Laurence about the nightmare she'd had and every detail about the bloody incident in the shower. Kenya knew that something was trying to kill her. She showed her husband the deep scratches and bruises on the back of her neck so he wouldn't think that she was inflicting the pain upon herself. Laurence never imagined his wife's depression would be as severe as it was. She was at a point where she couldn't be left alone.

"I hate this fucking place. It's wicked and haunted," Kenya said, wiping tears from her red eyes.

"What?"

"I have nothing but terrible memories of this town. I'm grown, and crazy shit is still happening to me."

"Tell me what happened," Laurence said as he took his eyes off the road and turned to look Kenya in her distant eyes.

Kenya suddenly became uncomfortable. She turned in her seat so she could stare out the passenger-side window. A frigid chill shot through her body that caused her to shiver as if she'd jumped in Lake Michigan in the middle of January. She closed her watery eyes. Graphic images of blood, a pink razor, and black fingernails digging and tearing into her skin flashed across her mind. Fear and terror consumed Kenya. She took a deep breath and began slowly telling her story about the small town of Redgrass.

In 1987, Ronald Reagan was the leader of the free world. The antidepressant Prozac became available to Americans, and a postage stamp was $0.22. The internet, iPhones, and social media were not household names as of yet. This was the first year that 7-year-old Kenya Snow and her older brother travelled down to Redgrass. Their parents drove them down to the quiet town to spend the summer with their uncle, his wife, and their six kids. Kenya and her brother were more than happy to spend the summer away from home playing and having fun with their cousins.

Every morning, breakfast was on the dining table for the kids. The smell of fried eggs, bacon, toast, and pancakes flowed throughout the four-bedroom home. After breakfast, the children would run outside and play in the summer heat. They usually stayed outside playing games with the neighbors until the sun went down.

One hot, sticky afternoon, Kenya and all of the kids were playing a game of hide-and-seek in the backyard of an abandoned house. They were warned countless times by the parents in the neighborhood to stay off of the vacant property. The three-story home was covered with thick bushes and weeds, and the grass was so high that it made the yard look like a forest. It didn't take long for the kids to build up the courage to jump over the tall red picket fence and roam around the decaying house.

Kenya counted slowly as the kids scrambled to find their hiding places. Before she could get to ten, someone yelled out that they saw a man standing in the broken window upstairs. Everyone ran frantically toward the picket fence, screaming. As Kenya began climbing the red fence, she felt something slimy crawl up her pants. She thought it was a worm, so she kicked her leg, hoping that it would fall out of her jeans. When the boneless creature began wrapping its warm body around her thigh, Kenya realized that it was a snake. She screamed at the top of her lungs before falling back into the tall sea of grass and weeds.

As Kenya kicked and cried out for help, the snake seemed to be tightening its grip around her thin leg. The bright sun was blinding her vision, so she closed her eyes. When she opened them, a tall man was standing behind her head. Kenya instantly panicked and went into a frenzy. She screamed and screamed.

Kenya shut her crying eyes again. She didn't want to see what the man standing over her was going to do with her. Something pulling at her leg forced Kenya to look around the deserted backyard. Her friends and cousins were all standing over her trembling body. Through the shining sun, she could see her brother, Andrew, ripping her pants leg with a knife. Kenya let out a terrifying shriek as Andrew killed the long snake and pulled it from her throbbing leg.

Kenya was silent on the way to the hospital. She had no energy left in her little body to cry, kick, or scream. But that all changed when the nurse attempted to give her a tetanus shot. Something happened to Kenya when she saw the needle that was the length of a beer bottle. She suddenly had a vision of the snake crawling up her leg and jumping up to bite her in the face. She fell to the floor kicking and screaming hysterically. The nurse and her aunt failed in their attempts to calm her down. When the security guard ran in the room, Kenya was kicking wildly at the air, scratching and ripping the skin off her face as she hollered for someone to "get it off me."

7-year-old Kenya Natalie Snow was put in a straitjacket and sedated. That was the only way to calm her down and stop her from tearing the skin off her face.

"So that's why you're petrified of snakes?" Laurence asked, pulling into the garage of the hospital.

"Yes! I think it's beyond fear," Kenya stated.

"You were watching a show about snakes trying to conquer that fear?"

"No. I will never look at a snake."

"When I walked into the room, there was a show on with . . ." Laurence stopped. He didn't want to worry his wife with anything else.

Laurence and Kenya sat in silence for a few minutes before walking through the emergency room entrance. They were both trying to comprehend the eerie events that had taken place.

Kenya was mentally and physically drained when she left the hospital. After receiving twenty stitches to close the wound in her armpit, she was given three separate shots: a muscle relaxer, a painkiller, and an antibiotic. Kenya closed her eyes and began snoring softly as soon as the Ferrari was out of the hospital parking garage.

As Laurence drove, he thought about the story his wife had told him and about her bloody incident in the shower. A million questions went through his mind. Was she suicidal? How severe was her depression? Was her condition going to get worse? Before Laurence could think of another question, an intense pain punched him in the stomach.

The Ferrari swerved to the right as Laurence tried to fight the excruciating pain that seemed to be pulling his insides apart. He gained control of the steering wheel again as he wondered what the hell was wrong with his stomach. For some odd reason Laurence thought that a cigarette would ease the burning in his gut. The urge for a cigarette instantly became a necessity. Laurence pulled over to the first gas station he saw.

When Laurence stepped out of his vehicle, the throbbing in his stomach increased. He bent over and vomited uncontrollably. After releasing everything that was in his stomach onto the concrete, Laurence slowly strolled into the gas station.

After lighting the menthol cancer stick, Laurence inhaled deeply. He began to choke from the thick smoke. The next pull he took was much better. Laurence smoked two cigarettes in a row and realized that there was no more pain in his abdomen. Something was wrong, and it began to disturb him. Laurence drove his sleeping wife home while he continued to indulge in his newfound addiction.

Chapter Twenty-eight

What Kenya didn't tell Laurence was that several years after the horrific incident in Redgrass, she started having nightmares. On the night of her thirteenth birthday, Kenya was in her bedroom watching a cult horror movie called *Spangler's Massacre*. Watching scary movies and eating popcorn with her brother was one of her favorite pastimes, but on the night of her birthday, Kenya was all alone. Her brother was downstairs in the basement with his friends playing video games.

Kenya's day had been perfect. She'd partied and celebrated with her family all afternoon and evening. They ate ice cream and cake, played music and danced, and showered Kenya with plenty of gifts to celebrate her birthday. One of her gifts was *Spangler's Massacre*. Kenya's teenage eyes lit up when she saw the videotape. She couldn't wait for nighttime so she could go in her bedroom, turn the lights out, and watch the gory slasher movie.

Kenya sat up in bed, hugging her pillow as she watched blood and guts being spilled across the TV. She even covered her eyes when some of the scenes became too graphic. But when the psychotic killer walked into a roomful of hissing snakes, Kenya screamed hysterically at the top of her lungs. Tears fell from her eyes as she covered her face with her pillow. When Kenya's parents ran into her dark room, she was shaking and screaming frantically.

It took hours for Kenya's mother to calm her daughter down. After Kenya finally stopped yelling and crying, she gave her a sleeping pill. Her mother hoped it would help her sleep through the night. Minutes after taking the sleeping pill, Kenya was under her blanket in a deep sleep. Her mother took the slasher movie out of the machine and threw it into the garbage can.

Kenya had jumped up out of her sleep at the crack of dawn. A nightmare about biting and hissing snakes crawling all over her bed and on top of her forced Kenya to wake up. She stood in the middle of her room screaming and tearing the skin from her arms with her fingernails.

The image of the deadly snakes on the TV screen traumatized Kenya. The sleeping pills were useless. And sleeping in the living room wasn't helping either. The nightmares about the biting snakes attacking her were becoming more horrific and graphic. Kenya began waking up in the middle of the night, ripping the skin from her face and arms as she screamed in terror. A week passed when Kenya's parents decided to take their only daughter to a therapist.

The therapist explained to Kenya and her parents that what she was experiencing was normal. She said a traumatic experience as a child always reappeared in our lives later in some form. Kenya was diagnosed as having severe post-traumatic stress. The doctor prescribed anxiety medication for her. And Kenya was not to watch any horror movies or sleep alone until the visions and nightmares were out of her head.

A month later, 13-year-old Kenya Snow was back to normal. Her mother didn't have to sleep in the bed with her anymore, and she didn't have to take medication once a day either. Most importantly, the creepy nightmares of snakes attacking her and crawling all over her were over. Kenya felt like a normal teenager once again.

The last visit to the therapist's office for Kenya and her parents was on a Friday evening. The doctor saw how refreshed and happy the little girl looked. And she saw the relief and joy in her parents' eyes. She did warn them that the nightmares could recur from time to time. That was perfectly normal in these cases, especially with kids. The doctor also told Kenya to stay away from any movies, magazines, or books that might have images of snakes in them. The sight of a snake would only cause her to have a relapse. She needed a lot more time to deal with her fears and the terrifying experience that she suffered years ago down in Redgrass.

Dr. Debra Hall told Kenya's parents that the anxiety medication was no longer needed. Too many kids were becoming addicted to pills because they were taking them when they really didn't need to. Dr. Hall then looked Kenya in her eyes and told her to stay away from horror films. Her mind was too fragile to constantly put graphic images of violence and murder into it. Kenya's mom assured the doctor that her daughter was done with scary movies and medication. She didn't know that the pills she'd told Kenya to throw away were hiding in the back of her sock drawer, along with a bottle of sleeping pills.

One night, Kenya was in her bed watching cartoons. She turned past the movie channel several times and saw that they were having a scary-movie marathon. Kenya couldn't resist the temptation to watch the movie that was on. She got up from the bed and walked into the kitchen. It was midnight and everyone was asleep. Kenya grabbed a small bag of chips and poured some juice in a cup. She walked back into her room and closed the door.

Kenya decided to take two sleeping pills and one anxiety pill, just to make sure that she would fall asleep and not have any nightmares after watching the movie marathon. After swallowing the three pills, Kenya jumped into bed and turned to the horror film. Chills ran through her body as the gory slasher flick petrified her. Kenya watched the entire movie and was still wide awake. She got out of bed and walked back to her sock drawer. Kenya swallowed another anxiety pill. As soon as she crawled back into bed, she was fast asleep.

An hour later the scary-movie marathon was still playing on Kenya's TV screen when she jumped out of her bed screaming. A horrific nightmare about being chained to her bed and snakes falling from the ceiling attacking and eating her flesh woke Kenya up in a panic.

When Kenya's parents ran into her room, she was standing in the middle of the floor, screaming hysterically with no clothes on. She was viciously tearing into her skin with her fingernails, trying to get the invisible snakes off of her.

Chapter Twenty-nine

Laurence tossed and turned in his sleep until he finally opened his eyes. It was near daybreak. He decided to go downstairs to the kitchen and have a cigarette or two.

Laurence couldn't remember much of his dream, or nightmare. Most of it was foggy and dark. The part of his dream that he did recall made him cringe. Laurence could clearly see his mother holding his hand and walking him down the hall of his elementary school. There had been no kids running and playing in the quiet hallway. No teachers paced the floors either. The only noise that Laurence could hear was the buzzing of the dim lights and the clacking of his mother's heels against the hollow floor.

Laurence had felt his skinny legs trembling as he watched his mother slowly turn the knob on the classroom door. He'd been nervous. Being the new kid in class was always terrifying and embarrassing, especially the first day. Laurence wanted to snatch away from his mom and run out the door, but the firm grip that she had locked around his hand wouldn't allow him to move.

The old door had made a loud creaking sound as it opened. There were no students or teachers in the classroom to greet Laurence and his mom. The cold, dim room was filled with caskets. Laurence had gazed up at his mother in shock.

She'd looked down at her small child with blood running from her eyes and mouth.

Laurence was relieved when his eyes had finally popped open. As he sat in the kitchen and puffed on his cigarette, Laurence thought about his parents. He wished they were still living and still married. How nice it would be to sit down with his father and watch a baseball game or drink a beer with him. It would be just as nice to sit down at the kitchen table and eat some of his mother's cooking.

Laurence's daydream was interrupted by a stinging pain that stabbed him in the stomach. The intense pain almost knocked him out of his chair, but then it slowly subsided after he took a long, hard drag from his burning cigarette. That was the strangest pain reliever in the world. Laurence assumed that the unknown pains he was experiencing were temporary, so there was no need to go to a doctor for an exam. And taking any type of pain pills was definitely out of the question. As long as the cigarettes stopped the torturing pangs in his stomach, Laurence was going to smoke them.

The dark sky was now bright orange with streaks of blue and purple running across it. It was time for Laurence to get dressed and get his day started. He had a business meeting in Chicago at noon, and he wanted to be on the highway by nine. A few weeks had passed since Kenya's accident, or incident, and she seemed to be doing better. Laurence felt comfortable leaving her alone while he went out and took care of some personal business. He put his cigarette out in the ashtray and headed back upstairs.

Kenya vaguely remembered her husband leaving the house. She thought Laurence kissed her goodbye, but she really couldn't recall. Kenya's dreams and reality all seemed to be the same lately. The bright sun shone in her face as she looked around the quiet room. Kenya wanted to be in the dark and go back to sleep. She got up and closed the curtains. Her head was throbbing and pounding like she'd run it into a brick wall. Kenya felt terrible. Since her horrific episode in the shower, she had eaten very little and slept most of the days away. The nightmares were becoming more and more graphic. But when Kenya wasn't asleep, she was miserable, tired, and depressed.

Kenya's headache was getting worse by the second. Not only did her head feel like it was about to explode, but she was also physically drained. Kenya had no energy to do anything. All she wanted to do was crawl back in bed and close her red eyes. Kenya gazed nervously around the dim room before creeping into her walk-in closet.

The massive closet was illuminated when Kenya hit the switch on the wall. Designer jeans, dresses, and blouses hung neatly throughout the sweet-smelling room. Kenya's overwhelming collection of shoes, belts, and purses were arranged meticulously in the rear of the closet. She stepped to the back of the room and quick-ly unzipped a yellow purse that was hanging behind a wall of different-colored bags. Pain pills, sleeping pills, and antidepressant medication were inside the leath-er garment. Kenya looked around the quiet room before dumping the pills into the palm of her hand. She dropped the bottles back into the purse before zipping it back up.

Overdosing or permanently damaging one of her or-gans didn't concern Kenya. She was in pain, and she wanted it to go away. She swallowed two sleeping pills, one antidepressant tablet, and two Vicodin. Soon she would slip into a dark place where there were no night-mares, no headaches, and no one trying to kill her. Kenya was about to turn the light out in her closet, but she paused when she saw her reflection in the full-body mirror.

The voluptuous, curvy figure that Kenya once possessed was now gone. The frail woman she stared at in the mirror almost made her heart stop. In the last three weeks, Kenya's appetite had been little to nonexistent. When she did try to put something on her stomach, it wouldn't stay down. Not only was she vomiting food, but Kenya was spewing out large amounts of blood, too. And to make matters worse, she was experiencing a severe case of dysentery.

A hand touched Kenya's shoulder. She screamed as a chill travelled down her spine. Kenya had to squint in the mirror to see who was standing behind her. The person touching her shoulder was no stranger. Her ex-boyfriend Damien was standing behind her with a very unpleasant look on his face. Kenya closed her eyes and opened them again. Damien was still there.

"I'm sorry," Kenya whispered to Damien.

There was no response. The reflection in the mirror showed rage in Damien's eyes and face. Kenya closed her eyes tightly this time. When she opened them, she was in the closet all alone. Kenya didn't know if she was going crazy or just having creepy hallucinations. Rest was what she needed. But she was afraid to turn around. Kenya took a deep breath. The pulsating pain in her head was now flowing throughout her entire body. She frantically ran out of the walk-in closet and slammed the door.

Kenya climbed in her bed and pulled the blanket over her head. Seconds later she was in a world where nothing existed but darkness.

Chapter Thirty

At exactly 11:07 a.m., three intruders entered Laurence's home. The three men, wearing black suits, black gloves, and white masks, were carrying navy blue duffle bags on their shoulders. An automatic firearm rested on the hip of each man. They were instructed to kill only if absolutely necessary. And the professional thieves were to leave the house as they found it. How could they ever be identified if there was no evidence that they were ever there?

The unknown intruders had thirteen minutes to get as much money out of Laurence's house as possible. The boss of the entire operation sat patiently in his car, reading a *Business Weekly* magazine and watching his stopwatch on his iPhone. He held an automatic handgun in his right hand, while an identical weapon sat on the passenger seat. At 11:20, and not a minute later, the boss was going to put his vehicle in reverse and leave Laurence's home. He didn't give a damn if his guys were in the car or not. They knew very well what the consequences were for not finishing a job on time.

The three masked men took their shoes off at the front door and scattered throughout the quiet house. A man as wealthy as Laurence had to have a safe somewhere in his home. They now had twelve minutes to find the money and get out. The thieves searched everywhere. They quickly looked under paintings on the walls, rugs, and all throughout the basement. They found nothing.

The boss took his eyes off the article he was reading and glanced at his phone. Nine minutes remained.

Two of the masked men continued their search downstairs while the third criminal headed upstairs. He pushed open the master bedroom door and scanned the massive room. Someone was in bed, asleep, wrapped up tightly in a blanket. The shoeless thief pulled his gun out and checked the closets and bathrooms for anyone else. The person in bed was alone.

The thief pulled the blanket from over the sleeping person's head. A beautiful woman was sleeping like a rock while he stood over her with his gun pointed at her face. Time was ticking. Seven minutes remained. The intruder touched Kenya's shoulder with his leather glove. She didn't move or make a sound. That was strange to him. Any other woman would've jumped up screaming and frightened to death after looking at a white mask with red eyes hovering over her.

The burglar checked to see if the beautiful woman lying before him was dead. There was a pulse. Maybe she was sleeping off a long night of drugs and alcohol? The giant criminal couldn't care less about the stranger in the bed. He pulled the covers back so he could see the rest of her. She was half naked, wearing only a small white T-shirt and some green panties. The thief rubbed his hand over her breasts and stomach. There was still no response and no sound coming from the woman. She was out cold. Before he could violate Kenya any further, he stopped and sprinted out of the master bedroom. One of the other thieves had whistled twice from the kitchen. They finally found what they came for.

The boss folded his magazine and placed it in the glove compartment. Only four minutes left now. He grabbed his cup of coffee and sipped slowly from it. His coffee had cream, sugar, and white tequila in it. The boss turned the radio on. The DJ on the lite rock station was giving an updated weather report on the scorching temperatures.

The safe was behind the fridge. The masked gunmen filled their bags with money until the safe was empty. There was a bright light shining inside the safe that they paid no attention to. They now had less than three minutes to be out of the house. Once they closed the safe, the intruders would put their shoes back on and exit Laurence's home. There was one problem. The safe wouldn't close. What the three men didn't know was that unless they had the six-digit code and the orange master key, the safe was never going to close. And that meant the bright light would continue to shine.

Time was ticking. There was no time left to figure out why the damn door wouldn't close. The masked man who had seen where Laurence slept at night slammed the refrigerator against the wall. You could hear some of the contents inside crashing to the bottom. The other two men paused and stared at him. A minute and a half remained. The angry criminals put their black shoes on and walked out of the quiet house. One of the guys drilled the knob back on the door while the other two thieves loaded the duffle bags in the trunk. The boss and his boys drove out of Laurence's driveway with $300,000 in cash.

Chapter Thirty-one

Food was the only thing on Laurence's mind. On his way to Chicago, he stopped off the highway and ate at a local diner. There he ate, like a wild beast, three double cheeseburgers, two hot dogs, French fries, lemon cake, and stuffed chicken breast with mashed potatoes. Laurence washed all of his food down with a large root beer float and two tall glasses of homemade lemonade. For some unknown reason, the more Laurence ate, the hungrier he became.

After their long and exhausting meeting, Laurence and the three other potential investors decided to go out for pizza and drinks. Once again Laurence ate as though it were his last meal. He ravaged a platter of Buffalo wings and ate seven slices of deep-dish pizza. The other businessmen were amazed at Laurence's outrageous appetite. They laughed and joked with him as he continued to satisfy his increasing need for food and alcohol. Laurence drank twelve shots of tequila, four beers, and three mixed drinks. He walked out of the upscale pizzeria drunk but still craving more food and liquor.

The sun began to set across the purple sky and head west. The temperature in Redgrass was now ninety-one degrees. The draining, intense humidity continued to loom over the small town. Laurence pulled his Ferrari into the garage and shut the engine off. Food and sleep were the only thoughts on his tired and drunk mind.

Laurence turned one of the kitchen lights on. While walking toward the refrigerator, he stepped in a puddle of water. Laurence stared at the water on the floor as he quickly sobered up. Something didn't feel right. He glanced around the spotless kitchen. Someone other than his wife had been in there. Laurence noticed that the refrigerator was not centered. It was too far over to the left. He folded his arms and closed his eyes as rage began to boil inside him.

Laurence was furious. When he yanked the refrigerator door open, a cracked glass pitcher full of sliced lemons fell to the floor. Some beer bottles, pop cans, and plastic cartons of juice also fell on the wet floor. It took some time, but Laurence managed to push the stainless-steel appliance away from the wall. His eyes turned red when he saw the door to the safe swing open.

The safe was empty. Someone had come into Laurence's home and walked out with a lot of money. If they were smart, the thieves would be above the clouds right now on their way to another country. Laurence knew better, though. He was certain that they were somewhere close, counting his money, drinking, and laughing about their big heist.

Laurence stuck his hands inside the spacious safe and pulled up the back panel. Two automatic handguns, several large stacks of money, and a hand-sized video recorder sat behind the dark wooden panel. The small round hole that was cut out of the panel was specifically designed for the camera to record any activity inside the safe. Laurence grabbed both guns and the camera. He put one of the guns on his hip as he headed upstairs to his bedroom.

Laurence stopped at the threshold of his bedroom. The master bedroom was just as dark and quiet as the hallway. Terrible thoughts began to run across his mind.

Was his wife lying in their bed dead in a pool of her own blood? Or was she somewhere being raped and tortured by the men who invaded his home? The bloody scenes of Kenya were stuck in Laurence's head. He couldn't erase them. He stepped into the bedroom to deal with his reality.

Laurence hit the light switch on the wall with his middle finger. Nothing in the room seemed to be out of place. Kenya was lying in bed on her stomach, with her face smashed into the pillow. Laurence didn't see any blood, but that didn't mean that she wasn't dead.

Laurence turned his wife over. She didn't move or open her eyes. He called out Kenya's name and shook her in an attempt to wake her up. There was still no response. She was lost in a colorless world where nothing existed. Laurence became irritated. He knew Kenya was secretly taking sleeping pills and other unnecessary medication. Why else would she be sleeping all damn day? The pills also explained Kenya's horrifying nightmares and hallucinations.

"Wake up, Kenya!" Laurence demanded.

Kenya still didn't blink an eye, nor did she move a muscle. Laurence lost his temper. Before he knew it, his hand was wrapped around his wife's throat. He cursed and blamed her for letting someone come into their home and empty out his safe.

Laurence knew he was wasting his energy on the wrong person. He pulled his hand from around Kenya's neck. If she hadn't been in a coma-like state, she would more than likely be dead right now. Laurence was sure of that. Kenya needed to sleep off whatever medication was in her system. They would have a long talk when she came back to earth.

A hard drink and a cigarette were what Laurence needed. Hopefully it would calm him down, because the rage inside of him was beginning to boil over. After he checked the bathroom and closets in the master bedroom for intruders, Laurence headed back downstairs. He was going in the basement to watch the video from the safe.

Laurence stood in front of his smart TV, holding a pint of tequila in his hand. He unconsciously kept pressing the rewind button on the remote control. Three masked men taking stacks of money out of his safe played over and over again on the large screen. Laurence was livid. The thieves in the video didn't know it yet, but they were going to die a slow and very agonizing death. The sweet thought of revenge wiped the frown from Laurence's face. He took a long drink from his bottle of tequila before sitting down on the couch.

Laurence lit a cigarette. He studied and dissected the short video like a scientist studying chemicals and formulas in a lab. Several things caught his attention. The robbers were all wearing identical gold watches with big faces. They were obviously on a tight schedule, because all three men kept checking their wrists. Although none of the masked men said a word, one of them kept hacking and clearing his throat like a walnut was lodged in it. The obnoxious snorkeling and hacking noise didn't distract any of the thieves from their mission. Once the safe was empty, there was a loud crashing sound, and then the screen went black.

"I can't fucking believe this!" Laurence shouted as he threw the remote control at the television.

Laurence drank what was left of his tequila. Who knew where he lived? And who knew about the secret safe? The few people who knew where he and his new wife resided would never steal anything from him. Whoever boldly came into his home knew nothing about Laurence and what he was capable of. Laurence puffed on another cancer stick as he thought about the people he'd come in contact with in the last few months. The only thought that made any sense to him was the Ferrari dealership. That was definitely a good place to start his inquiry.

Laurence grabbed another pint of tequila from the wet bar. He sank back into the black leather sectional and thought about the money that was stolen from his safe. Within minutes, the square-shaped bottle was empty, and Laurence's eyes were closed.

Chapter Thirty-two

The Chicago skyline was a beautiful view at night. Kenya stared out the restaurant window at the bright lights and buildings as she waited for Damien to join her at her table. The upscale restaurant was full of people engaged in conversations while eating and drinking. Kenya began to get nervous as she checked her phone for any missed calls or text messages. Damien was over an hour late, and she hadn't heard a word from him. She dialed Damien's phone number. The automated voicemail came on after one ring. She left a concerned message before ending the call. Kenya needed a drink to calm down.

"Can I offer you an appetizer or a drink while you wait for your guest to arrive?" asked a waiter politely.

Kenya took her eyes away from the window. "Yes, I'll have a tropical-pineapple Long Island."

"Sounds good. I'll be right back with your cocktail, ma'am," replied the waiter while adjusting his silver bow tie.

Kenya was running out of patience with Damien. She decided she would leave if she didn't see his face by the time she finished her drink. How dare he have her sitting at this table all alone for over an hour and not give her a courtesy phone call or answer his damn phone? Kenya was definitely going to let him know how rude and inconsiderate he was when he showed up.

"Here is your tropical-pineapple Long Island, ma'am," the smiling waiter said as he placed a tall, slender glass in front of Kenya.

"Thank you."

"My pleasure. I'll be back shortly to check on you," the well-groomed waiter announced before running off to serve another guest.

Kenya twirled her yellow straw around in her glass as she glared around the dimly lit room. Everyone was laughing and having a good time. She was the only person in the elegant restaurant drinking and sitting all alone. Kenya began to sip her strong and fruity elixir while continuing to survey the crowded room. She froze when she saw Laurence sitting across the room with another woman.

The woman sitting across the table from Laurence was wearing the same black dress that Kenya was wearing. Her long black hair flowed down her back, but Kenya couldn't see her face. The woman was facing Laurence and watching him while he ate like a lion in the jungle. There was a mountain of raw steak piled up on Laurence's bloody plate. He was grabbing the thick chunks of meat with two hands and devouring the steak at an insane pace. Kenya couldn't believe what she was witnessing. The man she was looking at was an animal, not her husband.

Kenya set her straw on the table and gulped her drink straight down. She needed another one. When she turned to call for the waiter, Kenya almost fell out of her chair. Damien was standing right in front of her. There was a hole the size of a half-dollar in his forehead.

"I didn't hear you walk up. Where did you come from?" Kenya asked, staring puzzled at the huge hole in Damien's head.

Damien didn't respond. He just sat down and stared at Kenya with hatred in his eyes.

"What happened to your head? And why are you giving me such an evil look?" Kenya asked with concern in her voice.

"She's going to make you pay for what you did to me!" Damien whispered.

Kenya's body turned into an icicle. Fear caused her heart to sprint at a rapid rate, and it wouldn't allow her to talk. She sat with her mouth wide open, staring through the hole in Damien's head. Kenya had a clear and direct view of Laurence and his guest. Blood dripped from his red lips as he continued to savagely eat the uncooked steak. Kenya was so terrified of what she was watching that tears began to fall down her face.

Damien whispered, "It's going to be very painful."

Kenya took her attention away from Laurence. Her mouth was so dry that it hurt to swallow. She stared into Damien's menacing eyes. "I am so sorry! I never wanted things to turn out the way that they did. Please forgive me?" Kenya asked.

Now there was no expression on Damien's stoic face. "It's too late."

"Why? Why is it too late for you to forgive me?"

"You let him do this to me," Damien said quietly, pointing to the hole.

"I'm sorry, Damien, but I couldn't change his mind. And why are you whispering?" Kenya asked as tears continued to pour down her face.

"Because she doesn't want me talking to you," Damien said as he looked over his shoulder and around the restaurant.

"Who doesn't want you talking to your ex-girlfriend?" Kenya asked with suspicion and a slight attitude.

Damien folded his arms. "She's standing right behind you!"

Kenya's flesh trembled uncontrollably as if she were lying in a pool full of ice cubes. Her heart pounded faster and faster as she digested Damien's last words. Long and razor-sharp nails dug deep into her neck before Kenya could turn around to see who or what was behind her. She yelled out a shrill of terror and pain. Damien sat with his arms folded and watched quietly as the lady in the black dress tortured and tormented his ex-girlfriend.

Blood poured and sprayed from Kenya's neck as the nails continued to claw into her skin. She waved her weak arms, cried, and screamed out for help, but no one in the noisy restaurant noticed her. It was like she was invisible or a ghost. Kenya begged Damien to save her. She got no reaction from him either. He just stared into her eyes and watched her suffer.

Kenya could clearly hear the sound of flesh being brutally ripped from her neck. Warm blood flowed down her chest and onto her dress. She tried to grab the thin arms that were attacking her and pull them off, but the woman was too strong. Kenya was at her mercy.

"I am very angry with you. You murdered one of my children," the lady in black whispered into Kenya's ear.

Kenya wanted to tell the evil woman that she didn't kill Damien, but no words came from her mouth. She could do nothing but scream as the pain in her neck intensified.

"I'm going to take your eyes out as your punishment!" the lady threatened Kenya.

Damien stood up and walked away from Kenya without saying a word. Kenya cried out and pleaded for him to come back, but he was gone. Everyone in the restaurant had vanished. The room was eerily quiet now.

The lady in black snatched Kenya's face and squeezed. Her helpless body jerked as the woman carved a deep circle around her eye with one of her stinging finger-nails. The wicked woman took her long black fingernail and engraved another circle around Kenya's left eye. When she was done, she let her face go and walked away.

The entire restaurant went dark. Kenya rubbed her eyes to see if they were still there. Thankfully they were, although her hands were smeared with blood. Nothing could be heard in the pitch-dark room but Kenya's heavy breathing and erratic sobbing. She stopped screaming for a moment to see if anyone else was still in the room with her. When Kenya looked in front of her, there were bright green eyes staring directly in her face.

Kenya gasped and screamed louder than she'd ever screamed before. The green and menacing eyes were on the face of a snake. The slithering creature didn't hesitate. The snake opened its wide mouth, showing all of its deadly teeth, and attacked Kenya's left eye.

Kenya hollered and called out for someone to help her. Her loud screams echoed in the silent restaurant. Kenya's throat burned as she screamed and screamed.

And then finally she was awake.

Chapter Thirty-three

Laurence jumped up out of his drunken sleep. Revenge and his stolen money were the only thoughts on his mind. He planned on killing everyone who was involved with stealing his $300,000. Laurence had a strong feeling that someone at the dealership knew about the heist. There was no time to waste. According to his iPhone, it would be six in the morning in six minutes.

When Laurence stood up, a powerful and electrifying pain shot through his stomach. He fell down on the floor in torturous pain. Laurence suddenly felt queasy and sick, like he had eaten spoiled meat. He jumped up and ran into the bathroom.

Laurence knelt down in front of the toilet and vomited. He hacked up everything that was in his gut for over four minutes straight. The pain was unbearable. When Laurence tried to stand up and rinse his mouth out, the need to vomit came back stronger than before. He was back in front of the toilet, vomiting uncontrollably. Large amounts of blood and food spewed from his mouth.

The cold water ran as he rinsed his face and mouth in the sink. The queasy sensation in his stomach was gone, but the excruciating pain was still there. It felt like someone was running a blow torch through the lining of his stomach. Laurence glared in the mirror. Nothing was going to stop him from getting his money back. He didn't care how sick he felt or how many times he threw up blood or food. A body bag was the only thing that could stop him from finding the three guys who broke into his home.

Laurence turned around when he heard a horrifying scream. It was his wife. He walked out of the bathroom and grabbed the two pistols off the bar. Laurence cautiously headed upstairs to his bedroom as the screams from his wife continued.

When Laurence stepped in the bedroom, Kenya was sitting up in bed, shaking and screaming out for someone to help her. Kenya's hands covered her eyes, but Laurence could see blood and tears dripping from her face. He had to squint to make sure that he was looking at skin dangling from the sides of his wife's neck. Kenya's bloody and mutilated neck looked like a wild coyote had attacked her while she was sleeping. Laurence ran over to his wife and hugged her.

"It's okay, I'm here!" Laurence said, as he scanned the cold room.

Kenya sobbed on her husband's broad shoulder as she held on to him tightly. The dark room was beginning to brighten as the sun rose.

Laurence placed his guns on the pillow. "Tell me what's going on. Why are you doing these things to yourself?"

"You think I would do these harmful things to myself?" Kenya asked in a hurtful tone while crying.

Laurence let Kenya go and held her wet hands while staring directly into her eyes. He was irritated and upset when he discovered perfectly round circles carved around his wife's eyes. "If you didn't do this, then who did?" he asked impatiently.

"Someone evil spirit is doing this. She is trying to kill me!" Kenya answered quickly.

"What? You think a spirit is trying to kill you?" Laurence asked. He could hear his voice raising another octave.

Kenya wiped the tears from her face. "Ever since we came here, she's been after me. I dream about it every night."

"Who is she?"

"I really don't know, but I dream about her trying to kill me."

"It's those damn pills you're taking. They're making you suicidal and driving you insane," Laurence said with anger in his voice.

"I haven't taken—"

"Stop lying! Whatever you are taking is turning you into a completely different person. You sleep all day and have very little energy to do anything."

"I'm scared. You know I wouldn't do these evil things to myself. The pills help take some of the pain away," Kenya said with fear in her voice.

"Three men came into our home yesterday and stole the money out of the safe," Laurence said with rage in his eyes.

"What!" Kenya shouted.

"You heard me. Three strangers were in here robbing us while you were in your sleeping coma."

Goose bumps crawled across Kenya's flesh as an icy chill shot down her spine. "I am so sorry. When I try to wake up, I can't."

"Don't be sorry. If you'd been up, they would have killed you," Laurence said coldly.

"You know who did this?"

"I'm about to go find them and kill 'em," Laurence said as he stood up. "We'll deal with all of this madness when I come home."

"Stay here with me. I don't want you to go, Laurence!" Kenya cried.

"I don't have a choice," Laurence said. His patience had run out. He walked into the bathroom and closed the door.

Kenya's head pounded like she had been drinking cheap whiskey all night. The deep gashes on her eyes and neck burned like a raging fire. The room began to rotate in slow motion. And then it began to spin around and around, faster than an out-of-control bowling ball. Kenya fell back onto the pillow and closed her eyes. Once again, she was surrounded by darkness.

Chapter Thirty-four

Laurence stood in the hot shower thinking about his wife's condition. Her mental health seemed to be getting worse every day. Kenya was in denial about her addiction to whatever medication she was taking. Why else would she be hallucinating, harming herself, and sleeping all day? Laurence made a promise to himself to bring Kenya to a rehab clinic after he found the person who stole his money.

Laurence's thoughts quickly switched from his wife to murder. He planned on putting a bullet in the head of everyone involved with coming into his home and stealing his money. To enter a man's home without being invited was the ultimate sign of disrespect. There was a wicked grin on Laurence's wet face as he thought about torturing the thieves before he put them to rest.

The bathroom door made a creaking noise as it opened. Laurence opened his eyes and snapped out of his visions of blood and murder. The door closed. Laurence expected to hear Kenya's voice, but there was nothing. Running water was the only sound that could be heard in the huge bathroom. But when Laurence closed his eyes again, he heard a voice.

"Your life is mine," the soft voice whispered.

A chill shot through Laurence's naked body as he looked up at the ceiling and around the circular walk-in shower. He could hear clearly every word the voice said. Laurence recognized the voice as the same whisper he'd been hearing. Was it real? Or was he simply losing his mind? Laurence was terrified of either possibility.

He quickly washed and rinsed the soap off his body. He could feel his heart beating faster than normal as he stepped out of the shower. Laurence gazed around the bathroom. He was alone, but he could feel a presence in the room with him. Something strange was happening to him. Laurence just didn't know what it was. He got dressed, walked past his sleeping wife, and left the quiet house.

Chapter Thirty-five

Kenya opened her eyes. The bright sunrays shining through the window made her red eyes burn. Kenya didn't know what time it was, but she was sure that her husband was gone. She saw the psychotic look in his eyes when he talked about finding whoever had broken into their home and stolen their money. Kenya was worried about Laurence and feared that something bad was going to happen if he went searching for the thieves. But he was stubborn and vengeful, and she didn't have the energy to try to talk him out of it. Kenya did have plans on talking to Laurence about moving out of Redgrass when he returned home. Their lives had dramatically changed for the worse ever since they'd arrived in the small town.

Kenya wiped her damp face and neck with her hand. The pain that caused her entire body to ache made her cringe and moan in agony. The morbid nightmare of an evil woman trying to rip the flesh from her body flashed across Kenya's mind. The images of the witch torturing her collided with gory visions of Damien falling in a pool of his own blood. Kenya thought of blood, snakes, murder, and a woman with black fingernails that were deadlier than any knife.

Kenya jumped out of bed when she thought about the letter that Damien had written her. Maybe Damien was trying to tell her something in the letter that she hadn't understood the first few times she'd read it. The room was slowly spinning, and Kenya's vision was fuzzy as she walked into her closet.

The doorknob was the only thing that stopped Kenya from falling on her face. The massive headache that overcame her caused Kenya to lose her vision momentarily. She grabbed the doorknob before she fell. Kenya was on her knees, gripping the doorknob tightly and trying to regain her composure.

"Somebody, please help me," Kenya whispered, and she took a deep breath.

The throbbing headache that made Kenya fall was still there. She opened her eyes. The room wasn't black anymore, but her vision was still blurry. Kenya pulled herself up by holding on firmly to the door handle. She stood still for a moment trying to regain her equilibrium. Kenya's legs felt weak and unstable as she let go of the doorknob.

Kenya walked over to her bench where she'd left her brown purse. The purse was not there. Kenya was certain that after she read the letter from Damien, she'd put it back in her purse and set the purse back on the designer bench. And then Kenya looked up at the ceiling as she thought for a second. She really wasn't sure what she'd done with the letter or the purse. Her memory lately was becoming just as foggy as her vision.

Kenya glanced around the wide closet. The purse was nowhere in sight. Then she smiled as she looked under the bench and saw it sitting on the floor. Her mother had always told her it was bad luck for a woman to set her purse on the ground. Kenya snatched the purse up off the floor as her mother's words played in her head.

"I know I didn't set this purse under this bench . . . or did I?" Kenya asked herself. She was trying to convince herself that she wasn't losing her mind.

The purse was unzipped. This was strange to Kenya because she distinctly remembered zipping the bag up after she put the letter back inside of it. Maybe Laurence was the one who unzipped her purse and carelessly left it on the floor? Kenya knew that was very unlikely, because he never went into her closet, and he had more pressing things on his mind than invading her privacy.

Kenya stuck her hand in the leather bag. She didn't feel the letter. She bent over and searched through it, but still she couldn't find it. She then rummaged frantically through the deep purse with both hands. There was still no letter. Kenya angrily turned her brown bag upside down and dumped all of its contents on the bench and floor. She slung the empty purse across the room in a rage. Grocery receipts, feminine products, credit cards, and loose change scattered everywhere. Kenya became hysterical when she didn't see the letter on the ground.

Kenya screamed furiously as she ran and snatched her clothes from the hangers. She tossed the clothes on the floor before knocking all of her purses off the rack. Kenya then wildly knocked all of her shoes off the racks and onto the floor. She grabbed a high-heel boot and slammed it into the full-body mirror. The sound of the glass cracking caused Kenya to snap out of her rage. She sat down on the carpet, breathing hard and sobbing. Kenya was afraid of what was happening to her.

The closet was a disaster. Clothes were scattered all over the floor as some still dangled from the hangers. High heels, boots, sandals, and other women's shoes were piled up on top of each other in the middle of the floor. Kenya was embarrassed by her behavior. If her husband came home and saw how she'd destroyed her closet, he would really think she was going crazy. Kenya had to clean her mess up before Laurence came home.

While picking up the quarters and pennies beside her, Kenya noticed a photo on the ground. She grabbed the picture and stared at it oddly. She knew this photo. It had been taken when she and Damien had been sitting on the porch of his parents' house. Damien was smiling, but now no one sitting next to him. Kenya's jaw dropped and her hand trembled as she stared at the photograph. Her image had been completely erased from the picture.

"What the hell!" Kenya blurted out as she touched the photo to make sure she was gone.

Kenya couldn't believe what she was seeing with her own two eyes. It was like someone had taken an eraser and deleted her from the photo. Kenya knew that that was impossible. There was no logical explanation for the missing image. Damien's eyes stared out at her as he smiled brightly. He seemed to be enjoying the idea of his ex-girlfriend slowly losing her mind.

"I'm not going crazy!" Kenya whispered as she swayed back and forth.

Kenya continued to stare at the creepy picture in disbelief. Maybe she was hallucinating and seeing things that really weren't there? She closed her eyes and took a deep breath. "I'm not going crazy!" she repeated in her normal speaking voice.

The long, deep breath seemed to calm Kenya down. Her heart was still thumping faster than usual, but she wasn't as shaky and nervous as before. She opened her red eyes and stared at the eerie picture. Terror overcame Kenya as she sat shivering from the chills that sprinted throughout her body.

Kenya was now staring at a photo of Damien and Laurence sitting on the porch together and smiling like they were childhood buddies. The picture instantly fell out of her shaking hand. Tears dripped onto the photo as Kenya picked it back up to make sure that it was real. Laurence and Damien were smiling at her as tears poured from her face.

"I'm not going crazy!" Kenya yelled out. Her eyes were still glued to the image of her husband and ex-boyfriend sitting together.

"I'm not going crazy!" Kenya yelled out again as she crumpled the photo into a ball like it was a piece of notebook paper. "I'm not going fucking crazy!" She opened the wrinkled picture and tore the photo of Damien and Laurence into a thousand pieces. Her screams of rage could be heard throughout the entire house as small pieces of the distorted picture fell to the carpet.

"I'm not going fucking crazy!" Kenya shouted one last time as she stood up and walked toward the door. She didn't realize that she was walking backward. Kenya turned the lights out and slammed the door shut as she stepped out of the closet.

Chapter Thirty-six

Laurence weaved his shiny Ferrari in and out of traffic like a professional stunt driver. Driving his new toy on the highway at a ridiculous speed made him feel like a kid again. The power and speed of the foreign car made adrenaline flow through Laurence's body. He watched other drivers on the road stare in envy as he zoomed passed them. Laurence didn't care about anyone on the road with him or even the police. He was willing to run over or drive through anything that got in the way of his mission.

Both of Laurence's hands were firmly gripped on the steering wheel as he continued to drive as if he were on a racetrack. He sat up straight in the bucket seat, trying to ignore his overflowing bladder. It couldn't be ignored much longer. Laurence wasn't going to make it to the dealership without emptying his bladder. He quickly switched lanes and made a sudden exit off Highway 9.

The first gas station he saw was abandoned. The vacant filling station was old and decrepit, with weeds growing up the rusted building and dirty boards covering some of the broken windows. Laurence cruised by the moss-covered gas station and drove several miles down a deserted road before pulling in front of a tavern. The small bar had a green neon sign on the door that read OPEN.

Laurence turned the ignition off and climbed out of his sports car. He instinctively surveyed the area around him. The bar was sitting in the middle of nowhere. There were no other businesses or any other sign of life near the isolated tavern. Laurence could see nothing but tall trees and a winding road that seemed endless. The bright sun blinded his vision as he pulled his sunglasses off and stared at the two vehicles parked beside him. A sparkling black cargo van and a muddy brown pickup truck were sitting next to Laurence's Ferrari. *Only a few customers must be inside,* Laurence thought as he walked to the door and stepped inside.

The nauseous smell of cheap cigars smacked Laurence in the face as soon as he stepped into the bar. He looked around for a second and saw nothing but mirror-covered walls. A sign about five feet in front of Laurence read RE-STROOMS. Without hesitating, he followed the blue sign and stepped into the men's room.

The washroom was surprisingly clean. The fresh lemon scent of cleaning products filled the air, causing Laurence's stomach to turn and cramp. The walls were oddly painted bright pink and yellow. The owner of the place apparently wanted the men's room to resemble a ladies' room.

Laurence walked up to the urinal and unzipped his pants. As he began to empty his bladder, he could sense that something was wrong. Laurence looked down. He was filling the urinal up with blood.

The blood continued to flow as Laurence stood in disbelief. He wasn't in any pain, and he had never experienced anything like this before. Whatever was going on with Laurence's body was a mystery. He finished urinating, or bleeding, then zipped his pants back up.

Laurence turned on the hot water and then pressed down on the soap dispenser. The soap's fragrance of cucumber instantly gave Laurence a headache and made his stomach cramp. The intense odors of the cigars, the cleaning products, and the hand soap all seemed to suffocate Laurence. He bent over and vomited in the sink.

Warm and salty blood flowed down the drain as Laurence continued to vomit. Nothing but blood was being released from his body. First, he was urinating blood, and now he was vomiting blood. The vomiting finally came to a halt.

"What the hell is wrong with me?" Laurence said to the frustrated man in the mirror.

Laurence rinsed his mouth with cold water, trying to get the putrid taste of blood out of his system. The cold water wasn't working. He could still smell and taste the warm blood. A drink would remedy the problem. Laurence wiped his hands and mouth with a paper towel, then walked out of the colorful bathroom.

The mirrors in the bar made the place seem a lot bigger than it really was. Laurence walked through the narrow hallway, made a right turn, and sat down at the bar. He was the only patron, despite the cars out front.

"Welcome, sir," a short elderly woman greeted Laurence from behind the bar.

"How you doing?"

"Great. And how are you on this beautiful day?" the gray-haired woman asked.

"I'm fine. Just stopping for a quick drink."

"You don't look fine. Is everything all right?" She rubbed her stylish buzz cut.

"Just a little fatigued. I could use a shot of your finest tequila," Laurence said as he glanced around the quiet bar.

The bartender smiled. "Coming right up."

The tavern was decorated with a pool table, an old jukebox, a massive flat-screen TV, and some round tables. There wasn't much room for anything else.

The petite and attractive old lady set a tall shot glass in front of Laurence, along with a napkin with fresh lime slices on it. She poured clear tequila in his glass until it was running over. "The first one is on the house, mister."

"Well, thank you. My name is Laurence," he said. He grabbed the glass and threw the alcohol down his throat.

"Nice to meet you, Laurence. I'm Gretchen, owner and operator of this place," the bartender said as she grabbed a bottle of white wine from below.

Laurence slammed the glass on the counter and grabbed a lime slice. As he bit into it, the smell and taste of blood in his mouth seemed to vanish. "Pleasure to meet you, Gretchen. I'll take another one."

Gretchen smiled as she refilled her customer's glass until it was overflowing. "Why haven't I seen you in here before?" she asked, grabbing a wide glass and filling it up with wine.

"This place is hard to find. I didn't know it existed," Laurence explained before picking up his glass and drinking down another shot. The smooth tequila felt like water going down his throat.

"Me and my first husband bought this place forty-five years ago. Since then, many of the businesses off the highway have come and gone, but I've managed to keep these doors open. There used to be a sign right before the exit telling you to stop in and celebrate with us," Gretchen claimed before sipping her wine.

"I'll take one more. So, you run this place by yourself now?"

Gretchen set her glass down and picked up the bottle of tequila. She poured liquor into Laurence's glass until it ran over for the third straight time. "Yes, I'm all alone now. All of my husbands are dead and gone."

Laurence wanted to ask her how many husbands were dead, but he knew that would be overstepping his boundaries. He glanced at his watch. It was time to get back on the road and go pay Mr. Car Salesman a visit. Laurence smiled at Gretchen before emptying his shot glass.

"My first husband, Earnest, got his brains blown out right over there in that corner," Gretchen said as she turned her head to the right and stared in the corner for a moment, reliving the murderous scene. "Two men came running in here at four in the morning with guns in their hands. Earnest and two of his friends were at a table drinking and playing poker. I was standing right here. One of the men asked my husband if he had twelve thousand dollars he owed. As soon as he said no, they shot him in the head twice and ran back out of here."

Laurence instantly thought of his father. "I'm sorry to hear that," he said as he pulled a stack of money from his pocket. Laurence handed Gretchen three crisp bills with Benjamin Franklin's face on them. "Keep the change!"

"Well, thank you, Mr. Laurence!" she said, smiling. She then stared at Laurence oddly.

Laurence put his neatly folded stack of money back into his pocket. He noticed the peculiar look Gretchen was giving him. "Is there something wrong?"

"You have blood running out of your ear," the bartender said, shocked.

Laurence tried not to panic. He put his hand over his left ear and felt warm blood gushing from it. "I need a towel!"

Gretchen quickly reached under the bar and grabbed a white towel. She threw it at Laurence as she stared at him with her mouth wide open. Laurence placed the towel on his ear to stop the massive bleeding. His right ear began to burn. When he touched his burning ear, blood instantly began to pour. Gretchen instinctively threw him another towel.

The white towels covering Laurence's ears were soaked with blood. "I don't know what's wrong with me!" he said with fear in his voice.

"You need to get out of here and go see a doctor," Gretchen advised Laurence.

"I will. Thank you for the drinks and the towels," Laurence said as he calmly walked out of the bar, leaving a trail of blood on the floor.

After Laurence shut the door and stepped back into the humid morning air, he heard a loud and horrifying scream come from inside the bar. It was Gretchen. He wasn't going back inside the empty bar to see what she was screaming about. Laurence dropped the wet red towels on the pavement and got in his car. He drove away from the bar without looking back.

Gretchen slowly got up from the floor. Her heart beat faster than normal as her arms and legs trembled from fear. She looked nervously around the quiet bar. The woman she'd seen in the mirror was gone. Gretchen reached under the bar and grabbed an automatic weapon. When she looked up, the woman wearing all black with the long black hair was standing right in front of the bar, facing the windows. Gretchen yelled out as she cocked the gun and fired. She closed her eyes and fired again and again. When she opened her eyes, the woman was gone and her mirrors were shattered from the bullets she'd fired into them.

Chapter Thirty-seven

Laurence drove down Highway 9 with his windows down. Blood was no longer gushing from his ears. The hot morning air blew across his face as he puffed on a cigarette. A talk radio program was playing on one of the satellite radio stations, but Laurence paid no attention to it. The horrendous pangs in his stomach seemed to be pulling his insides apart. The cigarettes would usually alleviate the pain, but this time the cancer sticks did nothing. Laurence knew something serious was going on with his stomach, he just couldn't put his finger on it. He decided to fast for twenty-four hours. That was going to be torture considering how hungry he was at the moment.

There were only a few cars in the parking lot of Jim's Exotic Motorcycles & Sports Cars. *Perfect timing*, Laurence thought as a grin appeared across his weary face. He intentionally pulled into an employee parking spot next to an all-black Mercedes-Benz. Was this the same vehicle that Mr. Beverage had told him was sitting in his driveway?

Yesterday, when Laurence let his garage door up, he saw Mr. Beverage across the street mowing his huge front lawn. The 80-year-old retired basketball coach was in excellent shape for his age. He'd told Laurence that the secret to his great health was exercise, no red meat or pork, and lots of sex.

"Good Morning, Mr. Beverage!" Laurence had said, trying to mask the anger in his face.

Mr. Beverage had let the handle on the mower go, and the motor quickly stopped. His smiling face and red tank top were dripping with sweat. "Beautiful day, young man. How are you doing?"

"I'm good."

"You don't look so good. Is everything all right?" Mr. Beverage had asked, wiping sweat from his wet face.

"Did you see anything unusual around my house yesterday?" Laurence had asked.

Mr. Beverage had looked at Laurence, then scratched the silver stubble on his face. "I can't say I did," he replied, looking up at the blue sky.

"No new cars or faces?"

"Now that I think about it . . . You know I'm getting old. There was a black car with tinted windows parked in your driveway," Mr. Beverage had said. He could see the anger in Laurence's face.

"You know what type of car it was?"

"It was a Mercedes. Looked like one of those fancy cars they drive the president in."

"Did you see anyone get in or out of the car?"

Mr. Beverage had wondered what this Q&A was all about. "I didn't see anyone. I went in the kitchen to make a fresh batch of lemonade and a sandwich. When I looked out the window again, the car was gone."

"Thank you, sir. I have to get going. I'll come over and talk with you later," Laurence had said. He extended his hand to his neighbor.

Mr. Beverage had wiped his moist hand on his khaki shorts before shaking Laurence's hand. "Those license plates had my mother's birth year on them. I couldn't see the letters, but I know the numbers were one, nine, zero, five."

"Thanks for everything, Mr. Beverage," Laurence had said while walking away.

"Anytime, young man. Be careful out there!" Mr. Beverage had replied. He'd turned the lawn mower back on and continued whistling as he manicured his grass.

It was no coincidence that the black Mercedes Laurence parked next to was identical to the one that Mr. Beverage described. Laurence got out of his Ferrari and walked to the rear of the Benz with the black rims and limo tint. He shook his head and smiled when he saw the custom plates that read JIM'S 1. Laurence took one last pull from his cigarette before tossing it on the ground. He then casually strolled into the dealership with his old Black Widow revolver on his hip.

A beautiful young woman greeted Laurence as soon as he stepped through the doors. "Welcome to Jim's Exotic Motorcycles & Sports Cars! How can we help you today?"

Laurence smiled. "I'm here to speak with Robert Fishman."

"I'm sorry, he's in a meeting right now. Can I assist you with anything?" the smiling saleslady asked.

"This is actually a personal matter about a Ferrari he sold me. How long will he be?"

"He should be out in ten minutes. You can wait for him in his office if you'd like."

"Thank you very much. That sounds good," Laurence said. He followed the young lady with the sweet-smelling perfume.

Laurence tried to get comfortable in one of the stiff chairs that sat in front of Robert's cluttered desk. The office was a complete mess. There were empty water bottles and balled-up paper overflowing from the trash can. Stacks of books and copy paper were scattered throughout the office, as well as boxes with dates marked on them. There were several certificates and licenses on the wall. And there were numerous accolades hanging up for salesman of the year. The computer on Mr. Fishman's desk was surrounded by files and papers. The out-of-order desk was also decorated with pens, clipboards, car keys, and car-buying magazines.

Laurence saw a long, sharp letter opener sitting on a pile of mail. He grabbed the utensil and placed it on the desk in front of him. As Laurence glanced at the digital clock on the wall, he heard footsteps from behind. He smiled as Robert entered the office.

Chapter Thirty-eight

Kenya was awakened by the bright sun that shone through the bedroom windows. The tremendous pain in her body started at her head and traveled down to her toes. Kenya could sense that someone else was in bed with her. When she turned her head, there was a dead snake lying right next to her.

Kenya's entire body became paralyzed from shock. The brown six-foot-long snake's mouth was wide open, but its eyes were closed. Kenya's eyes grew wider and wider as she stared at the reptile's deadly teeth. Seconds later she finally let out a loud and horrifying scream.

The grip that Kenya had on her thick hair was so tight that it was beginning to tear out. Her mind was telling her to get up and run out of the house, but she couldn't move. Fear possessed her. Kenya continued to scream and yell out, but there was no one around to help her.

After minutes of continuous and terrifying screaming, Kenya stopped. She was so petrified of the dead snake that her body continued to convulse erratically. Kenya somehow found the courage to jump up from the bed. She lost her breath when she looked down at the shining hardwood floor. Dead snakes were scattered all over the bedroom floor. Their mouths were wide open, displaying demonic and razor-sharp teeth. Kenya's fragile and tortured mind couldn't take any more surprises. Her red eyes closed as she fell backward. There was a loud thud as Kenya's unconscious body hit the floor.

Chapter Thirty-nine

Robert Fishman walked into his office holding a yellow legal pad and a clipboard in his left hand. His right hand was firmly gripping the handle of a piping-hot coffee mug. The cheerful smile on his bald face quickly evaporated when he realized who was waiting in his office.

"Good morning! Good morning!" Robert said, placing everything that he was carrying on the crowded desk.

Laurence's blood was beginning to boil. He wanted to take his bare hands and snap Robert's neck into two pieces. Laurence took a deep breath. "Same to you!" he said with vicious rage in his eyes.

Robert extended his hand to Laurence. "How's the Ferrari?" he asked, waiting for Laurence to shake his hand.

Laurence was never going to shake this bastard's hand. He sat up straight in the uncomfortable chair and folded his hands. "You know I'm not here to talk about no damn car! Why don't you sit down?" he said calmly.

Robert took his eyes off Laurence and smiled as he stared at his right hand hanging in the air. This asshole had some nerve to come in his place of business and disrespect him. "How can I help you, sir?" Robert asked, sitting down in his black leather chair.

Laurence was suddenly struck by a ferocious pain that electrified his stomach. He closed his eyes for a moment as he swallowed the vicious pain. "Someone stole five hundred thousand dollars from me yesterday!" Laurence said, reaching in his pocket for a pack of cigarettes and a lighter. He knew that $300,000 was the amount taken, but he wanted to see what Robert's reaction would be if he said a larger number.

Robert's body language altered at Laurence's words. He grabbed his steaming coffee mug off the desk and sipped from it. "You know, in the state of Illinois it is illegal to smoke in public facilities," he said sarcastically.

Laurence ignored Robert and lit his cancer stick. He took a hard pull from the cigarette and blew the smoke up into the air. "Don't try to change the fucking subject! You heard exactly what I said. Someone came into my home and stole five hundred thousand dollars from me!"

Robert grinned. "I'm very sorry to hear that, but how can I help you?"

"You can explain to me why that black Mercedes in your parking lot was sitting in my driveway yesterday!" Laurence demanded before taking another long pull from his burning cigarette.

Mr. Fishman drank the piping-hot coffee until the mug was empty. He slammed the cup on the desk and then wiped his lips with his hand. "What the hell are you trying to insinuate? My business is selling cars, not home invasions, sir!"

The more Robert talked, the angrier Laurence became. He didn't know how much longer he was going to be able to listen to him lie and bullshit about his money. "You and two other clowns came into my home yesterday wearing white masks and black suits. I have it all on camera," Laurence said with a wicked grin on his face.

Robert rubbed his hand across his bald head. The evil look in Laurence's eyes was beginning to make him uncomfortable. "I was in here doing paperwork all day yesterday, sir. And as I said before, my business is selling high-end vehicles."

Laurence could see in Mr. Fishman's body language that he was nervous. Why would he be nervous if he didn't do anything? As far as Laurence was concerned, the word "guilty" was stamped across his forehead. "You have exactly ten minutes to put my money in front of me, or I'm going to burn this building down and kill everyone in here," Laurence said calmly.

Robert could feel his heart thumping faster and harder. Things could get out of hand if he didn't calm this situation down quickly. "I don't have your three hundred thousand dollars, but I have a friend—"

Laurence dropped what was left of his cigarette on the brown carpet and then jumped up from the chair. "What the hell did you just say?" he barked angrily at Mr. Fishman.

"Calm down! Just calm down, sir! I have a friend on the police—"

"You said *three* hundred thousand. I never said that amount!" he said with hostility in his voice.

Robert's mouth opened, but no words came out. Laurence had heard all he needed to hear. He grabbed the sharp letter opener off the desk and stabbed it through the back of Robert's hand. Mr. Fishman yelled in agony as Laurence pulled the letter opener out and brutally stabbed him again. Blood poured from the two wounds in Robert's hand.

Mr. Fishman didn't have a chance to defend himself or get up and run out of his office. Laurence was standing beside him before he could even think about pulling the piercing letter opener from his bleeding hand. Laurence palmed Robert's bald head with both his hands and bashed his face into the thick wooden desk. Blood splattered and poured from Robert's mouth, nose, and forehead.

The rage inside Laurence caused him to black out. He closed his red eyes and continued to smash Robert's face into the desk like a deranged killer. Laurence didn't hear the office door open, and he certainly didn't see the two men who ran inside the office.

One of the men carried a pipe wrench, while the other guy held a 9 mm pistol. The man gripping the pipe wrench swung it at Laurence's head with the force of a baseball player swinging at a fastball. The unexpected and powerful blow to the head caused Laurence to fall to the floor. Blood ran from the deep gash in his skull. The two men stood over Laurence as he drifted into a sea of unconsciousness.

Chapter Forty

Kenya struggled to open her burning eyes. She stared up at the ceiling trying to remember where she was. The huge knot on the side of her head that throbbed and pulsated brought her memory back. Kenya attempted to touch the bump on her head, but her right arm wouldn't move. She tried moving her left arm, and that was lifeless also. Kenya tried raising her legs and moving her feet. Everything was unresponsive. She attempted to raise her head off the floor and turn it to the side. Again, nothing! A sudden surge of panic and fear overcame Kenya as she realized that her entire body was paralyzed.

The sun shone brightly through the windows as Kenya's eyes surveyed the room. Dead snakes were still lying everywhere. Kenya's first reaction was to scream for help. But when she opened her mouth, no words came out. She swallowed and tried to scream out again. Nothing but air came out of Kenya's mouth. She closed her eyes and cried as she realized the helpless state that she was in.

The sound of thumping footsteps opened Kenya's eyes quickly. Her breathing became heavier as she looked around the room. Kenya didn't see anyone, but the eerie clacking sound against the hardwood floors was getting closer and closer.

The banging footsteps came to a halt. There was complete silence in the home. Kenya's eyes continued to nervously roam around the cold room. No one was there. But when she looked up, someone was standing right behind her head.

Kenya's efforts to scream and move her limbs were once again futile. She was at the mercy of the person standing behind her.

The woman, who was wearing black high heels and a matching dress, kneeled down behind Kenya. She whispered softly into Kenya's ear, "You will never use these eyes again. They're mine now!"

The evil lady dug her razor-sharp black fingernails deeply into Kenya's eye sockets. She savagely pulled both of her eyes out and stood up. The lady in black stared down at Kenya's lifeless body with a wicked grin on her beautiful face.

Within seconds, Kenya's eyesight was gone. She couldn't feel anything, but she knew that the woman in the black dress had taken her eyes. Kenya was hoping that the wicked woman put her out of her misery and pain. A door slammed shut. And the sound of high heels clanking against wood slowly faded into the air.

As the burning sun headed westward, a dark and gloomy shadow loomed over Kenya and Laurence's home. Kenya's heart raced and vibrated uncontrollably as she waited in the quiet bedroom for her husband to come home.

Chapter Forty-one

Laurence sat in the barber's chair, watching the TV mounted on the wall. A baseball game was playing on the flat screen. Hair fell on top of the blue apron Laurence was wearing as the barber shaved his head. Laurence could hear his stomach rumbling and growling over the animated voice of the sportscaster.

"Son, before we go to the game tonight we have to stop and get you something to eat," Laurence's dad said. He was sitting in the chair next to Laurence with his eyes closed as the barber trimmed his hair.

"I ate breakfast before I got here," Laurence stated.

"Your stomach sounded like you haven't eaten in months."

"I don't know what's wrong with me. I ate ten pancakes, plus bacon and sausages. And I had a bowl of grits to go with my scrambled eggs and biscuits."

"Damn, you ate like a wolf and you're still hungry! Is there something going on that I should know about, son?"

Laurence hesitated. "I'm fine. I'll be even better when we get something to eat."

"That doesn't sound right to me. Maybe you should let a doctor check you out," Laurence's dad said with concern in his voice.

"I don't like doctors. And I definitely don't like hospitals," Laurence said firmly.

"You are more stubborn and foolish than I. We'll talk later about this matter when we have more privacy."

"Yes, sir," Laurence replied.

Laurence had no intention of telling his dad, or his mom, about the severe stomach cramps he was experiencing. If he told them about the excessive vomiting and bleeding, they would do nothing but worry. Some things Laurence had to keep private.

A bell chimed as the door to the barbershop swung open. Kenya walked in with Damien right behind her. There was a puzzled expression on Laurence's face as he watched the two enter the small shop.

"How is my beautiful daughter-in-law doing today?" Laurence's dad greeted Kenya.

"I'm good, Dad. We just came by to see your son for a second," Kenya replied, smiling.

Laurence was furious. "What the hell is he doing with you? I thought I killed him months ago."

"You did. He came back to give you an important message," Kenya said, looking at Damien.

Tears dropped from Damien's eyes as he began to speak. "You murdered me and my family. They were all I had. She is very angry with you. Your life is in her hands now."

"Who is she?" Laurence asked.

Damien grinned. "You will find out . . . very soon!"

"What have you done, son?" Laurence's dad asked with concern.

Laurence turned to look at his father. His eyes were still closed as the barber continued to trim his hair. "I took care of a serious problem."

When Laurence turned back around to ask Damien a question, he was gone. And Kenya was heading for the door.

"Goodbye, Laurence!" she said as she opened the door and walked out.

The barber squeezed Laurence's neck and whispered into his ear, "I want your life."

Laurence didn't have a chance to look up at the barber or jump out of the chair. All he saw was a sharp and shiny razor before it sliced him across the throat. Blood squirted into the air. Laurence gagged on his own blood as the razor sliced his neck again and again.

Chapter Forty-two

Cold water splashed Laurence's face, bringing him back to reality. He opened his eyes, but his vision was so blurred and foggy that he couldn't see anything but a bright light. Laurence tried to move his arms and realized that he was restrained. The handcuffs around his wrists were locked so tight that they were digging into his skin. Laurence attempted to move his legs and realized that they were shackled together, too. A thick metal chain was locked securely around his ankles and the chair he was sitting in.

"Time to wake up, Mr. Laurence Caine!" a voice yelled out.

Laurence blinked several times as the ice-cold water dripped from his face. His vision was no longer cloudy. He could see that he was in a spacious garage, sitting in the middle of the floor, strapped to a pole with handcuffs and a chain. He wasn't in a small barbershop sitting next to his father and getting his throat cut open by the barber. The last thing Laurence remembered was bashing the salesman's head into the desk.

Robert Fishman appeared out of nowhere, holding Laurence's Black Widow revolver in his hand. "How was your little nap, sir?"

Laurence could feel blood running from a wound on the back of his head. He smiled as he stared at Mr. Fishman, who was standing about four feet in front of him. A white bandage covered in blood was wrapped around his left hand. His black and purple right eye was swollen shut. And the open gash in his forehead was the size of a tennis ball. "How is your hand?" Laurence asked sarcastically.

Robert smiled. Three of his teeth were badly chipped from Laurence smashing his face against the desk. "It's doing great. Actually never felt better."

Robert walked behind Laurence's chair. He cocked the revolver, grabbed Laurence's hand, and fired a shot into his palm. Laurence screamed in agony. Mr. Fishman cocked the Black Widow again and shot Laurence in his other hand. Laurence screamed again as the pain from the bullet pierced his bleeding hand.

"Now let me ask, how are your hands doing, sir?" Robert asked with a sly grin.

Laurence took a long and deep breath and managed to utter, "Much better now."

"I'm insulted. You were going to kill me with this old piece of shit right here," Robert stated, staring at the Black Widow. "Now I'm going to kill you with it, sir!"

"You can't kill me! I died a long, long time ago!" Laurence replied.

Robert gave Laurence a puzzled stare. "You said there was a camera in the safe. Where is the video?"

"I lied just to see what your reaction would be."

Robert grinned. "I don't believe you. I will have someone burn your house down later tonight. That way, any evidence of any kind will be destroyed."

The recurring pain in Laurence's stomach was beginning to wake up. The burning sensation that ripped through his abdomen made him nauseated. "Why didn't you kill my wife?"

"Your wife?" Robert asked curiously.

The confused look on Robert's face and the tone of his voice let Laurence know that he really didn't know that

Kenya was in the house while they were robbing it. Laurence decided to see how much the salesman knew. "My wife was upstairs the entire time you and your boys were in my house."

Robert's bald face turned red as he listened to Laurence talk. "That's a lie. The house was empty."

"My beautiful wife gave one of your boys seventy-five thousand dollars to walk out of our bedroom and forget that he ever saw her. Why do you think it took him so long to rejoin you boys?" Laurence exaggerated convincingly.

Robert had heard enough. "You boys get your asses in here right now!" he screamed into the air.

Laurence kept talking. "My wife said your boy had a big gold watch on and that he was rubbing all over her and taking her clothes off like he wanted to rape her."

"Shut the fuck up!" Robert barked at Laurence. Three men quickly walked in the garage following his outburst.

The three men, who were all slightly over six feet, were all wearing red polo shirts that read "Jim's" on the pocket. One of the guys looked like he was in the gym weightlifting five days a week. None of the men gave the appearance of being a criminal. Laurence couldn't believe that he had been robbed by some damn car salesmen.

"Which one of you bastards tried to rape my wife?" Laurence asked angrily.

"I told you to shut the fuck up!" Robert yelled as he walked in front of Laurence and smacked him in the mouth with the butt of the revolver.

Laurence spit blood and several teeth out of his mouth. The salty taste of blood made his cramping stomach twist and turn in horrific knots. A cigarette would ease some of the deadly pangs, Laurence thought.

Robert was beginning to lose control. He stared at the revolver for a moment, then cocked the hammer on it.

Someone was lying, and he hated being lied to. "You guys told me the entire house was clear!" Robert said, pacing back and forth in front of his men.

"Boss, no one was in that house!" one of the thieves said with confidence.

"Mr. Ferrari here says that his beautiful wife was in her room and she gave one of you money to act like she was invisible."

Laurence had a smirk on his face as he realized that Mr. Fishman was never in his home. Now it was his story versus the thieves'. This scene was about to take a terrible turn for the worse. Laurence continued to spit large amounts of blood from his mouth as he watched and listened.

"Who checked the master bedroom?" Robert asked while pulling a pair of sunglasses out of his pocket with his wrapped hand. He put the dark shades on to disguise his swollen and bruised eye.

The muscular thief spoke. "I went upstairs to check all of the rooms, boss!"

"And was there a beautiful woman in the master bedroom?"

"No!"

"And she didn't give you an incentive to keep your mouth shut about her?" Mr. Fishman asked while looking at Laurence.

The muscular thief angrily blurted out, "He's lying, boss. Let's kill him and dump him in the lake!"

"Tell your boss how you took your mask off and showed my wife your face before you were going to rape her. The money was the only thing that stopped you," Laurence said, disgusted.

Robert and his other two partners in crime all looked at the bodybuilding thief in disbelief. Taking your mask off on a job was forbidden, and there were no exceptions to this rule.

"That's what took you so fucking long up there. You were—"

Robert quickly interrupted one of his men. He had heard all he needed to hear. "I'm going to ask you one more time. Was there a beautiful woman in that bedroom?"

James, the weightlifter, hesitated before he answered. "Yes, but she . . . she was sleep, so I left her there, and I didn't tell the boys because we were running out of time."

Mr. Fishman was livid. He took his sunglasses off and slung them across the garage. "Pussy and money will make a man lose focus. The pursuit of money and pussy will cause a man to make irrational and unintelligent decisions. This is not the first time that Mr. James here has let pussy interfere with my business, but I can assure all of you that it will definitely be the last!" Robert angrily stated, pacing the floor.

Robert stopped in front of James. He aimed the Black Widow at his burly chest and fired a shot. The powerful bullet knocked James down on the concrete. Robert pulled the hammer back on the pistol and aimed it at his partner's head. He squeezed the trigger, and James closed his eyes as blood flowed from his head and chest.

Chapter Forty-three

Robert Fishman had inherited his dad's exotic car business in the late nineties. Not only did Robert receive the family business, but he also inherited his dad's criminal mind.

When business was slow, Robert's father would host poker games at the local pool hall and then pay someone to rob the games. Robert's dad, Jim, was also the town's loan shark. He loaned out thousands of dollars and charged ridiculously high interest rates that he knew people couldn't afford. Many of Jim's clients had to turn over their vehicles and expensive jewelry to him, and in some cases the title to their homes. Jim Fishman was a con artist and a thief who would do just about anything for money. His sons were the same way, except they wanted more money and more power.

Robert was in total control of the car dealership. His older brother, Will, was a silent partner. Will was an accountant working for a large advertising agency in Chicago. They were being swindled out of hundreds of thousands of dollars each year by the conniving bookkeeper. Robert supplemented his income by stealing from his clients.

After Laurence drove off the dealership lot with his sparkling new toy, Robert went straight to work. A man who could afford to spend six figures on a car and not think twice must have some cash tucked away in his home. Robert went into his messy office and Googled Laurence Caine.

Laurence Caine was the owner of the upscale club/restaurant chain Club 38. He was a partner in a lucrative video game production company and a board member for a small independent film company. The multimillionaire's father was murdered during a drug deal gone bad in the late 1970s. And then there was more tragedy for Laurence. The bodies of his wife and her brother were found badly burned inside of a stolen car. The car was found by Chicago police in a dark alley on the south side of town.

Robert continued reading as he sipped on his mixture of coffee and tequila. No suspects were arrested for the brutal crime, and there were no witnesses to the murder or to anything involving the car parked in the alley. The case was closed.

Robert knew that Laurence would be his biggest payday yet. The most he and his team had taken from a home was $30,000. Robert considered that peanuts. It was time for a big heist and a huge payday. Robert grinned as he read the article on Laurence Caine again. *What a wealthy and interesting man.*

Chapter Forty-four

Rain began to fall from the dark sky. Kenya listened to the raindrops as she lay on the floor in a state of shock. She couldn't see the dead snakes, but Kenya could feel their creepy presence all around her. Terror overwhelmed Kenya as she thought about Laurence never coming home. How long would it take for someone to find her?

A door slammed shut down on the first floor. The loud bang made Kenya's heart almost jump out of her chest. Kenya knew that the evil lady was back to finish what she started. Another door slammed shut.

Kenya opened her mouth and screamed. She was surprised to hear her voice echo throughout the quiet room. Kenya was even more surprised when she realized that her feet and legs were mobile again. She was disappointed when she touched her face and her eyes were still gone. Something hissed and slithered passed Kenya's head.

Kenya quickly sat up. The painful shriek she yelled out caused her entire body to convulse. There was another hissing sound. Kenya instinctively turned her head, but she saw nothing but darkness.

Something slimy and warm crawled on Kenya's naked leg. She threw it off of her as she screamed out for help. Another snake hissed as it crawled up Kenya's other leg. Before she could grab the spineless creature, it sank its sharp teeth into her leg. When Kenya jumped up, the long snake wrapped its body tightly around her leg. She ran around the dark room frantically screaming as she tried to remove the biting snake from her leg.

Kenya stumbled into the love seat and fell to the floor. The hissing sounds in the room were ringing in her ear. The dead snakes were alive and hungry now. A snake crawled on Kenya's arm and savagely bit her shoulder. She jumped back up and ran around the room yelling hysterically.

Kenya tried to yank the slithering snake from her arm, but the creature was too fast. The snake was already wrapping its thick body around her neck and hissing wildly. Kenya knew her body was going into shock, and soon her heart would stop from fear of the snakes. She didn't want to be eaten alive. That would be torturous.

Kenya screamed in horrifying agony as the snake that was wrapped around her leg dug his vicious teeth into her skin again. She ran as fast as she could through the dark room and jumped out the window. Kenya screamed out for help into the humid night air.

Kenya wiped the steam from the bathroom mirror with a small white cloth. The woman in the mirror had tears in her eyes. Kenya held her left hand up and gazed at the fifteen-carat diamond wedding ring that shone and glistened. She put her hand back down as the tears began to roll down her face. Kenya thought about the phone call she'd made before getting into the steamy shower.

After the newlyweds made love again, Laurence decided to go downstairs and gamble. He took a quick shower, dressed, and walked out of the deluxe suite with a glass of cold tequila in his hand. The crap table and blackjack table were calling his name.

Kenya sat at the foot of the bed thinking about Damien. She decided to give him a call and see how he was do-

ing. Kenya grabbed her phone and dialed Damien's number. There was no answer. She listened to his voice on the voicemail. Kenya dialed the number again. No answer. The sound of Damien's voice made Kenya sad. The reality that he would never answer the phone again caused Kenya to throw her cell phone across the room. She grabbed her purse and ran into the bathroom, then slammed the door shut.

A beige towel was wrapped around Kenya's body as she stared at the woman in the mirror. The woman in the mirror was sobbing uncontrollably now. The violent image of Laurence shooting Damien in the head kept playing over and over in Kenya's mind. The fact that she watched the entire murder take place made her feel sick. Kenya gagged and began to vomit in the sink.

"I'm sorry. I'm sorry," Kenya cried out as she lifted her head from the sink.

The loud banging sound of the gun being fired rang in Kenya's head. She had a massive headache as the sound of the gun going off continued to rattle and disturb her. Kenya reached into her purse and pulled out a bottle of sleeping pills. She opened the bottle and poured a countless number of pills into her mouth.

Kenya turned the faucet on and drank the cold water until she swallowed all of the sleeping pills. She let the water run until all of the vomit was washed down the drain. Kenya continued sobbing as her head pounded. She walked out of the bathroom and crawled back into the king-sized bed. When Kenya closed her red eyes, all she could see was Damien lying in a pool of blood.

"I'm sorry, Damien. I'm so sorry. Please forgive me!" she cried out as sleep slowly came over her.

Glass shattered and fell as Kenya's body crashed to the wet pavement, breaking her neck.

Chapter Forty-five

"Is there anything else I need to know?" Mr. Fishman calmly asked the two remaining thieves.

"No, sir," one of the men spoke out.

"No, but what are we going to do about the wife?" the other thief asked.

Robert smiled as he turned around and looked at Laurence. "After we get rid of Mr. Rapist and Mr. Ferrari here, then we'll go put a bullet in the beautiful wife's head."

"Don't forget to burn the house down before you leave!" Laurence said with a sly grin.

"I hate you rich city boys! Y'all always come down here thinking you gon' take over my town and live like a king. Not on my watch, sir!" Robert said with animosity in his voice.

Laurence laughed at Mr. Fishman. He laughed even harder when he saw how irritated and angry Robert was becoming. The two thieves watched intently as their boss became completely unraveled.

"What the fuck are you laughing at?" Robert asked loudly.

"You and these clowns you got working for you! That money you stole from my safe was less than fucking peanuts to me. Three hundred thousand dollars . . . Stick to selling cars or start robbing liquor stores," Laurence said with sarcasm.

Robert stepped in front of Laurence. "What the hell did you just say to me?" he asked with rage in his voice.

"You didn't hear me? I said you guys are fucking amateurs!"

Mr. Fishman put the revolver on his hip. He then began to furiously punch Laurence in the face. He beat Laurence until his right hand began to cramp and throb.

Laurence hacked and spat up more blood onto the floor. The burning pain that was splitting his insides apart seemed to be getting worse by the second. "Before you walk away, there is one important detail that I forgot to tell you," Laurence said as his eyes began to swell.

"Shut the fuck up, dead man. This party is over!"

Robert walked up to his partners and whispered into their ears. Both men quickly disappeared from the garage. When Robert turned back around, he saw Laurence spitting up abnormal amounts of blood. And then Laurence began to vomit.

Robert cringed in disgust as he watched Laurence spew out blood and food all over the floor. He had never seen anyone vomit like this before. Blood and vomit continued to pour out of Laurence's mouth like a water fountain. Robert could see the pain and agony written all over his bloody face.

Minutes later, Laurence was done vomiting. His stomach cramped, burned, and viciously ached. Strong medication was the only anecdote for his pain at this point. A cigarette would only give him temporary relief. "Can I have a bottle of cold water? My stomach is on fire," Laurence wearily asked Mr. Fishman.

"I wouldn't give you a bottle of cold urine," Robert said harshly. "But I will put you out of your misery!"

"Thank you."

Mr. Fishman gave Laurence a strange look before he pulled the Black Widow from his hip. "You, sir, are a fucking psycho!"

Laurence closed his eyes and took a deep breath. He could feel whatever was in his boiling stomach starting to rise again. The hammer on the gun cocked. Laurence heard several footsteps before his body jerked from the impact of the bullet. He opened his eyes to discover blood running from a hole in his shoulder.

Robert threw the empty gun across the garage the same way he did his sunglasses. "You're going to die a slow and painful death. You deserve it!"

Laurence grimaced in pain. "I have something important to tell you."

Robert stepped directly in front of Laurence and bent over so that they were face-to-face. "I don't want to hear another word from you or—"

Before Robert could utter another word, Laurence was already lunging forward and gripping his ear with his teeth. Mr. Fishman screamed in horror as Laurence sank his teeth deeper into his bleeding ear.

Robert tried to pull away from Laurence, but he was no match for Laurence's brute strength. Blood sprayed and splattered everywhere as Laurence tore and ripped apart Robert's dangling ear. He was like a hungry lion on a piece of meat or a wild dog finally catching its prey. Laurence wasn't going to let go until the ear was completely severed. Blood filled Laurence's mouth as he continued to pull and yank aggressively on Robert's ripped ear with his teeth.

Skin tore and flesh ripped as Laurence snarled and growled like a dog. Robert screamed out for help as the sharp teeth sank deeper into his skin. Moments later a shot was fired, and Laurence fell back into his chair with Robert's ear in his bloody mouth. Robert was on the ground shaking uncontrollably and yelling out as he held his hand where his ear once was.

Chapter Forty-six

Laurence spat Robert's bloody and mangled ear out of his mouth. The bullet had hit Laurence on the side of his neck. As he drifted in and out of consciousness, Laurence's mind reverted to a dark moment in his life.

Laurence stood in complete shock as he watched the casket that carried his deceased father slowly be lowered into the ground. The screams and loud crying of his mother and other family members rang in his ears. Laurence didn't shed a single tear and said very little on that rainy and gloomy day. He walked away from the burial grounds feeling as though a piece of him had died along with his dad.

The passion and lust for life that Laurence had while his dad was alive disappeared. His motivation and energy for living vanished after burying his father. Laurence basically shut down from the world by locking himself in his bedroom. He went into deep depression and drowned all of his sorrows in alcohol and drugs.

Laurence's mom was worried that her only son was suicidal. She offered to get him help and counseling, but he refused every time. Laurence told his mom that he was all right and that he just needed time to grieve.

The tears that Laurence was unable to shed at his father's funeral were now flowing like a river. Laurence sat in his dark and quiet room, crying and drinking whiskey from a bottle most days. Not only was he drinking heavily, but he was also snorting cocaine. The dope and alcohol seemed to numb the pain that Laurence was in. But after he woke up from his intoxicated sleep, the pain was greater than before.

The destructive cycle of drugs and alcohol became Laurence's lifestyle for almost a year. He ate and slept very little during this period. The only time that Laurence even thought about going outside was to visit the liquor store and the neighborhood drug peddler. And then one night everything changed.

Laurence sat in his room on the floor, watching the nighttime news. The usual stories of crime, murder, and corruption were the headlines. Laurence was already drunk and high, but that didn't stop him from trying to get higher. He opened his second bottle of whiskey and drank it down like a professional alcoholic. Laurence then grabbed his plate of cocaine. He snorted the three lines that were neatly arranged on the white plate without pausing. Laurence slammed the plate back onto the floor as his red eyes rolled into the back of his head.

"Boy, what the hell are you doing?" a voice said to Laurence.

Laurence jumped at the eerie sound of his dead father's voice. He wiped his runny nose and watery eyes with his hand as he stared at the anchorman on TV. The excessive dope and alcohol were now causing Laurence to hear voices.

"Are you trying to kill your damn self?" Laurence's father said loudly.

Laurence jumped again, but this time he turned around at the sound of his dead father's voice. His dad was standing in the corner staring at him with a concerned look on his face.

Laurence was terrified and relieved all at the same time. He tried to stand up, but his drunken legs caused him to stumble back onto the floor.

"Just sit right there and listen to me, son!" Laurence's dad demanded.

"But, Dad, I have to tell you . . ." Laurence tried to explain as he wiped his leaking nose again.

"Just listen to me. Your mother needs you to be strong. You have to take care of the house, and you can't do that by wasting your life in here. I'm depending on you, so get it together and make me proud. I'm watching you, son!" Laurence's dad said, and he disappeared.

Laurence sat in complete shock. He wiped his red eyes and stared in the corner of his room with his mouth wide open. His dad was gone. Laurence finally stood up and stared around the dark room. Everything was moving in slow motion. Laurence needed some fresh air. He threw the whiskey bottles and his cocaine plate into the garbage. After dressing and grabbing his revolver out of the drawer, Laurence grabbed his jacket and went outside for a walk.

The drizzling rain and cool spring air felt better than any drugs or alcohol that Laurence had ever consumed. As he walked through the quiet neighborhood, Laurence thought about his father's words to him. "Make me proud," *and* "I'm watching you," *played over and over in Laurence's mind. It was time for him to stop feeling sorry for himself and get his life together. The more Laurence walked, the more he felt like he could conquer the world. The days of wasting time doing nothing were over. Laurence's visions of power and world domination were cut short by someone wearing a black ski mask.*

"Give me your wallet right now!" the masked man demanded as he pointed a sharp hunting knife at Laurence.

"What?" Laurence replied, startled. He quickly scanned the area to make sure that the robber was alone.

"Don't make me cut your throat. Give me your wallet right now!" the upset robber threatened Laurence.

Rain sprayed into Laurence's face as he stared the masked man in his eyes. He felt so alive. "Here it is," Laurence said as he reached around his back to grab the revolver.

Before the thief could say another word, Laurence was hitting him across his face with the butt of his gun. The man fell to the wet ground, moaning in agony as blood began to pour from his mouth. Laurence stood in front of the helpless criminal, a smile on his face. The adrenaline that flowed through his body was electrifying. Laurence cocked the revolver back as the robber begged him to spare his life. One shot was fired. Laurence cocked the hammer on the gun again and fired another shot into the stranger's chest. The thief stopped breathing.

Laurence put his gun on his hip as he quickly walked away from the murder scene. That was the first time he killed a man, and it was exhilarating. Laurence felt powerful, invincible, and full of life like never before. He continued walking and daydreaming as thoughts of conquering the world filled his mind.

When it was clear that Laurence had lost consciousness, the thief who had shot him took his handcuffs and shackles off before tossing his body onto the floor.

The two thieves were in a rush to get their boss to a hospital. They were afraid that he was going into shock and would possibly have a heart attack. He continued to twitch and yell out uncontrollably as massive amounts of blood poured from the hole that once was his ear.

One of the thieves pulled a black cargo van into the garage. He got out with a metal pipe in his hand and began to beat Laurence with it. He beat Laurence in the head, the ribs, and in the legs. The two thieves tossed Laurence's bloody body in the back of the van next to James.

The thieves assumed that Laurence was dead, so they decided to leave his body in the woods. They knew the coyotes would ravage and tear his body apart as soon as they smelled blood. One of the men tossed Laurence's limp body from the van while it was still rolling. James's dead body followed Laurence out of the moving van. Then the driver smashed on the gas and wildly sped off.

Laurence's body rolled and rolled in the dirt until it crashed into a tree, snapping his leg in half.

An old fisherman, who was camping out in the woods overnight, was disturbed by the loud sound of the van speeding off. He also heard the banging sound of Laurence's body hitting the tree. The old man grabbed his shotgun and flashlight and went to see who'd interrupted his sleep.

The old man with the gray beard found James's body first. He was dead. Several steps later he found Laurence's bloody body under a tree. Mosquitos and other nighttime insects already covered his body. There was still a pulse. The old man managed to slowly get the heavy bodies into his pickup truck. He drove both men to Redgrass Community Hospital and dropped them off at the emergency center.

Chapter Forty-seven

The red and blue sirens flashed and blared as two squad cars pulled into Laurence and Kenya's driveway. A 911 call by their next-door neighbor alerted the police of loud screaming and disturbing noises coming from the home. The two young officers exited their vehicles. One officer rang the doorbell while the second cop searched the front of the property. No one answered the door in the dark home, and everything was quiet and peaceful in the front of the property. The officers cautiously walked around to the side of the house. They both drew their weapons when they saw a body lying face down on the wet pavement.

The young cop wearing a thick mustache looked up at the window. The window was broken and shattered. The other cop checked the woman for a pulse. There was none. The lady lying in a pool of blood and covered with broken glass was dead.

"I'll go check the back of the house," the mustache-wearing officer said.

The other officer nodded as he grabbed his receiver and called for backup and an ambulance. He then grabbed his flashlight and pointed it at the broken window. There was nothing but darkness behind the shattered glass. The bright light scanned the rest of the house and the other windows. Nothing else was out of place or seemed abnormal. When the tall officer flashed his light back to the broken window, there was a woman staring down at him.

His nervous reflexes made his arm tremble, causing the flashlight to fall to the ground. Officer Aguirre picked his flashlight up and wiped the mist from his face. He flashed the light up at the window again, but this time there was no one there.

"The house is clear," Officer Johnson stated.

"I think I saw someone in the window up there," Officer Aguirre said.

Both of the young cops looked nervously at one another. This was their first time on an actual murder scene with a dead body.

"Or maybe this dead body in front of me is making me see things," Officer Aguirre explained.

"Maybe, but I have a feeling that this woman here didn't leap out of that window on her own," Officer Johnson said, running his flashlight up and down the dead body.

The officers immediately noticed the bite marks and torn flesh on the corpse. The woman looked like she'd been eaten by vultures or some type of animal. Fear was written all over the cops' blank faces as they stared at one another, speechless. The wailing sound of an ambulance approaching could be heard.

"This doesn't look right. Pick her head up," Officer Johnson said firmly.

Officer Aguirre bent down and lifted the head of the dead lady. The other cop flashed his light into her face. Both officers were frozen with terror when they saw that the eyes were missing from the butchered face.

"What the . . ." Officer Johnson uttered as he flashed his light away from the dead body. The ambulance and backup officers were pulling up as the two young cops flashed their lights at the broken window.

After the homicide detectives took pictures of the mutilated body and the entire crime scene, Kenya Caine's corpse was released to the town's morgue. Her body was placed inside a black body bag and zipped up before being lifted onto a gurney. The EMT workers rolled the gurney to the back of the medical vehicle and carefully placed it inside.

The emergency vehicle carrying Kenya's body arrived at the morgue. The driver quickly got out of the vehicle and opened the back door. Something looked different about the body bag. He climbed inside the truck, followed by his coworker. The driver curiously pressed down on the body bag. He felt nothing but air. Both workers stared at one another, puzzled. The driver slowly and carefully unzipped the body bag.

Kenya Caine's body was not inside of it. Stains of blood were the only remains left inside of the body bag. The terrified workers jumped out of the vehicle and slammed the doors closed.

Chapter Forty-eight

Laurence's eyes fluttered several times before they finally opened. His blurry and foggy vision was blinded by a bright light. The stinging light forced Laurence to close his burning eyes again. The monotonous tones of machines and monitors beeping and vibrating rang in Laurence's ears. He was in a hospital room, but he had no idea how he got there.

It was a struggle for Laurence to open his heavy eyelids again. A few minutes later they were open, and his vision was clear. Laurence scanned the small room. The flat-screen TV hanging in the middle of the wall was not on. There were two chairs and a table holding medical supplies and paraphernalia sitting to the right of Laurence. And the aroma of cleaning supplies and Lysol filled the air. The smell of hospitals always bothered Laurence. Why was he here? And how did he get here?

There was a light knock on the door before it slowly opened. A middle-aged nurse walked into the room, holding a chart. "How are you doing tonight, Mr. Caine?" she asked, taking a quick glance at the machines in the room.

Laurence tried to respond, but his throat burned and ached badly. When he opened his mouth, nothing but air came out. He needed a drink of water.

"Take your time. It's okay. I'll get you a cup of water," the nurse said, smiling.

While the nurse ran out to get a pitcher of water, Laurence looked at his arm. He saw three small tubes protruding from it. Laurence also noticed how little his arms were. He pulled the white sheets back and saw that his legs were just as thin. Laurence couldn't believe how frail and sickly he looked. He had to get out of this damn hospital as soon as possible.

The nurse came back into the room with a pitcher of water. She poured her patient a cup and checked over the tubes in his arm. "You seem to be doing very well, considering that you were in a coma for almost a month."

Laurence finished the cup of water. His throat felt no better. "I was in a what?" he asked. He didn't recognize the raspy and altered voice that came from his mouth.

"You came out of it yesterday. I'm not surprised you don't remember. You are very fortunate to be alive, Mr. Caine. You suffered a severe loss of blood and a fractured skull, which caused you to go under. And the bullet wound to your neck damaged your vocal cords, so you'll never speak as you did before."

It was painful for Laurence to talk. "How much longer do I have in here?"

"You will be here in ICU with us for another week, and then you will go to the rehabilitation unit on the west wing," the nurse said as she checked the bandage that was wrapped around Laurence's head.

Laurence didn't respond. He planned on leaving the hospital later that night.

The nurse grabbed her chart off the table. "Do you remember my name?"

Instead of saying no, Laurence just shook his head side to side.

"I'm Nurse Lauren Winter. And I must say, for a man who came in here with several broken bones, bullet wounds, and a fractured skull, you are doing excellent."

Laurence cleared his aching throat. "Has my wife been here today?"

Nurse Winter paused and squeezed Laurence's hand as she stared into his distant eyes. "I'm so sorry, but your wife died last month," she said with remorse.

The curvy lines on the heart monitor began to jump and accelerate as Laurence comprehended what Nurse Winter said. The machine began to beep faster and faster.

"Calm down and take a deep breath. Everything is going to be all right," Nurse Winter said calmly.

"How?" Laurence asked hoarsely.

The nurse continued to squeeze Laurence's hand tightly. "The police said it was an apparent suicide. Your wife suffered a broken neck after jumping out of your bedroom window, according to the reports."

Laurence closed his eyes and took a deep breath. He needed a cigarette and a bottle of whiskey. There was no way on earth that his wife committed suicide. Someone pushed her out of that window.

"Once again, I am sorry for your loss. You need to get some rest," Nurse Winter stated.

"Are you in any pain? Because I haven't given you any medication for pain since you came out of the coma."

Laurence wanted to tell the nice nurse that his entire body was in severe pain, but he knew that if he were sedated, he would be forced to spend another night in the hospital. "I feel okay right now," he lied.

Nurse Winter let Laurence's hand go and glanced at her charts. She quickly scribbled notes on her paper. "Good. Because morphine is very addictive, and if you don't absolutely need it, you should not put it in your body."

"Nurse, what's wrong with my stomach?" Laurence painfully asked.

Nurse Winter was surprised at the unexpected question. "Absolutely nothing. You are in pretty good health considering what you've been through. Now get some rest."

Laurence nodded. "Thank you."

"Buzz me if you need anything. Tomorrow we'll start your day off with a nice breakfast," Nurse Winter said before walking out of the room and closing the door.

Laurence smirked at the word "tomorrow." He was definitely not going to be lying in a hospital bed come tomorrow morning. But at the moment he was stuck here with unbearable pain travelling through his body. If the pain continued to increase, Laurence was going to need a heavy dose of morphine. He grabbed the remote control to the TV. Hopefully that would take his mind off the pain that seemed to be tearing his insides apart.

Laurence scrolled through the channels several times before stopping on an old black-and-white thriller. He set the remote control down and stared out the window. A dark silhouette of long tree branches and leaves were the only images that could be seen through the window. A voice spoke softly, causing Laurence to sit up straight in his bed.

"Your life will be mine soon," a woman whispered clearly.

Laurence could feel his heart beating faster as he looked around the dark room. He was all alone. But he did recognize the eerie voice that spoke to him. This was the same voice that has been speaking to him for over a year now. Laurence didn't believe in spirits or ghosts, but there was no other explanation for the strange events that were taking place in his life lately.

For some reason Laurence thought about Damien. He was a good kid who he really regretted killing. But the code he lived by wouldn't allow anyone to steal from him without there being severe consequences. Laurence vaguely remembered Damien telling him that his family was cursed, and that the curse was affecting his life. He paid the young man's story no attention then, but maybe Damien was telling the truth about a hex being cast upon his family.

"Am I being cursed for killing Damien?" Laurence asked aloud.

Laurence looked around the room as if he expected someone to answer his question. Of course, there was no answer. Laurence rested his aching head back onto the pillow and stared at the television. "Come and take my life if you want it!" he said with rage in his screaming voice.

Chapter Forty-nine

Laurence woke up in the middle of the night. He turned his head to see if his wife was still asleep. Kenya was not in the bed next to him. Laurence was all alone. He remembered that he was in a hospital room and not at home in his bed. The cold room was darker than normal. The curtains were closed, blocking the glow of the moon, and the TV was turned off. Laurence didn't recall turning the TV off, but he didn't remember falling asleep either. Laurence turned his throbbing head toward the door. It was strange that there wasn't any light shining at the bottom of the door. For some odd reason the lights were out in the lobby.

While Laurence stared into the darkness, pieces of the nightmare that woke him up began to flash across his mind. He tried to ignore the vivid images, but they would not go away. Laurence turned over and closed his eyes. He wanted to go back to sleep and forget about the dream, the hospital, and the excruciating pain that was torturing his body.

Minutes later, Laurence was turning back over and staring at the door again. He couldn't sleep. The nightmare began playing like a graphic murder scene in his head. Laurence closed his eyes.

He stormed into his mother's house with his black revolver in his hand. The house was dim and quiet. Laurence smelled the foul stench of cigarette smoke in the air. He ran into the kitchen, breathing heavily. No one was in the spotless kitchen. Laurence cocked his gun when he heard the sounds of laughter and chatter. The voices were coming from the living room.

What Laurence saw when he dashed into the living room was unexpected and a total shock. A huge pile of money was sitting in the middle of the floor like a mountain of dirty laundry. The talking and laughter ceased as soon as Laurence stepped into the room. All of the faces staring at him were very familiar.

Kenya and Damien sat closely on the sofa holding hands. And Laurence's mother and her second husband sat on the other end of the couch with burning cigarettes in their hands.

"What took you so long?" Damien asked as he stared at the pistol in Laurence's grip.

Laurence didn't respond to the question. When he saw his mother's husband and the smoke coming from the cigarette in his hand, his face turned blood red.

"All of your money is there. I counted it myself!" Kenya said with an attitude.

Laurence glanced at his wife, then turned his attention right back to his mother's husband. He was seconds away from making him swallow his long cigarette and putting a bullet in his head.

Laurence's mother puffed on her cancer stick and blew the smoke into the thick air. "You can trust me, son. All of your money is right there on the floor. We didn't touch one dollar of it. Count it for yourself if you don't believe your mother."

Laurence had no response for her. The truth was that he really didn't trust her or any other living soul on the earth. Laurence looked his mom in the face. Something was wrong with her. She didn't look like the woman who'd raised him.

"Where are your eyes?" Laurence asked as he stared in disbelief at the two black holes in his mother's face.

"She took them," Mother replied without hesitation.

"What!" Laurence snapped back.

"Watch your tone when you are speaking to your mother, son," the husband advised Laurence.

Laurence became filled with rage. He hated his mother's husband and everything about him. The sight of the portly man made Laurence's skin crawl. "What the hell did you just call me?" Laurence asked with anger in his cracking voice.

The husband took a long pull from his menthol cigarette. He smiled and shook his head playfully as he blew the thick smoke in Laurence's direction. "Calm down, kid. Come and have a smoke with your mom and me. Your wife told us that your new hobby is chain-smoking cigarettes."

Laurence was livid. His dark eyes stared at his wife with contempt. He was done talking. Laurence walked up to his mother's husband. Before the man could say another word or take one last puff of his cigarette, Laurence had put the gun to his head and pulled the trigger. Blood squirted into the air as the husband's body dropped to the floor.

Laurence went on a rampage. He cocked the gun and fired a shot into Kenya's face. That would teach her to keep her mouth closed and stop her from ever telling his business to anyone again. Her dead body fell next to the husband's. Laurence wasn't done yet. He turned and stared at Damien. The look of fear was written all over his face.

"Don't kill me. All of your money is right there on the floor. Please don't kill me!" Damien pleaded for his life.

Damien was wasting his breath, because Laurence didn't hear a single word he said. All Laurence knew *was that his money was short, and Damien was the man responsible for it. He had no sympathy for a thief. Laurence put the pistol to Damien's head. He pulled the hammer back and squeezed the trigger. Blood poured from the open wound as Damien's body crashed to the floor. Laurence cocked the gun again and put another hole in Damien's head.*

"You are a madman!" Laurence's mother yelled out.

Laurence stepped in front of his mother. He stared coldly into the two dark holes in her face. "They all deserved to die," Laurence said calmly.

"You are a lunatic just like your father was. I'm glad he's dead, and I'll be happy when you're in the dirt right next to him," mother said with anger in her voice.

Laurence was filled with rage that he couldn't control. He was devastated and hurt by his mother's cruel words. He closed his eyes as he put the gun to her temple. The Black Widow made a clicking sound as it cocked back.

Before Laurence could squeeze the trigger, his eyes opened.

Laurence tossed and turned in the cramped hospital bed. The surreal dream disturbed him more than he would admit. Laurence couldn't sleep, and he was becoming irritated. He opened his eyes again to a roomful of darkness. Someone was in the hospital room with him. Laurence could feel a pair of eyes watching him. He sat up straight in the bed and looked by the window. There was someone standing in front of the window. It was too dark to see if they were facing him or the wall. All Laurence could see was a shape.

The small shape that Laurence saw by the window moved. Her long hair seemed to blow in the cold air. Laurence was paranoid and frightened to death, but there was nothing that he could do or say. He was at the mercy

of whoever was in the room with him. The terrible pain in
Laurence's weak body wouldn't allow him to do anything
but lie in the hospital bed. He stared at the woman until
his heavy eyes closed and sleep came over him.

The witch didn't leave the dark room. She stood in
front of the window all night and watched as Laurence
rested.

Chapter Fifty

Laurence sat back in the inclined hospital bed, thinking about his wife. The image of her being thrown out of a window and falling to the ground was stuck in his head.

What he didn't know was that Nurse Winter conveniently left out the fact that her eyes were missing from her face when the police found her. The nurse also left out of her story that his wife's skin was mutilated and torn apart. She felt that type of graphic information was too much for his mind to digest.

Laurence tried to remember what happened after he bit Mr. Fishman's ear. Everything was a complete blank after that moment. He couldn't recall anything. What Laurence did know was that Robert Fishman and his boys went back to his house and threw his wife out of a window. He planned on leaving the hospital and killing all of them before the sun rose.

The more Laurence pictured his wife lying in a pool of blood, the angrier he became. It was time to leave the dark and quiet hospital. Laurence yanked the tubes from his arm. His muscles were extremely weak, and his body was in terrible pain. When Laurence tried to move his stiff legs, they remained frozen. He closed his eyes and took a deep breath. Before Laurence could open his eyes again, a voice whispered into his ear.

"I have your wife's eyes. Now I want your heart!" the soft voice said.

Laurence jumped and looked around the dim room. He heard the voice loud and clear but didn't see anyone.

"You killed one of mine. Now it's my turn," the voice whispered into Laurence's ear.

Laurence thought that the medication the nurse gave him was causing him to hallucinate. But Nurse Winter said he hadn't had any pain medicine in almost two days. The creepy voice now petrified Laurence.

The lock on the door turned and clicked. The monitors and machines in the cold room went out. Laurence's heart raced and thumped rapidly. He had no idea what was happening.

The clacking sound of high heels could be heard walking across the hollow floor. Laurence glanced around the quiet room, but once again there was no one. Moments later the light went out, and the room was pitch-black.

"Before I take your heart, I'm going to take your eyes," the woman whispered into Laurence's ear.

Laurence tried to call out for the nurse, but his hoarse voice wouldn't allow him to. The witch jumped on top of him and began to caress his face with her long black fingernails. She moaned excitedly as anger and hatred flowed through her body. The sharp heels of the lady's shoes dug into Laurence's legs, causing blood to drip on the white sheets.

Laurence's body jerked as the evil lady dug her sharp nails into his eyes. The stinging pain was unbearable. He screamed and screamed as the woman slowly carved his eyes out of his face. Laurence went into shock as blood poured down his stiff face. The vengeful witch showed no mercy as she began to slowly cut an incision by Laurence's heart.

In the dark hospital room, Laurence Caine yelled out in agony, but no one could hear his cries for help. The hospital was silent and still. Rain poured as thunder and lightning struck with ferocious fury. The evil witch smiled as she continued to slowly torture Laurence and tear his flesh apart. This moment was long overdue, and she cherished every minute of it. Blood dripped and fell to the floor as the night faded away.

Chapter Fifty-one

Nurse Lisa walked down the narrow hallway of Redgrass Community Hospital with her daily charts in her hands. Her first patient was a gunshot victim who had just come out of a coma. She stopped when she saw the name LAURENCE CAINE on the wall next to the wooden door. Nurse Lisa put on a pair of green latex gloves, which matched her crisp scrubs. Although she wasn't feeling as good as she normally did, Nurse Lisa put on a big, bright smile. An elderly nurse had told her that a warm and bright smile always made the patients feel better. She opened the door, and the radiant morning sun blinded her vision.

After Nurse Lisa stepped into the room and turned her head away from the blinding sun, she paused. Her clipboard fell out of her hand. It made a loud smacking sound as it dropped to the floor.

The entire room was covered with blood. Nurse Lisa's eyes widened as she stared in horror at the blood-soaked bed. The floor looked like someone had taken buckets of blood and poured it all over the ground. Blood was even smeared all across the walls. Nurse Lisa had never seen such a gruesome and horrifying sight.

Her heart pounded even faster when she realized that her patient was not in his bed. When Nurse Lisa looked closer at the bloody bed, she noticed a pair of eyeballs sitting on a red pillow.

She wanted to run out of the morbid room, but she couldn't move. Fear paralyzed her body from head to toe. The only thing that Nurse Lisa could do was scream for help. She screamed as if someone were trying to take her life. The room door slammed shut and locked behind her. The entire hospital could hear the loud and terrifying sounds of pain and torture coming from the bloody room.